Evelyn

A Middleton Novel

by John Wheatley

for Alma Wheatley

1942 -2013

A Hulme Hall Publication

PAPERBACK EDITION

The front cover is from a watercolour by Nick Wheatley, 1987

Part 1

Chapter 1

Who was Evelyn?

My mother talked of Evelyn, but in a hushed tone, which could have been disapproval, and in that little enclave of Middleton, in the middle of the 1950s, where Rectory Street joined Wood Street, there were lots of people who, in my childish comprehension of the world, merited the tone of disapproval. There was the Catholic family, the Butlers, who lived on the corner, for example. They were Irish, of course, as well as being Catholics. The father, Johnny Butler, was a big red faced man, and he was a motor-mechanic. When my father bought a Morris 10, in 1956, Johnny Butler was an affable consultant whenever it broke down, which was quite often. The son, Mattie Butler, was a bit older than me, but younger than my brother. He was slim and quite tall and he had a very open face which broke quickly into beams of laughter when anything took him that way, and I liked him. But they were Catholics, which wasn`t quite right, and it was nice of us to let our affection show.

And there was Miss Fitton, at number four Rectory Street – we were number ten – who wore a calliper on her leg and lived alone. Once, she asked me and a couple of kids I was with into the house, and gave us sweets, and when I gave an account of my day`s wanderings at home, I was told, quietly, but in no uncertain terms, not to go into Miss Fitton`s house again. I wasn`t told why, but I thought it might be something to do with her calliper. But I didn`t mind the prohibition. The sweets, which were caramels, like Toffo, which I really liked, were a bit soggy, as if they`d been there a long time and had had absorbed some of the damp which pervades an old lady`s house, especially one who lives on her own and has to wear a calliper.

But who was Evelyn?

And who was Merle?

Merle and Evelyn were often mentioned in the same sentence. And Marcia, too.

But I knew who Marcia was.

Marcia was my cousin, though she was quite a bit older, ten years, in fact, and Marcia, as I heard people say, was becoming such a lovely girl that she would break a few hearts before she was done.

Sometimes, when we had our first television, Marcia would look after us when my mum and dad went out, and she would snuggle me up against her so it felt cosy, as we watched what was on, and I wondered what it would feel like to have your heart broken, though I knew she couldn`t break mine because she was my cousin.

But the thing was that however nice Marcia was to me, she was friendly with Merle, and somehow, like the Butler family, and Miss Fitton, with her calliper, that wasn`t quite right.

The world extended beyond the junction of Rectory Street and Wood Street, to Cross Street which led down to Parkfield, and Silk Street where my gran and grandfather lived: my mother`s parents. And it extended down Wood Street to the town centre where my other grandfather ran a cobbler`s shop opposite the fountain in Middleton gardens. My grandfather and gran lived in the house which went with the shop, a big rambling building with three floors. They were my father`s parents.

Our house on Rectory Street had a garden front and back. Most of the houses I saw locally had only a yard at the back, and some had a front door which opened directly from the pavement. For this reason, and others, I grew up with the conviction that we were a little bit more posh than most other people in the neighbourhood. The house was also built of newer brick than most others and this added to my sense of superiority. It was all quite illusory. The house was part of a terrace of six houses, and they were pretty much utility houses, built just after the war, and in fact we did not own the house but rented it from a Mr Rhoyds, whose visits, I vaguely understood, were sometimes a cause of apprehension to my mother. But the newness was real. The house had a bathroom and a toilet upstairs, and it was less prone to the smell of dampness and the presence of mice than old houses, like that of my grandparents on Silk Street.

Toilets, of course, were important. The Butler house backed onto a yard, made up mainly of cinders, shared by a dozen other houses, and there were two toilets, each in its own brick house, like a sentry box, at each end. The toilet went straight down to the main drains about eight feet below, and as well as the permanent smell of drains and organic decay, there was the very real fear, as you were sitting there, that one false move could see you tumbling down to meet a dreadful fate below. I only ever went on that toilet once, and I felt that the Butlers had strained my good-will to the very limit by saying that I might use it.

7 Silk Street had a toilet in the yard behind, but at least it was a flushing toilet, and during the winter an oil lamp was kept burning there all the time, to stop the pipes freezing, and so there was a different smell that was not unpleasant.

My mother`s parents were older than my father`s parents, and there were more complications and illnesses on that side of the family. My grandfather, James, had been a calico printer at Schwabe's, in Rhodes, just a mile down the road, but he had been made redundant during the thirties. During that time, my grandmother, Alice, had had to take work in a factory, and that, according to my mother, had turned her from a young woman into an old woman.

They were a big family. Ernest, the eldest son, worked as a clerk at the Soudan Mill, and was married to Gladys, though they had no children, and the rumour was that she made his life a misery. Maureen, the eldest daughter, was Marcia`s mother, Bettie, the second daughter, had died from diphtheria when she was eleven, and they had found that it was her best friend at school who was the carrier. Eddie, another son, never married, but went to work in Blackpool, living his dream. Then there was my mum, Joan, and the youngest sister, my aunty Nancy.

And I haven`t yet mentioned John.

There was a framed photograph of John on the wall in the living room at 7 Silk Street, and you could say that it dominated the room. It was a portrait in his Royal Navy uniform. He had been on the ships that went up to the north of Russia during the war. I was named after him, and when he stared down at me from that portrait, I felt a certain weight of obligation.

Perhaps it was that that made the house seem, besides being a little bit musty from damp, daunting; the fact that my grandfather suffered from Parkinson`s disease, made it more so. He would sit in his armchair, with his hands shaking constantly, and you had to pretend not to notice it, which for a six year old was very difficult.

Before I went to school, my mum had to go back to work at Geigi, down through Rhodes, and I spent the days being looked after by my gran, behind the cobbler`s shop opposite the fountains in Middleton Gardens. The day always started off badly because to me my mother going to work was an act of betrayal, and I had to find some symbolic way of representing this. For example, if she took me into Redmond's next door, and bought me some chocolate fingers in a little white conical sweet bag, I would empty them on the floor and cry until she picked them up. Once this ritual was over, she would go off to work, and I would eat the chocolate fingers and would begin thinking what distractions the day would contain.

The best distraction was Monday, washing day. The equipment had to be set up first thing in the morning. A tub had to be filled with hot water, which meant the fire being stoked up to heat the copper behind, and then the washing went in, and here was the interesting bit because the dirty washing had to be thoroughly beaten about in the tub with a posser in order to release its dirt. The posser was solid circular disc of stout wood mounted on an equally stout broom handle. When the possing was done, the mangle was placed over the tub and the washing went through the ringer, on its way to the line outside. The entire operation took several hours, but the pay-off was that when the equipment was being put away, my patience was rewarded by being allowed to use the posser as a pretend steering wheel in whatever vehicle I fancied the chair where I was sitting to be.

Another minor, but no less pleasing distraction came each day at tea-time. Tea was set out properly, at four o`clock, on a white starched table cloth in the kitchen with slices of bread and butter, ham, fruit-loaf and so on. I would sit at the table, patiently waiting for my granddad to be called in from the shop, and also waiting for my gran to leave her glasses on the table which she invariably did. As soon as her back was turned I would pick up the glasses and make them into a motor-bike, weaving in between the cups and saucers and plates, until my gran turned round again and snatched the glasses from me. This was a bit of a ritual too. She always told me I mustn`t play with her glasses, because I would mark them or scratch them, but she always left them within my reach, and I always played motorbikes with them. I think she would have been as disappointed as I would if the ritual stopped.

Mainly, though, I spent my time in the shop. It was screened off from the small customers` entrance where my granddad served the customers, taking shoes, attaching stringed labels, handing back mended shoes, and having a bit of friendly chatter as he did so. Inside the shop, there were benches and lasts, and one big electrical machine with polishing wheels, and rotating brushes, and grinding wheels, which I was sometimes allowed to switch on and off by pressing the red or green button respectively. There were two pots of glue which were kept warm on a small gas burner, and hand-tools – hammers, pincers, knives. My granddad always had an assistant, and the one I remember best was called Horace, which I thought was a funny name, like someone in a comic. I liked to watch the two of them working, especially the way they sliced through thick leather with a knife to make the soles, and, most of all, the way they filled their mouths with nails, the standard way of operating when nailing on a sole, and one which I was strictly forbidden from imitating.

The world expanded. In 1955 I began to go to school at Alkrington County Primary School, following in my brother, Paul`s footsteps. Personally, I had always hoped I would go to the Parish School, where the neighbours Roger and Jimmy Mitchell went. It was a dignified square building, near the library and St Leonard`s church in the heart of Middleton, and I like the grey uniform with its red piping which the Parish scholars wore. But Alkrington, a mile up the hill of Manchester New Road, was thought to be more aspirational. Still known as Alkrington Garden Village, it was bordered on three sides by farmland, and open country, and it was where middle class folk lived and sent their children to school. So, it was there, according to our parents` plan, we went, and when my mother took me there on the first day, it was as big a betrayal, it seemed to me, as when she had gone off to Geigi, earlier in my infancy, leaving me at the mercy of Gran Warburton in the cobbler`s shop opposite the fountain. She had fondly told me that if I didn`t like it at school, I didn`t need to go again. That kidology was all right in the days prior, but on the day itself it was a big tactical error, because, as she might have known, I had not forgotten it.

"What if I decide I don`t like it?" I asked at the gate.

"I`ll wait here outside, just in case."

"All day?"

"Yes, all day."

I didn`t trust this – nobody stays outside a school gate all day - but felt that she had somehow regained the advantage.

"What will you do for food?" I asked.

"I`ll ask the lady at one of these houses to make me a sandwich."

Finessed by this, and other assurances, I took my first reluctant steps into the playground. Whether she was there at playtime, or lunchtime, I never knew, because I forgot to look, but she was there at half-past three, and with that I decided – though I didn`t know the saying then – to call it a draw.

Younger brothers who are close in age to their older brother – Paul was two and a half years older than me – have to find their own way of competing. Paul was good at technical things and had an inventive mind. He invented a way of closing a bedroom door from the outside so that it locked and no-one could get in. It was simple but brilliant. A piece of string was attached to the latch; you closed the door and pulled the piece of string, it closed the latch and then slipped away. Hey presto! My dad, after his anger had subsided, had to cut a hole in the door with a saw and reach through to release the catch from the inside.

I could not compete with that.

Paul also got orange boxes for thruppence from Jones` the greengrocer on Wood Street and did things with them. He made a bookshelf out of one which was still in service in his bedroom twenty years later. Other orange boxes he took apart, saving the wood for use in other projects - building a space rocket, building a stage set in the garden – his list of projects was endless. I once got an orange box from Jones`, and I hadn`t a clue what to do with it. In the end, I painted it, and asked Mrs Mitchell next door if she would be interested in buying it for sixpence. Much to my shame, she did. Awkwardly, I accepted my 100% mark-up but I wasn`t especially proud.

The opposite. I knew it was done from pity.

It was only when I learned my ability to kick a football that I discovered my freedom from Paul`s superiority. It was an area where he had neither skill nor interest. When my Uncle Roger took me to Old Trafford to see United playing, I was hooked. Football was my passport to independence.

I would set out from Rectory Street on Saturday, before my parents were awake, and would pick up my mate, Phil Hicks, from his house on Booth Street just off Manchester Old Road. If my timing was right, I would get a share of his breakfast; then, we would set out for the Town Hall fields, and watch the games going on there, kicking our own ball about along the side-lines or behind the goals. Afterwards, we would go up through Alkrington Woods, to see what was going on there. There was usually something. Once, we witnessed a Teddy Boy gang fight; once we saw a couple kissing very intimately and had to stifle our giggles, before breaking cover and running off.

I would get home at about five o`clock, exhausted and pretty much happy and ready for my tea. My parents rarely questioned where I had been; it never occurred to me that they might worry about me when I was out all that time; it never occurred to me that there was anything to worry about.

Once – I don`t remember the exact details, but I think it was when I was off school sick – I was looked after by my Gran Wilkinson at Silk Street. Because my granddad James was having a bad day with his trembling hands, she let me play in the seldom used front room. In one of the cupboards there, I found a display cabinet of medals with a photograph of a young girl with a coy smile, curtseying in a little dancing dress.

"Who`s that?" I asked.

"That`s Joan," she said. "That`s your mum."

My granddad Wilkinson, died in 1959.

A short time before he died, when he was confined to bed, I was sent up to see him.

"Not often you see your granddad in bed," he said.

I didn`t know what to say, but I was thinking that the word `often` didn`t come into it.

"Tell your gran I`ll have a glass of barley water."

Dismissed, I gratefully ran down the stairs to deliver the message. I realised, imperfectly at the time, but more clearly later, that I had been sent up so that he could see me for the last time.

Evelyn`s name, and Merle`s occasionally hovered in the air, in conversations which were not intended for my ears, but which nevertheless, were picked up on my radar. I was not especially curious then who they were, and I think it was the strangeness of the names that registered. There were lots of Maureens and Joans and Gladys and Nancys, but I didn`t know anyone else called Merle and I didn`t know anyone else called Evelyn, and so, even though I didn`t properly speaking know them, the names of Evelyn and Merle left a strange almost sensuous impression on my mind. But it was merely a childish impression, and in the feverish criss-cross of my play, the signals emitted by their names were quickly forgotten.

And then, a year after my grandfather`s death, in the summer of 1960, when he was ten and I was nine, I came across Charlie Wilkinson and it was then that the pieces of the jigsaw began to come together.

Part 2

Chapter 2

Imagine the hustle and bustle of a railway station. It is 1940, and the country is in the grip of war. On the platforms of London Road Station, in Manchester, troops in khaki make up a good part of the throng, moving between trains whose wheels hiss steam. Porters drag metal wheeled trolleys laden with mail sacks, and bales of newspaper, and then a shrill whistle is followed by a first heaving bronchial blast of smoke, and a train begins to labour, shunting, foot by foot, with disproportionate, almost heroic effort out of the station. Shunt. Shunt. Shunt. The air full of the hot smell of cinders. The soldiers returning on home leave, the younger ones at least, have a spring in their step, a cocky expectant look - a night on the town lies ahead, a night with the lads, on the beer - or with the wife, hurriedly married before going out, so that the nuptial bed has hardly yet been properly warmed. Amidst the dominance of brown and khaki, there is the occasional blue of a navy uniform, the white of a sailor`s collar, which reminds Evelyn, who is there with her sister-in-law, Maureen, of her husband, John, who joined his training ship HMS Eaglet at Liverpool three months earlier.

They are there to see off Herbert, Maureen`s husband of three months, who is setting off to join the 178th Field Regiment Royal Artillery. His destination is Aldershot, and from there - or at least so it is rumoured - after training, the regiment will be shipped to the Mediterranean to join the campaign in Africa.

"A bit of sunshine," Herbert quips. "Just what the doctor ordered."

"Goodness knows what your socks will be like!" says Maureen. "They`re bad enough at the best of times."

The guard`s whistle goes, and there are last minute hugs for those by the open sash windows of the door, and frantic blowing of kisses and fond waves as the train pulls slowly away. The departure is absolute – it is almost impossible to take in the enormity of the moment.

The two young women make their way back through the ticket hall, and onto the station approach.

"Let`s go into the Kardomah," says Evelyn. "Might as well make a bit of a day of it."

"Come on, then!"

The Kardomah Café is not a particularly exclusive establishment, but for two girls from a small mill town, unused to the urban sophistication of central Manchester, the fact that they are seated at a table with starched white linen, and with the nippies dancing attendance, makes it special enough.

"Poor old Ernest," says Maureen, caught up in the excitement of it all. Ernest, her eldest brother, has applied to the RAF but has been rejected from active service because of his poor eye-sight.

"Lucky old Ernest!" Evelyn retorts.

"Look at you!" says Evelyn putting her hand on Maureen`s tummy. Maureen is five months pregnant.

"I know. I`ve been trying to hide it, but it`s a losing battle."

"Why hide it? Is he kicking yet?"

"Is he kicking? I think he`s going to be a footballer!"

"You think it`s a boy, then?"

"Who knows? I think Bert wants a boy but I don`t mind. All I know is I`ll be glad when it`s over."

"It`ll be all right. Don`t worry. Like shelling peas!"

"I believe you. Thousands wouldn`t!"

"Trust me."

"Well, you should know."

"Shall we have another toasted tea-cake?" says Evelyn, clicking her fingers to attract the attention of the nearest nippie.

"Hark at you," says Maureen, laughing, "Lady Muck!"

Part 3

Chapter 3

There was a picture in Evelyn`s mind of Jubilee park, in 1934, the time she met John Wilkinson. It was Whit Monday, and she had been with her mother to watch the scholars walking through the town in the morning. It was one of those rare days of early summer, with the rhododendrons in full bloom, and a clear blue sky, and with everywhere the feeling of summer warmth and freshness. The town band was playing in the park, and with the factories and shops closed for the Bank Holiday, there were plenty of people in the park, enjoying a lazy time.

She`d walked up there with Harriet Lyons, and Betty Taylor, girls she worked with at the Tonge Mill, all three of them arm in arm, being frothy and full of laughter, and she had seen John sitting there on a bench, smoking a cigarette, whilst his young sisters Joan and Nancy, played on the grass, nearby.

"There`s Evelyn," called Nancy.

She knew the Wilkinson family from seeing them at church, in Parkfield, but the two little girls knew her from being a helper at the Sunday School, which she had done until just before Christmas.

"Hello, Evelyn!"

Harriet and Betty simpered and giggled, not because of the girls, but because of John, who was giving the three of them the casual once-over glance. He lifted his hand to raise his hat, with a kind of polite languor, and Harriet and Betty giggled even more loudly, with a giggle that was almost like a sneeze, as they hurried on, but Evelyn had already decided that she was in love with John.

They went on and stood below the bandstand for a time, then Harriet and Betty caught the eye of a group of lads they knew from the Tonge Mill, and wanted to follow them up the steps to St Leonard`s Square.

"I told my mam I`d be back," said Evelyn.

The girls didn`t object. It was a situation where one less girl was an advantage.

Evelyn walked back down the path, hoping that John and his sisters would still be there.

"Watch me!" said Joan, as she approached.

She caught John`s eye. He motioned her to sit beside him. Nancy, who had lost interest, was sitting on the grass behind, looking for a four-leaf clover.

Joan stood there, poised, on the path, waiting for the band to strike up, and as it did, picking up the rhythm, she began to do a tap dance, going through a pattern of movements, hands, legs, head and tapping feet that was so perfect that it almost made you want to laugh.

When she had finished, the people on the surrounding benches applauded, and Joan made a little bow, and then went off to help Nancy in her quest.

"She`s ever so good, isn`t she?" she said to John.

"She`s been having lessons, taken to it like a duck to water."

"How old is she?"

"Seven."

Evelyn nodded, impressed, and now that she was sitting there, there was no immediate reason for getting up.

"What do you think of this then, Evelyn?" he asked, a little bit cryptically, though she thought she knew what he meant.

"It`s nice. A break from work. Nice weather, too."

He didn`t reply. She wondered if he was weighing up her answer and finding it wanting.

"My dad`s been laid off."

"I`m sorry."

"He was a calico printer, down in Rhodes. Skilled craftsman. Been there since he was fourteen, never missed a day. Now they`ve finished him off. What do you make of that, Evelyn?"

"It`s bad," she said.

It was bad, but it wasn`t uncommon. Despite the happy face of the town on a warm Whitsuntide Monday, times weren`t good.

"No-one will take him on now. He`s a skilled man. Fifty years old. Too old to be a labourer. My mam has to work in his stead. They`ll always take women on, you see, won`t they?"

"We`ve found one," shouted Nancy.

The two girls brought forward a clover, carefully presented.

"That means good luck," said Evelyn.

"It was me who found it," said Nancy.

"No, it wasn't, it was me who found it."

"It was me."

"It isn`t really a four leaf clover at all," said Joan. "It`s a three leaf clover with another one shoved in. So there. No good luck at all."

"Spoilsport!"

"Come on, you two," said john. "I`ve had enough of you. Home."

"Not yet."

"Home!" John commanded.

"What do you think about going to the Vic one night, Evelyn?" he asked, as they were walking back through the town.

"Yeh, if you like," said Evelyn, with a lack of enthusiasm that came, not from lack of enthusiasm, but lack of self-belief. "That`d be nice," she added to compensate for this, though, in fact, her heart was dancing.

"Friday night then?"

"All right."

"All right. Seven o`clock, then. I`ll see you outside."

It was a day which was etched in her memory. As was the following Friday, when they met outside the Vic.

The film was `The Scarlet Pimpernel`, starring Leslie Howard and Merle Oberon.

Every bit of it was etched in her memory.

Chapter 4

On that day, in Jubilee Park, when she first talked to John Wilkinson and made a date to meet him outside the Vic, Evelyn Thomas was eighteen.

She was an attractive girl, slim though not without a figure. She had dark hair, dark arching eyebrows, strong lines on each side of her nose, and high cheekbones which sometimes gave her face a shadowy aspect, making the blue of her eyes stand out.

John was twenty two, had been apprenticed as a cabinet maker at fourteen, and had served his time, though not without a few scrapes, and at least one occasion when his father had been called in so that a proper formal warning could be given. Nevertheless, his master Henry Steadman took him on as a journeyman, aged 21, though so far he had progressed no further than that. He was a steady enough worker, but he had no passion for it – he admitted that himself – and couldn`t find any great ambition to get on. He`d talked of going in the Merchant Navy, to get away from it and see the world, but his father had always persuaded him not to, and his parents` hope was that once he got settled down and had responsibilities, he`d start to make headway.

The Wilkinsons had always been reckoned to be comfortable, as you might say, not well off, but certainly comfortable. Before he was laid off, James had a good job and was steady, and Alice was thrifty. They owned their own house, which was more than most could say, and though the three girls had to share a bedroom, and John had to share with his younger brother, Eddie, Silk Street was all right, and the house was nice enough. Of course, it had been four girls and three boys at one time, but Ernest, the eldest was now married, and lived up towards Mills Hill with his wife, Gladys, and

Bessie, Maureen`s younger sister, had died from diphtheria when she was eleven.

You wouldn`t normally think of John as the deep type, he was open and hearty, and had a way of casting cares aside, and that was something people liked about him. It was certainly something Evelyn liked. But sometimes he was moody and as she got to know him, Evelyn came to the conclusion that his sister`s death had left a deeper scar on him than he would admit.

It was one day when they were sitting in the parlour, talking, that his younger sister Joan told the tale.

"She was sitting in that chair," Joan remembered, "and she said, `don`t let them take me away, dad, don`t let them take me away, don` t let them take me away`, but she had to go to the isolation hospital and we never saw her again, did we, mum?"

"You don`t need to tell Evelyn all this," said Alice.

Joan looked momentarily on the verge of tears, as if suddenly aware that she had said something that wasn`t proper.

"It`s all right," said Evelyn. "I don`t mind you telling me."

Joan smiled glad to be exonerated.

When she looked at John, however, his hand was over his face, as if concealing something his manliness would not permit him to show to the world. But she, Evelyn, knew, and because of it, she loved him all the more.

But the Wilkinsons had always had the reputation of being solid and steady. There was a photograph which Alice showed her of their wedding group in 1909, Alice and her brother, James and his sister, all looking very young and very self-possessed, but the thing was, judging from the feathered hats and smart suits, and tailored gowns and the photographer`s sylvan background, it was a photograph of a couple who, if not affluent, had aspirations. Her own mother had no such photographs of her wedding. As far as she could tell her own mother and father`s wedding had been a very practical and uncelebrated event.

Now, however, it was clear that they had been through hard times.

Eddie, the younger brother, had left school to work as a masher at the Rhodes works, where his father had been, bleaching the fabric before it went for dyeing or printing, but he had not been there two years before all the processes were closed down and the men laid off.

There was no certainty in anything.

Joan`s dancing teacher had put her into a partnership with a boy, Jackie Adams, who was a year younger, and four inches shorter, but who was something of a prodigy. They were called `the two J`s` and they performed at a series of local venues and competitions, winning medals and trophies, and gaining a glowing reputation.

One day, a silver Armstrong-Siddeley pulled up outside 7 Silk Street, and its driver, a Mr Brotherton and his wife, introduced themselves. They had seen Joan dancing. They had been enchanted. They knew a little bit about her circumstances and wanted to help her to develop her talent. They were wealthy, very wealthy; they had no children of their own. They proposed to adopt Joan, to take her into their home as a foster child, and thereby to create opportunities for her which otherwise would be impossible.

Alice sat there tight-lipped.

"Does she know who you are?" asked James.

"Yes. She knows us."

"And have you said anything to her?"

"No. We didn`t think it proper without speaking to you first."

James nodded. "Quite right."

"She`s not going," said Alice, after they had gone.

"We`d better let her be the judge of that."

"We will not let her be the judge of anything. She`s eight years old!"

"Do you think she doesn`t know her own mind?"

"How can she? Talk sense, Jim."

Joan was called into the room.

"Do you know Mr and Mrs Brotherton, Joan?"

"Yes."

"And what`s your opinion of them?"

"They`re nice."

"You like them?"

"Yes, I like them. They`re all right."

"And what would you say if Mr and Mrs Brotherton wanted to take you to their posh house in Cheadle Hulme and bring you up? Would you want to go?"

"I hope you wouldn`t want me to go."

"We don`t. But we`re asking you what you want."

"They`re very nice," said Joan, "but I`d cry my eyes out if I had to go away from here and live with them. However nice it was."

"Are you sure of that, Joan?"

She nodded her head simply. And then, because they were looking at her, she nodded her head more intently.

"Right, then. Well, you`re stopping here then."

It was John who gave Evelyn his version of this story. They had walked down to Middleton Gardens and were sheltering from the rain.

"She wouldn`t budge," he said, laughing.

"Good for her."

"She`s got a bit of spirit, I`ll give her that."

He walked her back home under an umbrella and rested his left arm round her shoulder.

"I`ll go in through the back," she said.

By the back gate, as the rain pattered down on the umbrella, they kissed, slowly, and he slipped his hand inside her coat, onto her breast.

She knew then, or thought she knew, as she lay in her bed that night, with all the excitement of new experience coursing through her system, that, one day, they would be married.

Chapter 5

Ernest, John`s elder brother, was kind and considerate, a gentle soul, and apart from the two younger girls, who were free and unreserved in their affections, it was Ernest who was most welcoming when Evelyn began to appear on the scene. He had a tenacious loyalty to the family, and was inordinately proud of his brothers, especially John, who was three inches taller and who was generally admired for his good looks and athleticism.

He had been married for five years, to Gladys, but they had no children as yet. Ernest had met Gladys at a dance hall in Manchester, immediately coming under the spell of her outward charm and vivacity. She was from a good family in Moss Side, and told the girls that when she was a child they had liveried servants, but though no-one really believed that, no-one openly challenged it. It was just one of those family myths that cropped up occasionally in conversation. There was, as Ernest could confirm, a large house with gardens – though not with any present day servants – but the house had been inherited by her elder brother, and Gladys had become an inconvenient younger sister to be accommodated despite the displeasure of her brother`s wife. Ernest was her way out of this situation. He had a decent clerical job with, as they assumed, some prospects, and though she gave herself some airs and graces, having no money or prospects of her own, that had to suffice.

Maureen was the eldest of the Wilkinson girls, a year younger than Evelyn and to begin with she was stand-offish and suspicious. But Evelyn courted her, and gradually got under her defences until they began to share confidences and become friends.

But it was Ernest who tried to put Evelyn at her ease, in the first few months, and she began to like him straight away. He had a funny way of winking and making a click with his tongue, a bit like the way people call a dog, when he had something to say that he thought noteworthy, and it wasn`t long before she had perfected an imitation of him, which she would do to make john laugh, though it was not for anyone else.

On Friday nights, John had his night out with a few chaps from work, and others they happened across in the pub. They usually started at the Dusty Miller, in the centre of town, and then went on somewhere. Sometimes they went up Oldham Road way as far as the Old Cock, then back towards the centre via the Hare and Hounds, the Dog and Partridge, the Brunswick or the Railway, and then the Commercial; another alternative was to catch the tram down to Rhodes, where there were several pubs close together. A third variation was to walk up Wood Street to the Woodman and across to the Old Boar`s Head and other pubs on Long Street.

Maureen told her that in the past there`d been times when the lads had got involved in a bit of a roughhouse, and that once John had been brought home the worse for drink, and having been pulled out of a scrap, by the local bobbies. He had a bit of a reputation as someone who could look after himself, and Evelyn knew this had gained him some admiration amongst the girls she knew.

But he`d calmed down since those days, and she didn`t mind him having his night out, though she sometimes teased herself with jealous thoughts that some floozy out on a good time might set her sights on him. Respectable women didn`t go into the pubs. Her mother had never set foot in one, though sometimes on Saturday night, her dad would bring a bottle of stout home for her. It was the same with John`s mother Alice. The only time she`d been into a public house was to bring James home when Bessie had been taken ill.

Friday nights for Evelyn usually meant washing and setting her hair, a process that could take two hours. Her mother put in curling pins every night, and slept in them, but Evelyn didn`t like the thought of that. Sometimes in summer, when the men were out, the women talked at the back whilst the younger children played out, and it was a nice relaxed time. One evening she asked Maureen if she wanted to come round, and they sat in the front room and put the radio on and talked. If there was any doubt before, it now seemed they were the best of friends.

Evelyn had started off from school as a carder at Tonge Mill on the corner of Oldham Road; it was dirty work, which left you covered from head to foot in cotton fluff, but it was work and another wage coming into the house. Two years later, because she was a good worker, they`d moved her up to be a mule spinner which needed more concentration, and left you tired. It was a twelve hour shift, eight to eight, though eight to six on Friday, and eight to twelve on Saturday.

On Saturday afternoon, John played football for the Parkfield Church AFC, down at the Town Hall playing fields, and in the evening he took her out, usually to the cinema. Then, on Sunday afternoons, they walked out to the park or the recreation ground, or the cricket ground, depending on the weather.

It was one such Sunday, about a year after they`d been walking out together, that they got on to talking about the physical side of love and marriage. It was in connection with something that had been in the film they`d seen the previous night, and something one of the girls at work had been saying about her young man. It was a bit awkward at first, a bit embarrassing, but there was also a sense that they both wanted to take the conversation into that area. For Evelyn, sex had no real meaning. She`d been told, when her periods started, that she would start to get feelings that were linked with wanting to have children, and that was how she understood some of her own moods; and, like anyone else, she had seen dogs, and occasionally farm animals doing what her father referred to, with an ironic cackle, as the dastardly deed, but she could not make any true connections between the different bits of what she knew and what she saw, and what she felt.

"What do you think?" John asked. "Do you fancy having a go at it?"

"I don`t know if I`d know how."

"You just leave it to nature."

"Anyway..."

"Anyway what?"

"Well, it`s not just as simple as that, is it?"

"I can get something?"

"How do you mean?"

"To take away the worry, you know..."

"Oh, I see."

"Why, what did you think I meant?"

"I don`t know."

"Don`t go all moody on me."

"I`m not moody."

"Well, what are you, then?"

"I`m thinking. That`s all. You mustn`t rush me."

"No, all right."

They walked on homewards, along Mellalieu Street, in the soft evening light.

"You won`t go off me, will you?"

"Course I won`t," he said, and he slipped his arms round her shoulder. It was getting a little too light in the evenings for spooning by the back gate, not without the neighbours` kids catching them at it, but there was a little area of open ground just behind, shaded with trees, and they sat there for ten minutes, exchanging kisses which posed the same question they had been talking of before.

Nothing more was said directly for a few weeks, and then, just before the Wakes, John brought up the subject again.

"If you don`t want to, it`s all right, just say."

"It`s not that I don`t want to."

"Well..."

"But, well, where would we go?"

"We`d find somewhere."

"I`m not going in the woods," she said.

They both knew people who had gone into Alkrington Woods to find a secluded place for it. "So you can forget that one, if that`s what you mean."

"It`s not."

"Well, then!"

"We`re all going to Blackpool for the Wakes," he said.

"I know. Your mam told me. I`ll miss you."

"You don`t have to. I can come back."

"What do you mean?"

"I`ll tell my mam I`m coming home for my Friday night out. She`ll not stop me. Then we can have a bit of time together, you know, at our house."

"I`m not sure, John."

"Why not? It`ll be all right. Trust me."

He put his arms round her, and pulled her close, making her feel safe and warm. Then he kissed her and she didn`t want him to stop.

When the Wilkinsons went to Blackpool, the whole conversation they`d had begun to seem unreal, as if it had never happened.

"Meet me at the Redmond's Tea Shop at four o`clock on Friday," he`d said.

"All right, then."

Now it seemed like a joke. She would go there and he wouldn`t turn up. He`d still be in Blackpool, having a good time – he wouldn`t want to drag himself away.

She relaxed. It wasn`t going to happen.

But on Friday, she went anyway, down Wood Street to the town centre and Redmond's.

John was there. Her heart leapt.

They had a pot of tea, and then John said, quietly. "I`ve got something, you know, for protection."

He put his hand over hers on the table, and from that moment on she knew that it was going to happen.

And so it did.

And what was momentous about it was offset, almost entirely, by what was awkward, clumsy and messy. But not entirely so.

When Evelyn walked home, she was carrying with her a strangely light sense of having peered through a window into another world, a garden that she had never known was there, that she had not yet quite entered.

Her mother was waiting for her.

"Where`ve you been?"

"I stayed and had a bit of tea with John."

"And what would Mrs Wilkinson say if she knew you`d been in the house while she was away?"

"It was only a cup of tea. Anyway, John said he`d tell them."

Her mother looked at her father, who in turn looked uncomfortable.

Her mother waited until her dad went out the Albion for his pint.

"Well," she said, "has he said he`ll marry you?"

"What?"

"You heard me."

"I don`t know what you`re talking about."

"Don`t try and kid me. It`s written all over your face..."

"Well?" she continued after a long moment. It was that peremptory tone which left you nowhere to hide.

"No, he hasn`t."

"What?"

"Hasn`t asked me to marry him."

"You silly little fool. You silly little fool," she repeated, with more emphasis, when this elicited no response. "What were you thinking of?"

"I think he means to."

"You think he means to! He told you that, did he?"

"Yes," she said quietly.

"Don`t you understand the first thing about men, you silly fool! And what if you`re pregnant?"

She somehow couldn`t bring herself to say that John had taken precautions.

"You were pregnant with me, though, weren`t you? I mean when you and dad were married."

"Aye, I was, but I made sure I was engaged first, aye, and that everyone knew it."

"And that makes all the difference, does it?"

"Aye, it does. It may not be what God intended, but there`s plenty of women get with child wrong side of the vestry. Thing is, you make sure you`ve got your man before you do aught."

"I think John`d stick by me."

"Oh, you do, do you?"

"Yes."

"And what if he denies all knowledge of it?"

"He wouldn`t."

"And what if you`re not pregnant and he goes round telling all his pals about you? Bragging. Don`t think they don`t, you know."

"I know," she said, now almost browbeaten into simple acquiescence.

"Where`s your reputation then? You`re soiled goods then, aren`t you. No-one`ll look at you."

"Don`t tell my dad, will you?"

"Don`t tell your dad? What else do you think I`m going to do."

"Don`t."

"When do they get back. Mr and Mrs Wilkinson?"

"Saturday."

"Saturday. Right. Your dad`ll have to go down and have it out with them. That`s all there is for it."

A hot alarm began to trill in her nerves. She knew John would hate it if there was a fuss like that. Might even hate her, if he thought she was trying to set a trap for him. Her dad would hate it, too. He didn`t mind being the boss in his own house, but she knew he always shied away from confrontation with other people.

"Don`t tell him yet, mam. Let me have a chance to speak to John first."

"I don`t know about that!"

"It`s my life, mam."

"It`s your life, and you`re throwing it away. Well, don`t come crying to me when he makes a fool of you."

At that moment, the front door opened and her dad came back in. "What`s up with you two, then?" he said. "Faces like thunder."

"Nought," said her mum.

"Put the kettle on, then, Evelyn. Make us a pot of tea. Nice and strong."

"We`ll get engaged, then," said John.

"Are you sure?"

"Why not? We`re all right, aren`t we, you and me?"

Her heart danced with excitement and pleasure. It had been like a knot in her chest for three days, thinking of how to put it this way, and then that way, so as not to make him think she was angling for him, and now he had taken it so easily, just like that, with a warm, easy smile, as if it was all happening in a world lit by sunlight.

"Aren`t you going to propose to me then?"

"What, get down on one knee and all that?"
"That`s the way it`s done."
"Bloody hell. Go on, then."
"You`ll have to ask my dad next."
"Why. I don`t have to marry him an`all, do I?"
"You have to ask for his permission."
"Bloody hell! What if he says no?"
"My dad? You don`t know him. He`ll be more embarrassed than you!"

And that was how it happened. They were engaged, and Alice let him have a ring which had been her own mother`s, and he put it on Evelyn`s finger so that she could wear it and show people, and let them know they were betrothed. And after that they were allowed to be alone together in the house, to sit in the front room without being disturbed, and every so often, when everyone else was out, they went upstairs.

And then, one Friday, John went on a drinking spree with his pals which continued on Saturday so that he missed seeing her as planned, and when he called round on Sunday, she told him that the engagement was off. She didn`t see him until the next weekend, and then, significantly, it was Friday night that he called.

"Don`t be too hard on me, Evie. I`d had a proper bad week, and I was just blowing off steam. I`ve made a fool of myself, I know, but it`ll not happen again. I`ll knock it off."

"You say that!"

"I mean it. I`ve been feeling as gloomy as sin. I`ve missed you, Evie. I don`t know what I`ll do if you chuck me in."

"You`ll be seeing me on Friday nights from now on, then, will you?"

"I`ll do better than that. I`ll go and see the vicar about when he can fit us in, and we`ll have the banns read and all that."

"You`re mad!" she said.

“I might be mad, but I mean it.”

“But where will we live?”

Until now they had only talked of it in the vaguest of ways, of saving a bit towards making a start and renting somewhere, of putting things aside in a bottom drawer but it had still seemed in the realms of fancy.

“I`ll have a word with my mam about converting the front room for a bit,” he said.

“Or we could go to ours,” she said, now fully caught up in the scheme. “I`ve already got my bedroom, and there`s a little spare room too. I`m sure they`ll be all right with it.”

They were married at Parkfield Church two months later, with Ernest as John`s best man, and after a bit of a wedding breakfast at Silk Street, they set of on the train for a week at Morecombe. When they came back, they took up residence in the back bedroom at Wood Street, and their regular married life began.

Chapter 6

"You were making a bit of a racket last night!" said Evelyn's mother, one Sunday morning.

"I can`t help it if the bed rattles, can I?"

Her mother laughed. "Enjoy it while you can!"

But despite her mother`s insouciance, it put her off to think of everyone knowing, and she told John as much, the next time, when he asked her what was bothering her.

"Let`s get a place of our own, then," he said.

"How can we?"

"I was talking to a chap in the pub last week and he was telling me they`re looking to take men on at the Bleach Works at Simpson Clough."

"Where`s that?"

"Out through Heywood, between Rochdale and Bury. It`s nice out there."

"But you don`t want to do factory work, do you?"

"Why not? I`ll tell you, I`m sick of Steadman's. It`s all so stuffy and formal. And any hint of promotion, he puts me right at the back of the queue, and he`s got two nephews coming through now. I`ll be on the same money there when I`m ninety."

"You`re not serious, are you?"

"I am, the more I think about it. We could rent a cottage out there for next to nothing. Take our chance. Be on our own. Why not?"

"I don`t know, it seems like a big step," she said, though at the same time one part of her thrilled to the idea.

"We can think about it, though, can`t we?"

Thinking about it was as good as doing it. She could tell that straight away from the eager look in his eye. The following Saturday afternoon, he had a ride up to Heywood on the bus to have a scout around and speak to someone, and before the end of the month he had handed in his notice at Steadman`s and was taken on at the Simpson Clough Mill on Ashworth Road, in a hollow just below the Rochdale Bury Road, where the Cheesden Brook and the Naden Brook came together to supply the mill reservoir.

The cottage was part of a terrace on the steep part of Bamford Road, just above the big cotton mill at Hooley Bridge in the valley of the River Roach. The row of whitewashed cottages had been built for mill workers, but there were two or three that were vacant, and the rent was very reasonable. The rooms were tiny inside, and the furniture wasn`t up to much, but there was a little garden behind which had been kept nicely tended with flower beds and trellises. For a couple of days, Evelyn was home-sick, never having lived out of Middleton before, but she set to with a broom and a floor-cloth and a duster, and soon had the place ship-shape.

"I don`t recognise it," said John, when he got back from work that Friday night.

She showed him round the work she`d done upstairs, clean sheets and pillow-cases her mother had given her to bring from home, a mirror, a vase of flowers. She`d also managed to get the stove working and had made a stew with lamb and potatoes and onions, and she had bought him two bottles of brown ale to drink afterwards.

"You can walk up to the pub for an hour if you like," she said.

"Why should I want to?"

It was a soft October night, still warm at nine o`clock, so they sat outside and smoked a cigarette. He gave her a taste of his beer and she pulled a face, making him laugh.

Then, they went upstairs and made love, the first time that it had not been in someone else`s house.

"Now, that was something like!" said John, getting his breath back.

She agreed that it was. More than she had ever imagined.

And a short time later, it was so again.

The next morning he was a dead weight, lost to the world, and she had almost to drag him from the bed to set off in time for work. When he had gone, and she had tidied away the breakfast pots, she slipped back into bed and slept for an hour. When she opened her eyes, she found herself surrounded by the most beautiful stillness and silence. Remembering the night gone by, she felt transformed, as if she had been reborn into a world where physical happiness was the only rule.

"Your Evelyn`s got a shine in her eye," she overheard Alice saying to her mother. She had gone back to visit her mother for the day, and Alice had agreed to come over for a cup of tea. Evelyn was in the kitchen, washing the pots.

"Your Evelyn`s got a shine in her eye."

She was glad it was obvious. She wanted everyone to notice. Both families had said it was a mistake to move away, up to Heywood, but now they had to hold their tongues.

"Right," she said, coming back through and putting her coat on. "I`d better be getting off or I`ll miss my bus."

"Why don`t you stay over, love?"

"No, I`ve got his tea to make," she said, and in truth, she could not bear to be away from him, even for one night.

Rather than walk down Wood Street into the centre of town, she turned into Rectory Street, and then Durnford Street where she could catch the bus just beyond the Boar`s head, and save a farthing. The bus turned into Hollin Lane, past the cricket field, and then laboured up the hill to the top of Hebers, thence beginning the long gentle downhill run through farmland into Heywood. There had been more than a hint of frost in the morning, tracing the windows with its feathery designs, but now the afternoon was azure clear, with the distant prospect of the hills, rich in bracken, brought almost telescopically near.

"It`s beautiful," she said, quietly, to herself.

The bus, having left Middleton at four o`clock, was due in at Heywood at half past. The walk from Heywood to Hooley Bridge was twenty minutes. She had bought some sausages and potatoes in Middleton, and some milk, and butter, so she had no more shopping to do. That meant that she would have time, before John got back, at six o`clock, to set the fire going and get the house warming through, and have his dinner ready to go on the table.

Then, just on the outskirts of Heywood, the bus broke down with plumes of steam hissing from its front radiator. The passengers filed off to wait by the roadside.

"It`s no good," said the driver, wiping his brow with a rag. "I can`t do anything, I`ll have to wait for the next bus and then fetch an engineer out."

The conductor shrugged his shoulders and tipped his hat back on his brow. He was a conductor, his manner, said, it wasn`t his business to know anything about engines.

The next bus was quarter of an hour late, and then there was a question with the new conductor about whether his new fares would have to pay again.

By the time they got into the middle of Heywood, it was quarter past six. When she got back to the cottage, John was already home, sitting there in a bad mood which he took pains not to disguise.

"I couldn`t help it," she said, "I was in good time but the bus broke down."

"Your business," he said, emphatically, "is here, not there."

"I only went over to see my mother, and yours, as a matter of fact."

"That`s not the point," he said.

She found herself looking at him, wondering if she could quite believe he would be so unreasonable.

"You could have put a light to the fire," she said. "It`s all set."

"I didn`t know if it was worth it," he retorted. "I thought you might be stopping over. I was going to go up to the pub."

"Go on, then," she said. "Go there, if that`s what you want."

"Well, I might just do that, if you put it like that."

She went into the kitchen and then heard the front door slam.

She took a deep breath.

Then she went and set light to the fire, watching the little curls of flame on the rolled newspaper catch on to the coals, until they began to glow and light.

She sat on her knees before the hearth and watched.

It was no good putting the sausages on now, she knew, because they would be done and burnt before he got back.

She had never felt so depressed. And the worst of it was that she seen her own father like that, being petty and selfish, and she had thought John was different. She`d thought he was more of a man than that. And it made her sad because in one afternoon it had stopped being a new story of consummate love, and had become an old story of a man getting what he wanted, or to hell with it.

She peeled the potatoes and put them on to do slowly; once the fire was hot she would be able to do the sausages quickly in a frying pan on the hob. In the meantime, she put on a kettle to boil and then kept it simmering. Then she cut some slices of bread and buttered them. All this she did in a coldly detached state of mind, automatically, not letting herself think.

She turned on the radio and sat by the fire. If he was back by nine o`clock, she decided, she would cook his dinner for him; if not, she would go to bed and let him do for himself.

He wasn`t long. It was just after half past seven when the latch clicked and he came in.

"I just had one," he said, in the dogged voice of one who knows he`s in the wrong but isn`t going to go so far as to apologise.

“Take your boots off,” she said. “I`ll have your dinner ready in ten minutes.”

She kneeled in front of the fire, holding the pan over the flame until the sausages were sizzling in the fat. He came down and sat in the chair behind her, and put his hands on her shoulders. She felt a pleasurable tingling and wanted to give way to it, but there was still a wedge of resistance in her.

“I`ll go and mash the potatoes,” she said, getting up.

“That`s better,” he said, when they had finished the meal.

She poured him another mug of tea, and then went to the kitchen to wash the crocks.

“Put some coal on the fire,” she called.

“Right.”

By the time she was done, the flames had come through, and the room was pleasantly hot.

“Come and sit by me.”

She wanted to show resistance, but she did as he asked her, and soon she was nestling against him.

“We`re all right here, aren`t we,” he said. It was a statement rather than a question.

He was curling a strand of her air through his fingers.

“I thought we were.”

“Don`t be too hard on me,” he said. “Bad day there, today, not sure I`m suited to mill work.”

“Your dad warned you, but you wouldn`t listen to him.”

“I`ll stick it out, if you`ll stick it out with me.”

“You know I will,” she said, quietly.

The breach was made up.

“Shall I put some more coal on?” he said. “Or shall we have an early night?”

“Let`s have an early night,” she said.

Chapter 7

"There was a chap at work telling me, if you go on up, beyond the mill, up Ashworth Road, half an hour`s walk or so, there`s a pub, out in the middle of nowhere, well, up by a chapel, actually, but that`s in the middle of nowhere, too – anyway, I thought we might have a walk up there, on Sunday..."

"What to the chapel?"

"No, to the pub."

"John, I can`t go in a pub."

"Why not?"

"Because I can`t."

"Why not? Women do. We`re not living in the nineteenth century now."

It was a fine morning when they set out, the best of autumn, with the trees still full, a rich canopy of red and gold tinted leaves, and a warm October sun. They followed the course of the river to begin with. It wound quite extravagantly between meadows and steep shale banks, with woodland on the slopes above.

"Someone was telling me," he said, after they had crossed a fast flowing section of the stream on stepping stones, "there are six or seven mills further up the valley, water mills, all ruined now."

They came to a section of the river where it had cut through the exposed bedrock to form two or three deep basins.

"Deep enough for a swim."

"Rather you than me."

"I`m going to."

"John! You`re mad."

Nevertheless, he was stripping off, jacket, shirt, boots and socks, trousers, vest.

"We haven`t even got a towel."

"I`ll dry in the wind."

He plunged into the pool and let out a shout at the coldness and then laughed.

"Is it freezing?"

"It`s not so bad, when you get used to it."

"You`ll catch your death."

"Actually, it`s quite refreshing. Come on, you come in, too."

"Not a chance!"

"There`s no-one about."

"Not on your life!"

She sat on a boulder, and dangled her toe into the water.

"It`s icy," she said.

"You don`t know what you`re missing."

"I do."

"Come on, don`t be a chicken."

"Cluck, cluck."

"Come on."

He waded over towards her, and took hold of her feet as if to pull her in.

"Don`t you dare!" she said, standing up quickly and backing off."

"Come on, there`s nobody about."

"All right, then!" And with that, on a sudden impulse, she hurriedly unbuttoned her blouse, stepped out of her skirt, and pulled her shift over her head. Then she slipped into the pool, to her waist, and after a moment of gasping shock, lowered herself to her neck in the water.

He came over and held her close to him, from behind, with his hand around her waist.

"We`ll both get pneumonia."

He clasped his hands over her breasts, and kissed the crux of her neck and shoulders.

"You`re so lovely," he said.

She closed her eyes, and then opened them again, taking in the beauty of the morning and the surroundings. It was one of those special moments, she realised, a moment she would never forget.

When they got out of the water, they were both shivering. He rubbed her back vigorously with his jumper, and she managed to pull on her clothes.

"Come on, then," he said, when they were both clothed again.

"I`m glowing now, are you?"

"I am."

He took her hand and pulled her onwards up the path.

They re-joined the road, and walked on. The road wound slowly up the valley, passing through a small hamlet, with farmland and woodland bordering the road. Two miles further on a side lane led to a small church, and beside it an inn, the Egerton Arms.

"Are you sure it`s all right?" she asked.

"Course it is."

They went into the bar, and John ordered a pint, and a half of shandy. It was a woman serving at the bar, the landlord`s wife, and she was jolly, which made things easier. There was a dog, too, who sat looking up at Evelyn with big dark eyes, until the landlady gave it a saucer of beer from the drip tray, which it lapped up voraciously.

"I told you it`d be all right," said John as they were setting off back home.

"I feel a bit drunk."

"You`ve only had two shandies."

"I enjoyed it anyway."

They walked back in the hot afternoon sun, and when they got home, they both flopped into a chair and dozed. When she awoke, John was in the kitchen and there a crackling and a sizzling, and a smell of sausages cooking.

"You don`t need to do that," she said.

"Why not? I can fry a sausage as well as the next man."

"I`ve got some potatoes and carrots left over from last night. Shall we have those, too?"

They sat out in the back yard to eat. It was a soft October night, with big clouds and a warm breeze. They finished their meal, and then smoked a cigarette as the light slowly faded.

Then, drowsy and satisfied with the day`s outing, they went to bed early.

And that was the night when Merle was conceived. Of that, Evelyn never had any doubt.

Chapter 8

"I`ve someone to see down in Middleton," he said, one Friday morning. "I`ll go straight after work. Be back by nine."

"Will you want any tea?"

"No. I`ll pop over and see my mother. Get something there."

"All right."

She didn`t question him and didn`t feel that she should, though later she wished he`d said a bit more about who he had to see, or what it was about.

She didn`t feel much like eating at tea-time, but there was a bit of ham in the larder, so she cut some bread and made a sandwich, and brewed a pot of tea and sat by the fire, with the radio on, as it grew dark outside.

Eight o`clock came, and then nine, then half past, and then ten. By half past ten she knew that he wouldn`t come back now. She finished off and went to bed. He would have gone for a drink, she reckoned, with his old pals, that was probably the whole point of it, and she wouldn`t have minded so much, if only he`d been a bit more open about it.

He was back early the next morning, and brought her a cup of tea before she was awake. He was bright and breezy.

"I`ll just get a shave before I go in to work," he said.

"Why didn`t you come back?" she asked, going down to where he was lathering his face in the kitchen.

"I had a couple of drinks and missed the bus. Stayed at my mam`s. You don`t mind, do you?"

"You should have told me."

"I didn`t mean to stay over. I just got caught up in the conversation. They`re all saying we`ll have a war on before the end of the year. Tommy Wright and Jim Lund have already signed up for the army. That`s what I`d heard, that`s why I went down, you know, they were seeing them off."

She could have argued the point further, but the mention of war and men signing up, made a thrill of panic lurch through her bowels. Her mother had had two brothers, volunteers for the Welsh Fusiliers, both killed in Flanders. Her father had been in the 38th Division and had been through the Somme and the attack on Mametz Wood, and he never talked about it, except to say, sometimes, that whenever he thought about it the smell of death came into his nostrils. The remnants of all that had floated through her thoughts all through her childhood, an unspeakable terror that must never happen again. And they had grown into a false reassurance that it would never happen again, and now here was John talking about war on the horizon and saying that he was seeing off pals who were joining up.

He went off to work, and when he came back at dinner-time, his week`s work done, she had a pan stew ready for him, with some ox-tail which the butcher had kept for her.

"You won`t go will you?" she asked.

"Go where?"

"To war."

"It`ll probably never come to it. You know how people talk."

"I think I`m pregnant," she said.

He turned to her from his food, his eyes full of curiosity.

"Are you sure?"

"I`ve not seen the doctor but I`m two weeks late."

"Bloody hell," he said, with a mixture of surprise and pleasure.

"I`ll go and see Dr Gourley next week. See what he says."

"Right. Bloody hell!"

"Are you pleased?"

"Course I am. Well, it takes a bit of getting used to, though, doesn`t it?"

He finished his dinner, and they had a walk across to Queens Park.

"Let`s take a boat out, shall we?" he asked. So they went out for a half hour on the lake, and then sat watching the bowls.

"We`ll have to have a think," he said, "you know, about how to sort things out. Staying up here and all that."

"I don`t want to move back to Middleton. I like it up here now."

"I do, too, but you`ll need to have people about, your mother and so on."

"Not for a bit yet. Nearer the time, maybe, go back and stop with my mum for a couple of weeks. Or go into hospital."

"Have to see what the doctor says. Maybe we should get to know a doctor out here. Just in case."

"I`ll see what Dr Gourley says, anyway."

"Right."

They sat for a time, listening to the peaceful click clack of the bowls running into the pack, and the murmurs and laughter and small applause of the men playing their games.

The following morning she was sick. At first she thought it must be the remainder of the pan stew which she had eaten the previous evening, and then she realised that it was probably telling her what the doctor would confirm when she saw him.

She travelled down on the bus on Tuesday morning, and the doctor saw her straight away.

"Have you brought a sample?" he asked, discreetly. Dr Gourley had been their doctor since she was a child and she trusted him.

"Does John know yet? Have you told him?"

"Yes."

"Is he pleased?"

"Surprised, but yes, pleased, too."

"I should think so."

"Does that mean…?"

"Yes, no doubt about it, Evelyn. Congratulations."

She walked up Wood Street to see her mother.

"Your John was about Friday night."

"Yes, I know."

"Your dad saw him in the Britannia. You want to watch that caper, you know."

"I knew where he was."

"Aye, well," she said suspiciously, "mind you do! Give an inch and he`ll take a mile. They`re all the same, men are."

"Anyway, I came down to see Doctor Gourley."

"Why, what`s up?"

"There`s nothing up. I`m going to have a baby."

"You`re never!"

"I am. He says so."

"When?"

"June, he thinks."

Her mother put her hands to her lips, her eyes suddenly brimming with excitement.

"Oh, love!"

Sit down, mum, I`ll put the kettle on."

The following Sunday, they went down to see John`s family with their news. Ernest and Gladys were there, and Maureen with her young man, Herbert. John took Herbert for a pint at the Joiners` Arms, on the corner of Kemp Street, and Eddy, just eighteen, insisted on going with them. Ernest, under Gladys` watchful eye, stayed put. Joan, who had won a trophy the previous evening with her tap dancing partner, Jackie Adams, was full of her own excitement, but when Evelyn told them her news, James decided it was a suitable moment to bring out the sherry for the ladies, and a scotch for himself and Ernest.

Alice took her to one side, and squeezed her hand, with the same look of excitement as her own mother.

"It`s such good news I can hardly believe it!"

"I`m only just getting used to it myself."

"You will take care of yourself, won`t you?"

"Course I will."

In the room, Alice`s enthusiasm was more tempered, and she suspected that was for Gladys` benefit.

"Did you see her face?" she said to John, on the bus going home.

"How do you mean?"

"Everyone else was happy for us. She looked sour, Well, not sour but you know..."

"She always looks like that. Anyway, maybe she`s jealous. They`ve been married over four years, and nothing to show for it."

"She sometimes seems the sort who wouldn`t want to have kids."

"Do you think so? Well, maybe, but anyway, that`s enough of her. I`m not having her spoil my day."

"Nor me," said Evelyn, putting her arm through his and drawing close.

Chapter 9

It was a cold winter, but by the beginning of December her morning sickness had passed, and as her stomach began to show the first signs of swelling, she felt healthier and happier than she had ever been. Albert, the old man in the house next door, who was a fly-maker at the Hooley Bridge mill, brought her boxes full of broken shuttles to burn on the fire, supplementing the weekly coal delivery, and John sometimes came home with a sack of logs washed down the river as far as Clough Mill, so she kept the house warm. In the evening, she took a scuttle full of hot coals up to the little hearth in the bedroom, to take the chill off up there. She had got to know the local shopkeepers by now, and appreciative of her condition, they were generous in keeping a little bit to give her, a few sausages with the piece of brisket she bought for Sundays, some broccoli from the greengrocer`s own garden to go with the potatoes and carrots and onions which were the staple. A chap at work gave John a brace of rabbits which he had caught, and he brought them home. When she said she wouldn`t touch them, he skinned them himself, and after she had overcome her aversion she made a stew with one of them, and a pie with the other. Whenever the savings left a little bit extra in her purse, she would buy him a couple of bottles of brown ale to drink after his tea, and it always reminded her of that special night, back in July, just after they had first moved in.

"Mind if I go to see the game at Gigg Lane?" he said, getting back from work one Saturday dinner time.

"Who are they playing?"

"Blackburn. Local derby. A couple of chaps at work asked me if I fancied it. I`ll not go if you want me here."

"No, you go. When will you be back?"

"Seven. Eight at the latest."

"Shall I make you some supper?"

"No, I`ll get a pie at half-time. That`ll do me."

It was at half past eight that she began to suspect a repeat performance of his night out on the tiles at the end of October. He would have met up with some of his Middleton pals at the game, or in the pub before, and then would have gone back for a couple in the old haunts, and lost count of time. If they`d still been living in Middleton, she reflected, it wouldn`t have mattered so much; it would have just been like one of his Friday nights out with the lads, and he would have come home, later if not sooner, and if he was a bit the worse for wear, then so it was. But living out here made it different. Here she was on her own, with no company, and if he stayed out beyond a certain time, there was no way he could get back until the next morning. And the worst of it was that he had to lie about it, knowing full well that he was going to go out for a drink. By ten o`clock, when she went to bed, she`d worked herself into a fine state of anger and resentment.

And then, at what must have been one o`clock, or even later, she woke up and heard him in the kitchen below. One side of her was flooded with relief, that he was back safe and well; but on the other her anger at the way he took her for granted was still sharp, and she didn`t want him to come into bed, and have him snuggle up, breathing his beery breath all over her. She waited, determined to feign sleep if he came up. Five minutes, ten minutes passed, and it had now grown silent below. She went to the top of the stairs and could see that he had raked up the embers of the fire and put a log on that was now sending out a glimmering light. Hearing the steady rhythm of his breathing, almost a snore, she realised that he had fallen asleep in his armchair. She went back to bed and pulled the blanket up round her chin.

The following morning, she got up at six, dressed, and whilst he was still asleep in his chair, put on her coat and hat and set off to catch the bus back to Middleton.

"What on earth are you doing here at this time on a Sunday morning!"

"He stayed out again, didn`t come home until the middle of the night. Drunk."

"Did you have words? He didn`t hit you, did he?"

"No. He was just drunk. He fell asleep downstairs."

"Sit down and I`ll bring you some tea."

"What`s up?" said her dad, coming down in his vest and braces.

He listened to the tale.

"Well," he said, "you know what you can do, don`t you? You can get back on the next bus home and get back to your husband where you belong."

"Albert!" her mother remonstrated. "Can`t you see she`s upset!"

"I don`t care. She`s no business running back here."

"Don`t listen to him, love."

It was three o`clock in the afternoon when John turned up on the doorstep.

"Is she here?" he said.

"Aye, and what if she is?" said her mother.

"Can I come in and talk to her?"

"And what if she doesn`t want to talk to you?"

"Do I have to come in and take my own wife?"

"Don`t you raise your voice to my wife like that," said her father, stepping up to the door, and now responding to another instinct.

"All right, have it your way, then. She knows where she lives." And with that, he was gone, and her father closed the door and came back in.

"Don`t you worry, love," he said, with a wink – having now changed his position altogether. "He`ll be back."

It was true. He was back with his father in less than an hour.

"He`s got something to say," said James. "Can we come in?"

They sat together on the settee, father and son, with their hats in their hands. "Go on," said James.

"I was in the wrong," John said, meekly. "I`ve come to say I`m sorry and to ask you to come home."

"Sounds fair enough to me," said her father.

"Shut up, Albert," said her mother, and then, turning to James rather than John, "she`s got her condition to think of. She can`t be having all this fret and worry."

"No, you`re right," said James. "Are you listening to this, lad?"

"Happen she`d be better staying here for a few days," her mother went on.

"Right," said James, standing. "Well, we`ve said what we came to say. You`ll let us know when you`re ready."

"I`m ready now," said Evelyn. "I was upset, but I`m all right, now. I want to go home."

"Walk down to the Gardens," said James, when they had their coats on. "Take her home in a cab."

"Dad!"

"We`ll be all right on the bus," said Evelyn.

"You heard me," said James, "take her home in a cab."

It was about two weeks later that Charlie Breen turned up. He knocked at the door at four o`clock on a Tuesday afternoon.

"Mrs Wilkinson?" he asked.

"Yes."

"I thought it must be," he said, tipping his hat. "I`ve been wandering about a bit, to tell you the truth. He gave me directions, your John, I mean, but once I got out of Heywood I was a bit lost."

"You know my husband?"

"Your John, yes, of course I do."

"Is it business?"

"No, no. I`s a social call. Strictly social."

"He`s at work just now. He`ll be back at six."

"I`ll come back later, then, if you`d prefer."

"No, no, it`s all right, if he`s expecting you. Come in, I`ll brew a pot of tea."

"Music to my ears."

His breath was slightly beery, she noticed; he wasn`t drunk, but he`d come from somewhere where he`d been in a pub.

She was uncomfortable and suspicious, but she felt she ought to show hospitality to someone who her husband obviously knew in some capacity. She made a pot of tea, and he sat drinking it before the fire, and then fell asleep.

She was making a soup with vegetables and barley and a stock she`d made from some chicken bones left over from the weekend.

"Smells delicious," he said, waking up.

John came in, a little later.

"Charlie!" he said. "If you`re not off..."

"I`ll saw your leg off..." Charlie retorted, as if in some familiar recitative.

"This is Charlie," said John, by way of introduction. "We can stretch to a bowl of soup for him, can`t we?"

"Wouldn`t dream of taking advantage. I was passing by, just popped in to say hello. No, I`ll get off."

"Sit where you are," said John.

"Well, only if you insist."

"We do, don`t we, Evie, love?"

Later, they walked up to the Hare and Hounds, and she was glad to have them out of the house. She hoped that when John came back, Charlie would have gone, on the bus, to wherever he had to go to, but at half past ten, they came back together.

"It`s all right if Charlie stays over for a couple of days, isn`t it?"

She demurred, which he took as a yes.

She was up the following morning to see John off to work.

"Am I to make him any breakfast or anything?"

"I shouldn`t worry about that. He`ll probably sleep till dinner-time."

This proved correct.

"Any chance of a cup of tea?" he called, just after eleven o`clock.

His face appeared at the top of the landing, with a broad grin.

"I thought I`d have a lie-in," he said. "Didn`t want to be under your feet. Well, I know what a lot you have to do. Don`t let me stop you, by the way, just pretend I`m not here."

She continued with her work and left him sitting by the fire with his cup of tea.

"Is there anything I can do to help, any shopping you need?" he asked, later.

"No, I`m all right, really."

"Right, well, I`ll just have a bit of a walk out, then."

She suspected that having a walk meant going to the pub, but she didn`t mind; she was just glad to have the house back to herself.

"Who is he?" she asked John, later, when they had a moment together.

"Charlie? He`s just a likeable good-for-nothing, really, I suppose you could say."

"Doesn`t he have a job or anything?"

John laughed. "I doubt he`s ever done a proper day`s work in his life."

"How does he live?"

"His grandfather had a mill in Chadderton, there was some money in the family at one time, but I think Charlie`s father got through most of that, and like father like son. Anyway, he has an aunt, lives up on Alkrington somewhere, mad as a hatter, who subs him depending on what mood she`s in."

"So why has he come up to see us?"

"I bumped into him last time I was over in Middleton, knew him from the old days, you know; anyway, he`s on his uppers a bit at the moment, and I said he could stop here a couple of days."

"You didn`t say anything."

"No, well, I was already in the dog-house enough, if you remember; to be honest, I never thought he`d take me up on it."

"You`ll have to say something."

"There`s no harm in him."

"That`s not the point."

He stayed nearly a week. As John said, there was no harm in him, and sometimes he made her laugh with his quips and jokes, but even so, she didn`t like being alone in the house with him.

"I know this is asking a lot," he said, one morning, "and say no if it`s not in order, but do you think I could have a hot tub?"

The tub was kept on a hook, in the outhouse. She brought it into the kitchen, and stoked up the fire, setting it on to draw.

"The water`ll be hot now," she said. "There`s a jug to fill it with, and some soap, and a towel. I`ll have a walk to the shops."

"Unless you fancy giving my back a scrub," he joked.

"No, I don`t. You can scrub your own."

When she got back, he was finished, and he`d cleared up after himself. He`d had a shave and was combing his hair with some hair-oil, trying to make himself smart with a collar and tie, and a clean shirt he`d found somewhere in his bag.

"Right," he said, "I`ll get off then."

"Are you going somewhere?"

"I`m going to meet a couple of pals in Salford."

"Right."

After he had gone, she found that a ten shilling note had disappeared from her purse. She hoped it meant that he was gone for good. She decided not to tell John about the missing money.

"Where did he say?"

"Salford."

John laughed. "He means the races."

"What?"

"The Manchester Race Course, it`s in Salford."

"Oh, I see."

It was eight o`clock when he came back, a little bit tipsy, and insisted on taking John to the pub.

"He`s flush," said John, when they were in bed. "Backed a couple of winners."

"I want you to tell him to go."

"All right."

"No, I mean it this time, John. Tell him."

"All right, I said I would!"

The next day, though, before either of them was up, Charlie had gone. His bag was gone, and all his things. When John had gone to work, she stripped the bed in the spare room where he had been sleeping. Under the pillow was a note. It said, `thanks for putting up with me.` Next to it was a ten shilling note, and next to that, folded over, two one pound notes.

"Seems quiet without him, doesn`t it?" said John.

"You mean you`ve lost your drinking pal, and your excuse for going out every night!"

"Not me. I`m happy to stay in, just like this."

She`d bought three lamb chops, two for him and one for herself, with one of the pound notes Charlie had left. And as usual, when she had a bit extra, she`d bought him a couple of bottles of ale.

"Never mind staying in," she said, "you can take me to the pictures tomorrow night. We`ve not been for ages."

"All right, then."

They caught the bus over to Rochdale. The Odeon was showing `Wuthering Heights` with Lawrence Olivier and Merle Oberon, and on the way back, still feeling caught up in the aura of the film, she leaned against him, and he put his arm round her shoulder.

"That was grand," she said. "If we lived out over Knowle Moor, we`d be just like that. Cathy and Heathcliff."

"It`s only a film," he said, laughing.

But she didn`t listen. It didn`t matter that it wasn`t real.

Chapter 10

The plan was that she would go to stay at home in good time for the birth, but as it turned out, events took over. She had just lit the fire one morning, and was out in the yard filling the coal bucket, when her waters broke. She went into the house and sat down. It was ten days to her expected date but there was no doubt what was happening. When she began to feel distinct contractions, she decided she had to do something. There was no reply when she knocked at the house next door, but the old woman next to that was in, and she knew straight away what was happening. She sent her husband to find the mid-wife, and then came to the house to sit with her.

"You`ll be all right, lovie," she said. "I was twelve hours with my first. Mother nature knows what`s best."

After twenty minutes, the old man returned, saying the mid-wife was out on a call but would come as soon as she could. His wife then sent him down to Simpson Clough to tell John, and bring him home.

It was not long before the mid-wife arrived, on her bicycle, and the first thing she did was to brew a pot of tea.

"Now, then," she said, "that`s better. When did you start?"

Evelyn told her.

"And the contractions?"

"About every two or three minutes."

The mid-wife nodded, thoughtfully, and took another mouthful of tea.

"Will I have to go to the hospital?"

"I don`t think so," said the mid-wife. "Not unless you want to, love. There`s nothing they can do there we can`t do here, and we can keep the kettle going here, can`t we?"

It was about twenty minutes later that John came in, sweating and anxious, and out of breath.

"I ran all the way," he said.

"It shows!" said the mid-wife. "And there was no need."

"Is there anything I can do?"

"Yes, you can go back to work. There`ll be nothing happening here for a few hours yet."

John looked towards Evelyn, and she rolled her eyes mirthfully. The mid-wife was proving to be something of a character but her robust confidence was catching.

"Right," said John.

He came back again during his dinner-break, by which time the mid-wife had settled Evelyn into bed and was on her third cup of tea. He went upstairs.

"How is it?"

"All right," she said, though almost immediately a sharp contraction came, and she screwed up her face. "Don`t worry," she said, seeing the sudden look of alarm on his face. "Do you have to go back?"

"No, they said it was all right."

"Go and tell my mother, then. The mid-wife`s going to stay to see me through, but I`ll need someone after that."

"Right," he said. "I`ll get off right away, then."

As he left the room, another contraction came and she stifled a moan. The mid-wife`s footsteps were heard on the stair.

By the time John came back, Evelyn was sitting up in bed, with two pillows behind her head, nursing a baby girl. The midwife made a pot of tea for them all, and then said that she would get off home.

"You`ll not need me anymore just now, but I`ll call tomorrow morning to see how the baby`s feeding."

"Thank you."

"Good girl. You`ve done well. She`ll need sleep now," she said, turning to her mother, woman to woman.

The mid-wife had emptied a drawer to make up a little cot for the baby. Her mother made a fire in bedroom and took up residence in an armchair in the corner.

"What are you going to call her?"

"We haven`t talked about it yet."

"You must have some idea, though."

"I`d like to call her Merle."

"Merle. Where did you get that one from?"

James and Alice came over to see their first grandchild two days later. There was some `clucking` as John called it, between the two mothers, as if their maternal instincts prompted them to rivalry, and the child was fretful, though when James held her, she settled down.

"My word," said James, "you`re a bonnie one, aren`t you? You`re a bonny one, all right."

Her father came out the next day, and took John out for a drink.

"Are you all right, love?" he said. "Is there ought you want me to do?"

"Take my mam home, will you, dad? It`s been grand having her here, but I need to start doing for myself now."

In truth, she just wanted to be alone with John, to have him back in the bed again, to be normal. And she felt strong and well, well enough to cope on her own.

"I`ll do my best, love, but it`ll be a tall order."

It was too tall an order. Her mother stayed on another week, and in a way, as she admitted, it was for the best.

"Thank God we`ve got the house back to ourselves," said John, the night after she had gone. Her mother had left some liver and bacon, but John went out to bring fish and chips.

"That`s more like it!"

"Let`s go over to Middleton, next Sunday, shall we, and show her off to Joan and Nancy?"

"Aunty Joan and Aunty Nancy! I can`t wait. They`ll be as pleased as Punch!"

Chapter 11

September had begun, but the weather was so fine that it might still be high summer. Merle, seven weeks old, was lying on a soft rug, waggling her legs and arms in the air. Evelyn was sitting on her haunches, leaning over the baby. John was lying back, with the brim of his hat over his eyes, smoking a cigarette.

"Can you imagine anything better than this?"

"No," said Evelyn, simultaneously giggling at a funny look passing over the baby`s face.

They were in Carr Woods, a little further on from the tea-rooms, sitting on a patch of grass by the River Naden.

"What are you laughing at?" he asked.

"Nothing. I think she`s got a bit of wind. She has such a funny surprised look on her face sometimes."

He stubbed out his cigarette in the grass, and sat up to look.

"There," said Evelyn, giggling again. "Did you see?"

"That`s not wind. She`s smiling. She`s watching the birds, aren`t you?"

Recognising the deep tones of her father, the child waggled her legs a little more vehemently. They both laughed.

Evelyn leaned back and looked up at the trees, which made a wall of thick green luxuriance on each side of the little valley. Then she closed her eyes and listened to the rippling and gurgling and murmuring of the brook.

It was, as John said, beautiful. And so peaceful.

The child fell asleep and Evelyn put her back into the pram, to keep her out of the sun.

John lit another cigarette. "If there is a war," he said, "I`ll go in the navy. Safer there. You should hear the tales they tell of what the soldiers had to put up with in the trenches..."

"I`d rather you didn`t go at all."

"They say there`ll be conscription. There may be no choice."

"Maybe it won`t come to it."

"No, maybe not."

"They`ll sort something out."

She pulled the hood up over the pram, and rocked it gently. John went to stand by the brook.

"What are you doing?"

"Going across. Stepping stones."

"You`ll fall," she said, watching him balancing with his arms like a tight-rope walker.

"No, I won`t," he said, and at that precise moment he slipped. Both feet, and one trouser leg up to the knee, were completely soaked.

They both laughed again.

"Come on," she said. "I`d better get both of my children home."

That night, she baked potatoes on the fire, and she mashed some of it with milk and butter for the baby. They had some bread and cheese, and some onions which she had boiled and then left to stand in vinegar, together with two slices of tongue left from the previous evening.

"That was a meal fit for a king," he said.

"There`s a bottle of beer in the outhouse, if you want one," she said, "I put it out there to keep cool."

"It`s been a perfect day," he said.

Merle had to be fed again at ten o`clock. But as if she, too, was happy with the day, she went straight off to sleep again.

In bed, they lay quietly for a time, and then reached for each other, and made love.

A perfect day.

On the radio the next day, Sunday 3rd September, they listened to Mr Chamberlain, making the announcement that, no satisfactory reply having been received from Mr Hitler, the country had been, from eleven o`clock, in a state of war with Germany.

Chapter 12

They had excavated the ground at Market Place to make an Air Raid Shelter, and moved the market down onto the spare ground between Fountain Street and Oldham Road. Along Mellalieu Street, on the playing fields of the Grammar School, two mounds had appeared, covered in turf, which were designated as shelters for the pupils during the day, and the local residents at night.

Leaflets were circulated to all the houses in Middleton, explaining the importance of the black-out, and showing how it could be achieved in each individual household using ordinary materials.

Gas masks were distributed to all families, with special versions for infants and babies, and in the schools children had regular drills in gas-mask use. Every morning, at an appointed time, the town was haunted with the wailing of the air-raid siren, and then after a short period of time came the all clear. They were expecting Manchester to be bombed, especially the docks and Trafford Park, but nobody could be too careful.

John had presented himself at the Royal Navy recruiting office in Dover Street, by the Royal Infirmary in Manchester, in January 1940. He passed the medical exam, and three weeks later his papers arrived with instructions to report to HMS Eaglet in Liverpool. His initial training period was three weeks and after that time he was given weekend leave.

They had moved back to Middleton before Christmas, and were living once again with Evelyn`s parents on Wood Street. Neither of them was looking forward to this but they agreed it was best, and though Evelyn missed their special newly married life out in Hooley bridge, it was nice to be back at home over Christmas, near the family, and near John`s family, and she began to enjoy Maureen`s company, especially after

John had gone for his training. On New Year`s Eve, they went to a dance at the reception rooms of the new public baths on Fountain Street, Evelyn and John, Maureen and Herbert, making a foursome, and they all got tipsy and had a thoroughly good time. Herbert was a year older than John, and he had a good job as an overseer at the Soudan Mill, where his acquaintance with Ernest had first brought him into contact with the Wilkinson family. He was quiet but had a wry sense of humour, and it seemed to Evelyn that were it not for the war, he and John might well have become the best of friends. It had been his intention to volunteer for the army in the New Year, at the same time as John enlisted for the navy, but this intention had to be put on hold when Maureen found she was pregnant.

"Bloody hell," said John, home on his weekend`s leave, "does my mam know?"

"Not yet."

"What`s she going to do?"

"I don`t know. Don`t say anything. Herbert`s said he`s going to sort everything out."

That night, they made love, though with Merle being restless in her cot at the end of the bed, and with Albert`s coughing from along the corridor – his bronchitis has worsened a lot since they had last slept there – it lacked some of the carefreeness of their time at Hooley Bridge.

The next night, John went out to meet some of his old friends at the Commercial, on Oldham Road, and had to pull Eddie out of a fight with a drunken Irishman who said that Hitler would be welcome in his house whenever he came, sooner or later.

"I saw Herbert, too," he said.

"And what? You didn`t say anything, did you?"

"I didn`t, but he did."

"What?"

"He said they`re going to get married. He`s going to see them tomorrow, my mam and dad."

Herbert and Maureen were married at Parkfield Church in April 1940. Because of wartime restrictions, the wedding party was confined to immediate family, and Alice had prepared some sandwiches and cake at the house in Silk Street. John, who had managed to get leave for the weekend, was handsome in his Royal Navy uniform, and Eddie used the occasion to announce that he, too, had signed up for training with the navy.

The newlyweds spent two nights in Blackpool, and then went to stay with Herbert`s mother, a widow, at his family home on Green Street, behind Oldham Road. It was then that Herbert started talking again about registering for the army.

"Do you have to go?" said Maureen cuddling up to him in bed one Sunday morning.

"The worse thing is the waiting. They could call me up at any time, anyway. Might as well seize the nettle."

"It`d be nice if you were here when it`s born."

"We should stop calling it `it`," he said, putting his hand on her tummy.

"What if it`s a boy?" she said, going into a familiar routine.

"Edwin," he said.

"No, not Edwin."

"Simon, then."

"Not Simon, either. I like Stephen. Or Brian. That`s a nice name. Brian."

"It might be a girl, though."

"Joan."

"I`m not in favour of re-using family names."

"Why?"

"Oh, I don`t know, gives people something to live up to."

"Is that bad?"

"I don`t suppose so, but better to have your own name that you can put your own stamp on."

"What do you think, then?"

"If it`s a girl?"

"Yes."

He thought for a moment. "Marcia," he suggested.

"Marcia?"

"Yes."

"Where did you get that from?"

"I don`t know. Just a name in my head. Marcia."

"No. I`m not sure I like that."

"We`ll just have to stick with `it` then."

The following week, two of Herbert`s pals from work decided to cut to the chase and volunteer.

"If it`s what you really want to do?" said Maureen.

"No. I`ll hang on. Like you said, it`d be nice to see my son – or my daughter – before I go."

Ten days later, his call-up papers came through. He was to report to the barracks at Aldershot, at four o`clock the following Wednesday afternoon.

Part 4

Chapter 13

Leaving the Kardomah, they made their way to the bus stop on Cannon Street, where a number 17, a Rochdale blue bus was waiting.

"Let`s go upstairs and have a smoke," said Maureen.

"Go on, then."

A soldier, sitting in front, turned to ask for a light. He grinned and half-winked at Maureen as he struck the match and returned the box, but he turned back and didn`t bother them.

"What will you do, stay with Herbert`s mother?"

"For the time being, whilst I`m still working. Eddie`ll most likely be gone by the time I`m due. I`ll go back to my mam and dad`s then, I think."

They got off the bus in Middleton, and she waited with Maureen until the 59 Derker bus came, and then she walked up Wood Street. The postman had delivered a letter for her. Her mother had propped it up on the sideboard, and she knew from the stationery and the scrawled name and address that it was from John.

"Dear Evie, hope this finds you well..." She scanned the ten lines of the letter. He didn`t say much, but then he never did, it was not his style, and then she supposed they had to watch out over what they said, or the blue pencil marks would start appearing. At least he was well, and the tone of the letter was cheerful. It was as much as could be expected, though inevitably she was disappointed.

"What has he to say?" asked her mother.

"Oh, nothing much. He seems all right, though. Where`s dad?"

"Went for a lie down. He had a bad night."

She looked at her mother`s face. The mouth had the taut set look that betokened something hard that had to be faced up to.

"I`ve mashed up some carrots and gravy for her. She`s been good as gold."

Evelyn took Merle from her cot and started to feed her.

"What did the doctor say?"

Her mother`s mouth tautened a little more. She shook her head. "What he usually says. Lay off the fags. Well, there`s no chance of that, is there?"

"Perhaps he could try tipped."

"Says he can`t taste them."

After tea, she pushed Merle out in her pram, up to Top Wood Street, and then across, by the sand hills and the lodge to Parkfield church. Then she followed the road down through Archer Park and Kemp Street to Silk Street.

"Did he get off all right?" asked Alice.

"Yes. We stopped and had a pot of tea and some tea-cakes at the Kardomah."

"What`s the Kardomah?" asked Nancy.

"Shush," said James, who was trying to pick up the latest news of the war on the radio. Nancy`s face set into fixed and exaggerated sulk.

"Do you want to push her up and down the street?"

"Can I?" The sulk was immediately gone.

"Where`s Joan? Dancing?"

"Rehearsing. They`ve got a do in Oldham, some competition or other. She talks of nothing else."

"Maybe they`ll put her in the pictures."

"Over my dead body," muttered James.

"Any news, dad?"

"They`re talking of asking Mr Churchill to form a coalition! Praise the Lord and pass the ammunition!"

"How`s your dad, Evelyn?"

"No better."

"Oh, dear. He could do with getting to Blackpool. Get some sea air in his lungs."

"Oh, by the way. I heard from John today. Do you want to see?"

"Not if it`s private, love."

"Oh, you know John, he never says anything private!"

"Look at his handwriting, too. Terrible. Not as bad as Eddie, mind you. He doesn`t say where he is, then?"

"Well, they can`t really, can they?"

"I`ll walk up with you," said James, as she made to go.

"I`ll be all right."

"No, I`ve got to meet our Joan off the bus, anyway."

They walked over the Recreation Ground, past the bowling green, and then through the little streets to the junction of Cross Street and Wood Street. It was a pleasant spring evening. Just the time of year when it began to feel comfortable and easy being out as night began to fall.

"I`ll see you soon, then, love. Take care."

"Take care, dad."

When she went into the house, the doctor was there. Her father had taken a turn for the worse.

"If he gets through the night, we`ll see about getting him to the hospital tomorrow. I`ve given him something for the pain. He`ll probably sleep."

"Dad!" cried Evelyn, in sudden shock.

"Evelyn!" said her mother, sharply. "See to the child."

Later, when she went in to see her father, he was still awake and peaceful. His voice was quiet and gentle and there was a kind of light in his eyes which she had never seen before.

She squeezed his hand. "You`ll be all right, dad."

"Aye, maybe I will."

"Do you want anything? Can I get you something to drink?"

"A pint of bitter`d be all right."

"You`ll be having a pint again in no time, dad."

He smiled and closed his eyes and seemed to have drifted into sleep. Her mother came in to sit with him, and after she had checked Merle, Evelyn went to bed.

She lay for a while, listening tensely for any sound from the room where her mother was watching over her father, but a strange peacefulness seemed to have stolen through the house. She meant just to lie there, resting, for a time, and then go to relieve her mother so that she could get some rest, too; after a while, though, she felt her eyes growing heavy, and allowed herself to give way to the subtle temptation of sleep.

She dreamed of being in the cottage at Hooley Bridge. In the dream she had found a doorway on the landing which she hadn`t realised was there before, and going through it she had found another corridor with thick plush carpets, and rooms going off on each side. It had a slightly stale smell, as if the windows hadn`t been opened for some time, but it wasn`t unpleasant. Then, she went back, through the doorway, into the little bedroom and she was lying in bed, with John beside her. He had turned to her, his front against her back, like spoons as they said, and his hand had slipped under her arm, and was fondling her breast. He kissed her neck, and then, feeling all the gladness of wanting to make love, she turned to him. Only when she turned to him, it was not John who was smiling at her, but Charlie.

She woke up suddenly, with a snap, but before she could completely rid herself of the spidery web of the dream, she was aware of other voices in the house.

"Wake up, Evelyn."

"I`m awake. What is it?"

"It`s your dad, love," her mother said, quietly. "He`s gone."

"No!"

"Shush. Don`t wake Merle up. Come through and see him. Mrs Conroy next door`s come in. She`ll make us some tea. Then we`ll have to start getting things sorted."

Chapter 14

Maureen had a scare in the third week of July and they rushed her up to Boundary Park and decided to keep her in until the baby was born. A week of hot weather, lovely at first, but increasingly oppressive, had left the air in the town stale and full of smoke; in the carding room where she worked at the Albany Mill, always humid, the atmosphere was unbearable. It was just before the morning tea-break that she had a bit of a turn, feeling sick and dizzy. They took her to the rest-room, and gave her a cup of strong tea, then the overseer told one of the girls to walk her back to her mother`s. She`d been at home for half an hour, and said to her mother that she was feeling better, but when she got up to go out to the toilet she fainted in the doorway. Joan, home from school for her dinner, was sent to the telephone box on the corner of Kemp Street to call the Emergency Exchange, and twenty minutes later the ambulance bell was heard approaching. Joan was told to run up to Green Street to tell Mrs Jones what had happened, and then to come back and make sure there was something on the table when her father got back from work.

As it turned out, Alice was back herself. The hospital admitted Maureen, put her in a bed, and then told her mother to go home and let her get some rest.

"She seemed all right, but they said they`d keep her in just the same, keep an eye on her."

"Just as well," said James. "Best place for her."

"My teacher fainted at school once," said Nancy, not wanting to be left out.

"That was ages ago," said Joan, setting the record straight.

"It`s the weather," said James. "We need a good downpour and a bit of a breeze. Get the air cleaned up."

"We can go and visit tomorrow, they said."

"Can I come?" said Nancy.

"No, you can stay here. Joan`ll watch over you."

"I`m rehearsing tomorrow, dad."

"Well, you`ll have to tell them you can`t for once."

"I can`t. We`ve got a concert on Saturday."

"You`ll do as you`re told, young miss!"

"I`ll have a word with Evelyn," said Alice. "I`m sure she`ll come and sit with Nancy for an hour."

"Will she bring Merle?"

"I`m sure she will, love."

Maureen`s baby, a girl, was born in Boundary Park, on the 29th August, 1940. It was a difficult birth, but within twenty four hours the doctor told Ernest, who was in the waiting room, that they were well enough to have visitors.

James and Alice were the first, and the next day Alice travelled up to Oldham with Evelyn.

"How`s your mother now, love?" she asked as the bus pulled slowly up through Chadderton.

"Oh, she`s all right. She was coping till after the funeral, then she went to bits."

"We'll, it`s only to be expected."

"I don`t know. Sometimes she hadn`t a good word to say for him."

"Well, that`s wives and husbands, isn`t it? Twenty years, thirty years, day in, day out. It`s not all a bed of roses."

"No, I suppose not."

"If James went, I don`t know how I`d cope. Well, I wouldn`t."

"She likes it when she`s looking after Merle. It gives her something to do."

Maureen was sitting up in bed, bored and restless.

"She`s lovely," said Merle, looking at the baby in the cot by the side of the bed.

"Is she feeding yet, love?" asked Alice.

"Yes, and I hate it. I`m going to get them to make up bottles."

"No, you`ll not, madam! You`ll knuckle down to it!"

"Why. It`s only food, isn`t it?"

"Mother`s milk is nature`s food, and nature knows best."

"If nature knows best, she could have come up with something better than that."

"Don`t talk squit!"

"What do you think, Evelyn? Did you feed Merle?"

"Course she did."

"I had her at home. I had no choice."

"Anyway," said Alice, "first things first. Have you thought of writing to Herbert?"

"No, not yet."

After his initial training, Herbert had been posted to Rangoon, and his letters, like John`s, were concise.

It seems like a quiet spot, but the monsoon is like Manchester weather but twice as wet and twice as hot!

"And what about a name? Have you thought of that, yet?"

"Not really."

"She`s got to have a name."

"Marcia."

"Marcia?"

"That`s what Herbert wanted."

"Marcia," said Alice, as if trying it out for size.

"Marcia Jane, I thought."

"Marcia Jane," said Alice, as if still not sure.

"I think it sounds lovely," said Evelyn. "Hello, Marcia Jane," she said looking down at the child, who, at that moment, as if by some omen, opened her eyes, blue and wide.

All three women, seeing this, laughed.

They kept Maureen in hospital for the usual two weeks, to make sure the baby was feeding properly and putting on weight, and that the mother was fully recovered from the delivery, and then she went back to Silk Street, moving into the bedroom which had previously been John and Eddy`s. By this time, Eddy`s papers for the Royal Navy had come through, and whilst he was waiting to go on his training, he moved into the front room downstairs and slept on the settee.

John had weekend shore leave in September, and on the Saturday they called in at Silk Street and then walked as far as the river below Alkrington Hall. John wouldn`t speak much of his duties, but she understood that it was something to do with protecting the Atlantic convoys against air and submarine attacks. Maureen had written to Herbert telling him of Marcia`s birth, and four weeks later received a short reply saying how sorry he was to be so far away. Like John, he said little about the action, but he did say that there was no prospect of home leave in the foreseeable future.

Though pronounced unfit for active service because of his eye-sight, Ernest had been taken into the RAF in a clerical capacity. He was stationed at RAF Kirkham, a desk job which involved the logistics of food and medical supplies, and he was able to come home on weekend leave once or twice a month.

Evelyn always had a soft spot for Ernest. When Maureen mocked him, Evelyn would counter by saying that Ernest was the kindest and most good-hearted man she had ever known. And it was true. There was something reassuring and benign about the unassuming reliability of his considerateness, his self-deprecating smile, his willingness to help; they were qualities a sister-in-law might appreciate more than a wife, perhaps, because Gladys hardly tried to disguise her impatience with him, her inference being that the effort he spent being pleasant to other people might better be spent trying more assiduously to please her.

During October and November, Joan and her tap-dancing partner, Jackie – The Two J`s, as was their official name – had a number of engagements in the programme of variety entertainment being put on for the troops in theatres in

Oldham, Rochdale and Manchester. They were chaperoned by Miss Lyons, who was the dance school organiser, and they were paid expenses and a small fee for each performance.

When Ernest called at Silk Street on the night of 21st December, Nancy, full of excitement, told him that Joan had gone to dance in Manchester. It was when he was walking home along Oldham Road that Ernest became aware of an irregular booming noise in the distance and of lights flashing across the night sky. At first he thought it must be a thunder storm, and he pulled up his collar and quickened his step, thinking to get home before the downpour started. The booming and the flashing continued as he walked on, and by the time he reached the Hare and Hounds, a crowd of men was gathered, drawn outside by the disturbance.

"It`s that swine Hitler, isn`t it," one man said. "He`s bloody-well bombing Manchester, isn`t he?"

Ernest froze in his steps. Manchester was being bombed and Joan was in Manchester. His knees went weak and he felt that he was going to fall over.

"You all right, pal?" said one of the gathering. "You look like you`ve just seen a ghost."

"No, I`m all right. I just had a bit of a turn."

"Come in and have something for it. A brandy`s what you need pal."

"No," said Ernest. "No, I have to get back home."

He hurried on, back to Elm Street.

"Well, there`s nothing you can do about it, is there?" said Gladys.

"I should go back to my mam`s, see if she`s got back all right."

"And what good will that do? Either she has or she hasn`t, and there`s no difference you going there will make. "

"I`ll not rest."

"Well, you please yourself. I`m going to bed."

Ernest sat in the armchair, as the remaining embers of the day`s fire slipped into dust. Even now there was a dull rumble of noise. It was still going on. He went to the sideboard and, remembering the advice of the man outside the pub, took out the whisky bottle and poured himself a small glass. It burnt in his throat and then began to soothe. Another glass, he thought, and his desire to feel reassured would be appeased. Another glass and then another glass. If Ernest had learned one thing about himself, it was that if he allowed it, he had an endless capacity to indulge in the comforts of drink.

He resisted the second glass. Instead, he put on his coat and hat, and began to walk back to Silk Street.

James and Alice were still up. Joan was not there. James had walked up to the bus stops in Middleton Gardens, but had been told there were no more buses coming out of Manchester tonight. The reason was obvious.

"What are we to do?"

"Nothing we can do, lad. Wait till morning. Try to get some rest."

"Do you want to stay over, son?"

"No. I`d better walk back. I`ll call in the morning."

Once again, Ernest started off for home, down Kemp Street, then onto the Old Road. He cut across Jackie Booth`s field, crossing the river at the little footbridge, and emerged from Leiter Street, opposite the Commercial at the start of Oldham Road. Then, on a sudden impulse, instead of turning into Oldham Road, he kept on walking up the New Road, towards Manchester.

That there was something fatuous about his intention, something verging on the ridiculous, he was fully aware. He knew the centre of Manchester well enough to know the basic layout of the streets, the location of the railway stations and bus stops – well enough, in other words to find his way around in normal conditions. He knew it well enough also to know that the chances of finding someone at random in the grid work of streets were next to zero. He didn`t even know where the theatre or hall where Joan was performing was, or what its name was. But the compulsion, as if to take himself right into the eye of the storm, was paramount. To be doing something, however quixotic, rather than to be going home, to be lying in the sterile atmosphere of the bedroom, sleepless, was infinitely preferable.

He passed Victoria Avenue, and a little way beyond, where the road began to slope down towards Blackley, the skyline of Manchester, four miles distant, was alight with fire. Searchlights were still scanning the sky, through thick veils of smoke, though to judge from the relative calm, the German aeroplanes had returned, and the air-raid itself was over.

He walked on. Down into Blackley, then up the hill to Harpurhey, past Queen`s Road, through Collyhurst, and then into Ancoats and the outskirts of the city proper. At the top of Shude Hill, he stopped in his tracks at the sight of a building which had been caught by a bomb. People were clambering about amidst the smoke and the rubble, calling names, and on the pavement a young woman was weeping hysterically, in the arms of an old man who both comforted her and restrained her.

Ernest waited for the shock to pass, and for the strength to come back into his legs, and then walked on again, towards Piccadilly, and it was here that the true awesome scale of the destruction was evident. Flames, sixty feet high, were surging from the shells of five storey buildings, illuminating their windows and making them seem like demonic palaces of fire. Fire engines and police wagons and ambulances were driving around in a chaos of effort, bells clanking, wheels bumping over piles of broken masonry in the road. On the corner of Market Street, three firemen, on ladders thirty feet above the road, were playing hoses of water endlessly into the fire of a building which he remembered as having housed the café where he had once met Gladys in their courting days. Someone close to him in uniform was saying that a gas-main had been ruptured on the Tibb Street side, and that the whole area needed to be evacuated. Another man, a police sergeant, put his hand on his shoulder and advised him to move on.

He crossed to Portland Street, intending to go as far as Oxford Street, where there were several theatres he vaguely knew of. Fifty yards further on, the way was blocked where a shell had fallen directly on the road and people were being diverted down to Whitworth Street. On the corner of Whitworth Street and Oxford Street, the Palace Theatre was a shell, but it was dark and there were no flames, and he remembered reading in the paper that the Palace had been struck in one of the first raids back in the autumn. St Peter`s Square was a miniature version of Piccadilly, though there were fewer fire engines. People were out on the streets everywhere, all caught up in the same chaos, figures in a vision of hell. Ernest worked his way as far as Central Station, and then, because the road was closed again, found his way by the back streets onto Deansgate and then to Exchange Square, which was another cauldron of burning buildings.

Where on earth, he said to himself, could Joan be in all of this?

On Cannon Street, where the empty and abandoned buses were lined up, he sat on a bench, and pulled his coat around him. It was nearly four o`clock. Above him, the air was close and orange tinged in the darkness. He tried to think of a course of action, but even though he was shivering, he felt his eyelids growing heavy, and it was somehow easier to give way to that than to think. When he opened his eyes again, the air had grown thinner with the dawn light, and the smoke was acrid in his nostrils. He had stopped shivering. He let go again.

It was the throb of a motor engine which next woke him, and when he opened his eyes it was to see a bus pulling out of the bus station. Life was beginning to get going again. He stood up, stiffly, and stamped his feet to try to get some warmth back into them. Soon the bus stop area was filling up with people, mostly tired and disgruntled, having spent the night in shelters, and now impatient that the bus service was so slow to get going. The crowd was so big that when a driver and conductor turned up to man a bus, there was struggling and squabbling over who should be allowed to get on it. Deciding not to get involved in the fray, Ernest began to walk. There was nothing for it now but to get back, and just hope that Joan, like all these people, had managed to find her way to a shelter.

He turned into Hanging Gardens, then into Withy Grove and back onto Shude Hill. Here, the building he had seen in flames four hours earlier, was a blackened smoking ruin, now deserted. He passed Oldham Street. By the Goods Depot, he stopped as an engine shunted slowly over the track crossing the main Rochdale Road, and as he did so, a bus which had turned out of Oldham Street from Piccadilly stopped beside him, and taking his chance he grabbed the rail and jumped up onto the conductor`s platform.

"All right, pal," said the conductor, "shouldn`t let you really, but after a night like last night, bloody hell, I should have been home myself before midnight."

"Thanks," said Ernest.

The lower deck was full, and overfull with people standing. Ernest held onto the rail at the bottom of the stairs. The conductor continued to talk, glad to have found someone to chatter away to. His mind almost numb now with tiredness, Ernest paid only sufficient attention as not to be rude, nodding and muttering agreement. Images played across his inner thoughts, pictures of the night which had passed, the conflagration in Manchester, and at the same time he was vaguely thinking what he would do when he got back into Middleton, when he became aware of youthful laughter breaking the dull taciturnity of the bus. He could not see through the crowd, but he recognised immediately, or as soon as his credulity would allow it, that the laughter, light-hearted, girlish, and beautifully frivolous, was Joan`s laughter.

She was on the same bus as him, going home.

"You all right, pal?" said the conductor.

"Yes," Ernest muttered. "Yes."

"Looked as if you`d had a funny turn or something."

"No, I`m fine," said Ernest, his relief tempered now by a full realisation of the utter stupidity of his own night`s escapade.

The laughter came again, and peering through the standing passengers, swaying with the motion of the bus, he saw, momentarily, the back of Joan`s head, her beret, her scarf. No doubt about it.

At Queens Road, two men came down the stairs and left the bus.

"You`ll be all right up there now if you like pal, get a seat, have a smoke."

"Thanks."

He sat back in the seat, closed his eyes, and then, finding a packet of Capstan in his pocket, took one out and lighting it, took a deep drag down into his lungs.

Everything was all right.

He made his mind up that neither Joan – nor anyone else for that matter – would ever know that, in his desperation, he had walked into Manchester to look for her.

"Where have you been?" said Gladys, when he got back.

"I was bothered," he said. "Just slept in the chair downstairs, then walked down to my mam`s early on."

"And is she back?"

"Yes."

“I told you as much. You`re too soft Ernest. You`re like a creature with no shell.”

“You`re right. I`ll be harder from now on.”

“Some hope of that!”

Chapter 15

"Gladys is lucky," said Evelyn to Maureen one day. It was the beginning of December, 1942, and any hopes that the war might be a short term affair had receded.

"How do you mean, lucky?"

They were in the front sitting room at Silk Street. Merle, now three, was sitting quietly in the armchair, a rag-doll clasped against her shoulder, her eyes growing heavy with sleep. Marcia was sitting against a cushion in the corner of the settee, wide awake.

"Well, I mean that she has her husband here, at home, she sees him, every week or so."

"Don`t know if she`d see it that way," said Maureen, with a bubble of laughter.

"Don`t be cruel," said Evelyn. "She doesn`t realise how lucky she is."

"Do you know what I think?"

"Go on."

"I think Gladys would like Ernest to go away so that she could have a bit of a war-time fling."

"Or two."

"Or three."

They both laughed.

"Do you really think so, though?" said Evelyn, more seriously.

"She`s more or less said so to me."

"True?"

"True."

They sat in silence for a moment. Over the two years since they had been to see Herbert off at London Road Station, the two of them, Evelyn and Maureen, young mothers, wives whose husbands were away at war, had grown closer as friends, and their conversations included things which neither of them would talk to their mothers about.

"Would you ever do that?"

"No. But there are people who do, you know," said Maureen.

"I wouldn`t ever do that."

"Nor would I."

"You do miss it, though, don`t you?"

"Do you?"

"Don`t you?"

"Yes," Evelyn conceded.

"I never used to think about it at all, getting married was just about, well, you know, getting married, but Bert was keen."

"So was John."

"And once you`re used to it, well, you miss it, don`t you?"

"Yes," said Evelyn, quietly.

Maureen was right. It was something you missed. You missed it a lot.

They sat in silence for a moment, and then, catching one another`s eye, they both giggled. Marcia giggled too, or had the burps. It was the same thing.

"She knows what we`re talking about."

They both laughed. Marcia flailed her arms, and then went silent.

"I know that sign."

Maureen went to change Marcia`s nappy.

"Come on, little one," said Evelyn to Merle. "Time we were going home."

"Can`t I stay here with grandma and Marcia?"

"No, you`ve got a nice warm bed waiting for you at home."

"Will you carry me?"

"I can`t carry you all that way."

"Here," said Alice, as Merle got onto the push-chair, "put this round her legs, it`s a cold night."

"Goodnight, love."

"Goodnight."

It was a crisp clear evening, and in the sky over Cross Street, the stars were beginning to show. In the evenings at Hooley Bridge, she recalled, they sometimes sat out at the back, with their overcoats on, looking up and trying to identify the constellations, Orion, the Great Bear, the Pleiades, though in fact they only knew the names of half a dozen or so. Sometimes John would invent funny names and pretend they were the real Latin names of constellations. He used to say he`d go to the library and get a book out about it, but he had never got round to it.

Her mother had already gone to bed when she got back home. She was good with Merle, but apart from that, since her husband`s death, she seemed to live in some remote corner of herself, as if sleepwalking.

She lifted Merle, already fast asleep, from the push-chair and carried her upstairs to bed. There was a kettle over the hob, so she made some tea, and toasted a piece of bread over the glowing embers.

In bed later, she pictured again the days when they had lived in Hooley Bridge. It seemed so remote now that it might have been in a different life-time, and everything about it now was tinged with nostalgia. The walks along the Roach valley, the trek up through Ashworth Valley to the Egerton Arms, the picnics in Queen`s Park and Carr Woods – all now seemed so perfect, and trouble-free, and happy, but the memories could only be like that, she realised, when you accepted that it was gone, and could never come back again.

The sheets were chilled when she got into bed; she huddled herself up until she had made a small centre of warmth, and then slowly spread out trying to take the warmth with her. It was a big bed, too big for her alone; it was a bed which needed a man in it, a man beside her.

She missed John so much.

It was quite possible, she admitted, to torment herself with other recollections from the year they had spent at Hooley Bridge. She opened her eyes and looked up at the ceiling, thinking, and indulging herself, at first just in thought, then in a little more than just thought.

Later, she felt mildly ashamed. But it wasn`t long before sleep began to close around her, and with the tension gone from her body, she clung to the pillow, and felt vaguely happy.

Chapter 16

It was difficult to know what was really going on in the war. At the cinema, where Maureen and Evelyn sometimes went together, with Alice minding the children, the news reels showed film clips of troops, smiling and smoking, of vehicles advancing, of ships ploughing through the sea with aeroplanes crossing overhead, but with the orchestral music in the background and the high-toned voice of the announcer, full of very British bravado, it somehow made you feel a moral boost without feeling that you had actually discovered anything about what was happening. People cheered. It was a bit like being at a football match.

"Wouldn`t it be odd," said Maureen once, "if you were watching the Pathe News, and you suddenly saw John, or I suddenly saw Bert?"

"I suppose it must happen. Someone somewhere seeing someone they know."

"Must do, I suppose. Don`t know what the chances are, though."

James liked to listen to the radio, and sometimes he read them the newspaper headlines, but he too admitted to being as confused as everyone else about the overall picture and the progress of the war.

The only thing to become clear was that the war was everywhere: North Africa, Italy, Palestine, Russia, as well as France and Germany. When she had first learned that Herbert`s posting was Rangoon, and then Singapore, Maureen was pleased, picturing a lazy outpost of the Empire far away from the German tanks and the German warplanes, but when James told them that the Japanese had attacked Pearl Harbour, and that there was a theatre of war in the Pacific involving China and Burma, it began to take on a more ominous perspective.

"The good thing," said Ernest, "is that we beat off the Luftwaffe in 1940. If we`d lost that one, there would have been an invasion, not a doubt about it."

It didn`t feel likely that there would be an invasion; in fact, it was sometimes almost possible to think that life was just going on in an ordinary way. Most things, from a day to day point of view, were as ordinary as most days tended to be. There were rations, of course, and shortages, but most people had known that before, during the depression, so the deprivations weren`t new or unexpected. Even having your husband or your son away, and not knowing whether he was safe or in danger, dead or alive, wasn`t something you could think about all the time. It was there, like a nagging anxiety, of course, and sometimes it rose to grip at your throat in moments of panic, but you had to get on with things. Everyone said that – just got to get on with things – nothing else for it.

The one thing you couldn`t get away from was how few men there were about, young men that is. There were plenty of older men, of course, but when you saw young men, on the street or on buses, you tended to wonder why they weren`t out there, doing their bit. When she took the bus up to Green Street, with Marcia, to see Bert`s mother, Maureen came back with the tale that the bus had been driven by a woman, and that she had been frightened to death at the thought of putting herself and her baby daughter`s safety into the hands of a woman driver.

"Why shouldn`t a woman drive a bus?" said Evelyn.

"I don`t know. It just doesn`t seem right, somehow."

"I`d like to be a bus driver," said Joan.

"I thought you were going to be a dancer."

"I`m getting sick of dancing," said Joan, who was now thirteen. "I want to have my own life back."

In the Middleton Guardian, there were adverts every week, encouraging women to go to work in the mills and factories, in place of the men who`d gone off to war. Most women had worked as mill girls at some point, and some, like Alice, had had to go back when their men were out of work in the thirties. But most left to get married and have children, and it was generally regarded as a hard case if they had to go back. Now, however, it was being encouraged, almost as a moral duty, like keeping the blackout, or digging for victory.

Maureen and Evelyn went part-time at the Bridge Mill, just behind Jackie Booth`s field; it had been a dye works, but was now more of a machine shed, and the two of them were set on to work on fixed drills, drilling holes in metal cylinders enclosed in a sleeve which already had the pattern of holes drilled into it as a template. No-one would tell them what the cylinders were for – they said it was top-secret, classified information – but they suspected that the foreman was teasing them about this, having them on, a pretext for chatting them up under the cloak of his own self-importance, and they had a good laugh about it, but when people asked them about it, they said that they were involved in important war work.

Alice looked after the two little girls when Evelyn and Maureen did their shift, and when they got back, Marcia ran to her and threw herself into Maureen`s arms. Merle, now more sophisticated, sat in the chair, looking at a picture book, or pretending to be listening to the radio with James. Once, when they got back, she was sitting there with James` newspaper on her knee, moving her eyes regularly from side to side.

"Nancy`s taught me how to read," she announced. "We spent all morning on it."

"I only taught you A, B, C," said Nancy.

Watching Maureen attending to Marcia, Evelyn acknowledged, she was a good mother, a natural. She complained about other aspects of her life, and was impatient, bemoaning the responsibilities of having a child when the man was away, but when she was with Marcia it was as if some natural instinct took over, something very focused and protective and maternal.

Alice had made some soup for their lunch, with a marrow-bone the butcher had kept on one side for her, with rice and lentils, and a few potatoes. Having only a paved yard at the back, there was no room to grow vegetables, other than a few peas and beans on a trellis against the wall, but James sometimes helped Arthur, the old man who lived next door with his allotment, and so some extra provisions came to them that way.

When she got back home, Evelyn found her mother sitting half way up the stairs.

"What`s to do, mum?" she said, trying to disguise her alarm.

"I can`t remember," said her mum. "I started upstairs, and then I must have come over all faint and sat down."

"Come on, I`ll help you to your bed."

"I`m not going to bed at this time of day. I`ve got work to do."

"You can come and sit by the fire, then. I`ll make you a cup of tea."

She went into the kitchen but when she came back, her mother`s eyes were closed and she was fast asleep.

Merle, sitting opposite, looked up to Evelyn with wide questioning eyes.

"It`s all right," Evelyn said, "She`s just having a little sleep. Come into the kitchen with me. We`ll not disturb her."

By the next day her mum was more her usual self, and she reassured her daughter that she was perfectly well, but in future years, when she looked back on her mother`s decline, it was that day, when she found her sitting on the stairs, that always came to mind as the day when it had started.

Chapter 17

In October, when John`s ship was in Liverpool, he was given a day`s shore-leave, and came back for the night.

"You look well," said Evelyn meeting him at the door. His face was ruddy and a little rough as if chastened by the wind.

"Are you my daddy?" said Merle.

He picked her up and twirled her round. "Don`t you remember me?"

"A bit. I remember you used to give me sweeties."

"You`re a sharp one aren`t you!"

"Come on chuck," said her mother, "I`ll take you out for walk. Let your mum and dad have a bit of time together."

"But I want to be together too."

"Come on, get your coat on, missy."

He took her up to the bedroom.

"Bloody hell," said John. "I`ve missed this."

"So have I."

He was passionate and strenuous, but it was over quickly, too quickly for her, but she didn`t mind. She thought that perhaps there`d be time again before he went back.

He fell asleep, and she leaned on her elbow, her hand propping up her cheek, and looked at his sleeping face.

Suddenly, his eyes opened.

"What are you looking at?" he said.

"You. I`m looking at you, John Wilkinson."

He sat up, and put his arm round her neck, pulling her against his shoulder.

"I suppose I`d better go down and see my mam and dad."

"Yes. Do you want me to come with you?"

"No. I`ll just stop by for twenty minutes. Thought I might walk into town and have a couple of pints. Is that all right?"

"Yes, course it is," she said, though she knew it did not sound convincing.

"It`s like a prison, a ship," he said, sitting on the bedside, pulling on his vest, and lighting a cigarette. "You think of the open sea, and riding the waves and all that, but it`s like a sardine can. You live with other men`s sweat and filth. You can`t imagine it."

"It must be bad."

"The thought of having a bit of time, you know, with you, and then having a bit of a walk out, it`s like a pipe dream."

"You go," she said, now hiding her disappointment and sounding cheerful.

"I`ll not be late."

"Where are you, with the convoys?" she said, fastening the front buttons of her blouse, and then re-pinning back her hair.

"With the convoys, yes. Mainly. Can`t really say much more than that. Don`t really know much more than that. Someone said we`ll be going north, into the Baltic, and the Arctic, now that Russia`s isolated. The land of ice and snow."

"God, John, that sounds awful."

"Have to take my long-johns."

"Can I send you anything?"

"How do you mean?"

"Woolly socks, gloves."

"No, it`s all right. We get what we need. How`s our Maureen doing? Can`t imagine her as a mother."

"She`s good."

"With my mam`s help, I bet."

"No, she`s good on her own."

"What about the girls, do they get on?"

"Merle and Marcia?"

"Yeh."

"Oh, they`re great. Best of pals."

"Have to watch them when they get a bit older."

"Well, their dads`ll be back then, won`t they? Assert a bit of discipline. Lay down the law."

"Oh, aye! Has she heard anything from Bert?"

"Not much, really. A couple of notes. He`s out in the east somewhere."

"No chance of getting back then."

"Don`t think so."

He waited until Merle came back, and then took her out to the recreation ground for half an hour, and then walked on to Silk Street.

He was late back in. He`d met a couple of old pals at the Britannia, he said, and they`d made a night of it. And the following morning, he slept in, and then was in a panic about missing his train back to Liverpool.

"When will he be coming back?" said Merle.

"Soon," said Evelyn.

She had never felt so empty or so miserable in her life.

Chapter 18

Dances were held most weekends at the new baths on Fountain Street, the Co-op Hall, and other venues in the town. They were the subject regular correspondence in the Middleton Guardian, and opinion was divided. Some applauded the provision of entertainment in such dark times, the effort to raise the spirits and boost morale; others regarded them as an affront to decency, and to those who had sacrificed their leisure and liberty to fight in foreign fields etc. The editorial took the middle view, arguing that there was nothing wrong with people enjoying themselves, so long as it was done in a proper way, without excess. It was a well-known fact, it was added, that servicemen at home on leave often made up part of the number at such gatherings, and it would be a shame to deprive them of such well-deserved diversion.

A Christmas Dance was to be held at the new baths on the 20th of December, and Maureen was trying, one Sunday afternoon, when they were having tea with Alice and James, to persuade Evelyn that they should go there together.

"I don`t know," said Evelyn. "It wouldn`t seem right somehow."

"Why not? Plenty of girls go and partner each other these days."

"I don`t know," Evelyn repeated. "You lose the habit of enjoying yourself, don`t you?"

"Well, I don`t see why you should."

"I agree with Evelyn," said Gladys, who had joined them with Ernest some time before.

"No-one asked you," said Maureen, under her breath.

"Maureen!" said Alice.

"Well," said Gladys, quite prepared to take Maureen on, "I don`t know what it`s coming to if young married women with children go gadding about while their husbands are away."

"Maureen wasn`t talking about gadding about," said Evelyn, trying to mediate.

"Well, call it what you like. It`s the primrose path, if you ask me."

"Don`t be argumentative, love," said Ernest, uncomfortably.

"I`ll be what I like. I can speak my mind, can`t I?"

"Why don`t you go to the dance with Ernest?" suggested Joan. "Then you can keep an eye on everybody."

Gladys gave Joan a withering look, though she knew better than to make a comment to either of Ernest`s younger sisters. She sipped her tea in silence.

"I could cheerfully swing for that woman," said James, quietly, after they had gone.

"What does that mean, pops?" said Nancy.

"Nothing. Anyway, where has that come from, `pops`?"

"Everyone`s saying it," said Nancy, breezily, as she helped her mother clear the table.

"Right," said Evelyn, putting on Merle`s hat and gloves. "Let`s go home and see your nan."

"I`ll walk a bit of the way with you," said Maureen.

"Say thank you for having us to your gran and granddad, Merle."

"Thanks for having us."

"You`re very welcome," said James, who was always charmed by both of his grand-daughters.

"Goodbye, mum," said Evelyn to Alice. "Goodbye, pops."

Nancy squealed with laughter. James gave a look of mock indignation, and then smiled broadly.

"She`s such a hypocrite," said Maureen, as they walked back.

She helped Evelyn lift Merle`s push-chair up the steps to the recreation ground and they began to walk across.

"Can I have a go on the swings?" said Merle.

"Just one go," said Evelyn. "Two minutes."

“It`s true though,” said Maureen, as Evelyn pushed the swing lightly. “There`s nothing she`d like better than to have Ernest out of the way, and she`s jealous of us, just because we want to have a night out."

"Higher,” instructed Merle.

“If it wasn`t for Ernest, I`d give her a piece of my mind, proper speaking I would.”

“Higher!” Merle insisted.

“Well,” said Evelyn, “we`ll go, if you like.”

“Honestly? Do you mean it?”

“Why not? What harm can it do?”

“I`ll have a word with my mam about minding the kids. She`ll be all right with it.”

“I`ve no idea what I`ll wear.”

“Doesn`t have to be anything special.”

“Right, young lady,” said Evelyn, “home!”

“One more!”

“No, not one more.”

Maureen helped her carry the push-chair up the steps on the far side.

“Right, I`ll see you in the morning then.”

“Back to the grind.”

“Back to the grind.”

Chapter 19

As the winter drew on, the Pathe News showed some newsreel of the war in Russia – tanks and troops beleaguered by snow, and the story was that the Red Army had held up the German advance at Stalingrad. The Russians, who at the beginning of the war had been their enemies and Germany`s allies, were now their friends, it seemed. From his newspaper, James picked out a story of the French sinking their own battleships at Toulon to prevent the German Navy getting its hands on them, and another of the Japanese advancing into the Philippines. There was a vague hope that things would turn around during the coming months but there was still no real sense of the overall shape of the war, no light at the end of the tunnel.

It was now nearly six months since Maureen had had word from Herbert. She had tried to contact his Regimental Headquarters by telephone, but had got no further than an orderly to whom she had been passed by the telephone receptionist. He was kindly and considerate, but he could give no new information other than to say that the nature of the terrain where his Company was made communications difficult, and the best thing was not to worry too much.

There was no further talk of the dance at the baths until two days before it took place, and then it was Alice, who, sensing the dark mood into which Maureen was slipping, suggested that they should go.

"It`ll do you both good to have a night out," she said.

"What about Marcia?"

"I`ll look after her, and Merle. You can tell Evelyn. I know her mother`s not been so good recently."

"Are you sure?"

"Course I`m sure."

"I`ll ask her at work tomorrow, then."

"All right, then," said Evelyn, when Maureen told her the next day. "Why not? Let`s have a bit of fun for once."

Two or three girls from the Bridge Mill besides themselves were going, and they in turn knew others, most of them single, though one or two, like themselves, with husbands away in the forces.

"You look nice, mum," said Merle.

"Course she does," said James. "She always does."

"Come on," said Maureen, "let`s get going."

"I`ll walk you up there," said James.

"No, you`ll not!"

"I`ll walk up and meet you later, then."

"You`ll not do that either!"

"You see if I don`t."

"Stop teasing them!" said Alice. "Now get your coats on, and get off, the pair of you!"

There was a four piece band playing, and thirty or forty people in the room, most of them women. Of the men, perhaps a dozen, half were in uniform, and the others were men in their thirties and forties, some of them with their wives. There were a few Christmas decorations and lanterns with coloured lights placed around the hall, and a small Christmas tree on a pedestal to one side of the band.

"Shall we have a drink?" said Maureen.

"All right. What do you think?"

"I`m going to have a Cinzano."

"What`s that?"

"I don`t know, but I like the sound of it. You can have it with lemonade."

"All right, then, I'll have that too. But a lot of lemonade in mine."

"Right."

They found a table, meeting up with some of the other girls from the Bridge, and a mood of frivolity prevailed. The girls danced with each other, in turn, joking that they made better partners, at least as far as dancing was concerned, than the men.

"Hello, stranger!"

It took Evelyn a moment to realise that the voice was addressing her, and when she turned she found herself looking up at the smiling face of Charlie Breen.

"Hello, Evelyn."

She felt her face colouring, and turned to Maureen. "This is Charlie, a friend of John."

"Hello, Charlie."

"Hello, Maureen. How`s tricks?"

It was obvious that they`d met before, which made Evelyn feel even more awkward.

"Come and have a dance with me Maureen."

"Get on your bike!"

"Suit yourself. Evelyn?"

"Not just now."

He turned to the other girls, and didn`t have to try too long before one of them got up to have a dance with him.

"You want to watch that one," said Maureen.

"I know. John brought him to stay with us once."

"Well, you`ll know what I mean."

"I`ll get us another drink, shall I?" said Evelyn.

After nine o`clock, the band started playing Christmas music, and the mood became jovial and carefree. For half an hour or so, people were prepared to let themselves go a bit.

"Why aren`t you in uniform, Charlie?" called Deirdre, one of the girls from the Bridge. "Not a coward, are you?"

"Work of national importance," said Charlie.

"What`s that then? Looking after the girls."

"Something like that!"

Later, when Maureen and Deidre were getting drinks, and the other girls were dancing, Charlie slipped into the chair beside her.

"Have I done something to annoy you, Evelyn?" he asked.

"You stole ten shillings from my purse."

"But I put it back, and another two pounds. Good return that! Did you tell John?"

"No."

"Good girl. Well, a girl doesn`t have to tell her husband everything, does she? So, are you going to have a dance with me?"

"No."

"What harm can it do?"

She took a sip of her drink and shrugged.

"Come on, before the others get back. Don`t miss your chance."

"You think very highly of yourself, don`t you?

"Please yourself," he said, but he stood, and held out his hand, and she took it.

He wasn`t a great dancer, but he knew the basic steps, and he had a bit of swagger that made him seem better than he was. What Evelyn noticed most however, was the sense of his maleness near her, his breath which had a slight smell of whisky and tobacco smoke, the slightly dark musty smell of his clothes, and it made her feel embarrassed and uncomfortable, as if everyone in the hall was looking at her and thinking bad things of her. The dance had also made her aware that she was a little bit tipsy. She was glad when it was over.

She went back to her seat, where the other girls, also a little tipsy, were laughing and smoking as they finished their drinks.

"You looked as if you were enjoying yourself," said Maureen, archly, leaning over towards her.

"No, I wasn`t."

"Don`t believe you. Wait till I tell Gladys."

"Don`t you dare say a word!"

"Course I won`t. I`m only pulling your leg."

She squeezed Evelyn`s elbow and then put her arm round her and gave her a little hug. "It`s been nice, hasn`t it?"

"Yes," Evelyn agreed, squeezing Maureen`s hand. Across the room, she could see Charlie Breen, now lavishing his attention on another group of women. It was all a bit tawdry, somehow, and she remembered how John had described him as a likeable good-for-nothing, but nevertheless, when she saw him holding his hand out to invite another girl onto the floor, she felt a sudden pang of resentment.

"I`m going to get my coat," she said, a few minutes later. "Time to be off."

"Right," said Maureen. "I`ll just go to the Ladies. I`ll meet you in the foyer."

"Are you off then, Evelyn?"

It was Charlie, who had come over as she put her coat on.

"Yes."

"So soon?"

"Late enough for me."

"I`ll walk you back if you like."

"No, it`s all right. I've got Maureen with me."

"Oh, well, another time maybe."

Outside, it had been snowing. A thick white carpet lay across Fountain Street, stretching towards the Gardens, and fluffy snow-flakes were drifting in a lazy multitude through the air.

"Look at it!" said Maureen. "Should have brought our wellingtons."

"It`s lovely, though, isn`t it?" said Evelyn.

"I suppose you could call it that."

They linked arms and started to walk towards the Gardens.

"I`ll walk up to Cross Street with you," said Maureen.

"No. I'll be all right. You`re better going down by the Old Road."

"All right. I`ll see you in the morning, then."

She watched Maureen go and then began to walk up Wood Street. The few people who were out were walking up a track in the snow made by a car which had passed, rather than on the pavement which was still thick with snow.

"Wait on," she heard, from behind, and turning, she saw Charlie Breen.

"Just thought I`d see you were all right."

"I told you I was all right."

"You told me you were going home with Maureen."

"I didn`t know it had snowed like this."

"All the more reason for me seeing you to the door. Now then, take my arm. I insist."

They got as far as the front door, and then he said goodnight, tipped his hat, and turned to go. He didn`t, as she thought he might, try anything on. She was glad.

The house was in silence, and the fire had died down, but when she got into bed she found her mother had put two hot water bottles in earlier. They were luke-warm now, but they had taken the chill off the bed.

"Thanks mum," she whispered, pulling the blankets up round her chin. The tipsiness she had felt earlier had gone now, but in the warmth of the bed, she felt a nice glow, and slipped into a pleasant reverie about the evening.

She drifted slowly towards sleep, and then, half awake and half asleep, it seemed, she thought she was back in the house at Hooley Bridge. The door was there again, and again she went through it into the lush carpeted room beyond, where the funny musty smell was now mixed with the smell of whisky and tobacco. The carpet was white and deep piled like snow, and there were other rooms from which she could hear laughter, though she could find no doors into them, and the further she went on the deeper and colder the snow carpet became...

She woke up with a start and stared into the darkness. For a moment the images were so vivid and sharp that she fully expected, as her eyes adjusted, to find herself in the bedroom at Hooley Bridge. Then, the apparatus of the dream receded, and she remembered, with pure relief, where she actually was.

Chapter 20

The next day it snowed again, and when Evelyn arrived at Silk Street all the local children were out throwing snowballs. Marcia was in Joan`s arms at the gate, laughing at the goings on, and Merle, red-cheeked and excited was in the thick of it, throwing handfuls of snow, and dodging in and out of the alley next to the house.

Alice was in the kitchen baking a cheese and onion pie. Like most housewives, she had kept back a little of the ration each week to have something extra to put on at Christmas. James had cleared the yard of snow, and was out there now, chopping wood for the fire. Maureen was still in bed.

"Must have been a good do!" said Alice.

"Yes. Well, a bit of a change, anyway."

"There`s a pot of tea on the go if you want to take her one up."

Maureen sat up in bed when Evelyn came into the room.

"Recovered?"

"Yes, I`m all right, now. Had a hangover. Were you all right?"

"Not too bad."

"You must be more used to it than me."

"Less of that!"

Maureen took a sip of the tea.

"Mmm, that`s nectar."

"Life-saver, that`s what my mam calls it when I take her a cup of tea in the morning."

"What did you think of it last night, then?"

"Good. Enjoyed myself."

"So did I. Could do with more like that."

She finished her tea.

"Do you ever have dreams, Evelyn?"

"Not really," she replied, a little awkwardly. "Well, I suppose I do, but I never remember them."

"I`m the same usually, but I had a dream about Bert last night, well, this morning I suppose it was."

"And you remember it?"

"Yes. I dreamed that we were at the dance, and Herbert came in, in his uniform and everything, and we had a dance and then he said, don`t wait for me any longer, I`ll not be coming back again, and I told him to stop being daft, but when I turned back to him, he`d gone. What do you make of that?"

"You know what dreams are like."

"When I woke up my head was so full of sadness I could have slit my wrists, honestly. Like a great weight, it was. Then, when I woke up again, it was gone."

"There you are, then."

"I just hope it wasn`t a prophecy. Do you believe in things like that?"

"Course I don`t. I think dreams are just a load of squit."

"Good. So do I. Anyway, what did you think of Charlie Breen?"

"Didn`t think anything of him, really."

"Someone was saying he can get you stuff off the black market."

"Wouldn`t surprise me."

"He`s a bit of a spiv. Mind you, I wouldn`t mind some new stockings. Mine are like a patchwork quilt they`ve been darned that much."

"Mine, too."

"Are you getting up, madam?" came Alice`s voice up the stairs.

"I`m up," shouted Maureen. She puckered her nose and giggled silently.

"I`ll see you later," said Evelyn, moving to the door.

At the bottom of the stairs, Nancy was brandishing a letter which the postman had just delivered, rushing through to the kitchen. Evelyn followed her.

"Let`s have a look then, love," said Alice, wiping the flour from her hands with a rag.

The envelope had the distinctive trim of the Royal Navy.

"It`s from John," said Alice, half calling it out to James in the yard as she opened the letter.

"Hope this finds you all well," said Alice, deciphering John`s scribble. It went on for four or five lines, mainly Christmas wishes, and a reference to having crossed paths with Eddie in Belfast. Other place references were blocked out with the blue censor`s pencil, though when she looked at it later, Joan thought she could make out the word Murmansk.

"Happen there`ll be one for you, love, when you get back home," said James, detecting the look on Evelyn`s face.

"Yes," said Evelyn. "And talking of that, come on, young lady, it`s time we were getting back."

"Won`t you stay for a bite to eat?" said Alice.

"No, I`ll get back. My mum`ll have something on."

"Right."

"And thanks, you know, for looking after her."

"Oh, that`s all right, love. She was no trouble at all, were you pet?"

"No," said Merle, smiling coyly.

The snow was thick on Kemp Street and Cross Street, so they left the push-chair, and Merle had to plod along, lifting her little legs up above the snow.

There was no post when she got home.

"You know what it`s like when the weather`s bad," said her mother. "He`s probably not even got as far as Wood Street yet."

Half an hour later, however, the postman`s bike passed the window, going in the opposite direction.

"There`s a war on," said her mother. "I expect some letters get stuck for weeks before they find their way back."

"Yes, I know. It`s just, you know, seeing his writing like that, it made it seem that he was so close."

"Come on, love, don`t let Merle see you upset."

"No, I`m all right, now. It`s like you said. I`m sure there`ll be something soon."

Christmas came and went, however, without there being any word from him. She concealed her disappointment, reasoning it this way and that. In all the chaos, it wouldn`t be any surprise if private mail went missing, it probably happened all the time. And as he`d said himself, you couldn`t really say much in a letter, not anything special, anyway. At least she knew he was alive, which was a better situation than Maureen was in. If Maureen`s mother-in-law had had a note to say Herbert was alive and well, Maureen would probably be jumping for joy.

Chapter 21

In the news, they were saying that a German plane had been shot down by the anti-aircraft guns in Heaton Park. In Parkfield, everybody was saying that they`d heard a roar over the rooftops so loud that they were scared out of their wits. Those out on the streets said that it was a German plane flying low. They could see the swastikas, some people said. One youngster, standing at the corner of Cross Street and Kemp Street, eager to have the best tale, said that he had seen the pilot`s face as he flew over, and that he was grinning.

The popular version was that the German pilot, flying low to show off and put the fear of God in people, had met his match with the sharp shooting of the Heaton Park gunners. It was the war in a nutshell: German arrogance overcome by dogged British resistance.

James` opinion was different. The Germans weren`t fools; if the plane was flying that low, he said, it must have been in trouble already, engine failure or some other damage; he even ventured the opinion that the plane had probably just crashed into the hillside rather than being shot down by the Heaton Park men. But there was no way of proving that.

"How`s your mother?" Alice asked Evelyn, one Sunday when James and Ernest were debating the German aeroplane.

"She`s been getting out of breath. Says she can hardly walk up Wood Street without stopping two or three times."

"Has she seen the doctor?"

"No, she won`t. She says he just asks her the same questions and gives her the same pills."

"My mother was always a great believer in rhubarb."

"Rhubarb?"

"For purifying the blood. And keeping the lungs clear. I don`t know if there`s any truth in it, but she swore by rhubarb."

"I`ll tell her."

"Does she inhale at all?"

"Inhale?"

"Salts."

"I don`t think so."

"I`ll give you some crystals to take home. Put them in a bowl of hot water, then put a towel over your head, and breathe them in for ten minutes. Does you a power of good. Well, it does me."

"Well, anything`s worth a try, I suppose."

It was just after the doctor had called, two days later, that Joan arrived suddenly at the house on Wood Street.

"Three days of bed-rest!" her mother was saying, repeating the doctor`s prescription. "I can`t rest in bed for three days!"

Then came the knock on the door. It was Joan, and she had Marcia with her.

"My mam says will you look after her for a bit."

"Why what`s happened, love?"

"She didn`t want her to see our Maureen upset."

Evelyn saw the strained look on Joan`s face, and felt the blood draining from her own.

"What is it?"

Joan`s face quivered, and then crumpled into tears. "There`s been a letter..."

The letter, when Evelyn got to the bottom of it, was from Herbert`s regiment, and it said that he was missing in action. There was no further information than that. Over the coming days and weeks they all pondered that phrase, turning it over in their own minds, and bringing it up for family scrutiny.

Missing in action.

"He`s dead," said Maureen, at first.

"No," they said. "Missing in action, is missing, not accounted for. If they knew he was dead there would be a telegram."

Ernest was the one who sought most to put Maureen at her ease.

“It`s a vast area,” he said. “It`s all jungle and mountains, we can hardly picture what it`s like.”

“I don`t know how you know all this,” said Gladys.

“Shut up,” said Ernest, being sharper with her than any of them had known before.

“Ernest!” said Alice, who never liked sharp words.

James sat quietly in his own chair, pondering things in his own way.

Ernest went on. “There are no railway lines to speak of, no air reconnaissance, it`s like a thousand miles of no-man`s-land. It`s no tea party, I`ll admit, but if a man goes missing there, I`d say his chances of being found again are as good as anywhere.”

Maureen, sitting beside Ernest, and sobbing quietly into her handkerchief, leaned her head against his shoulder.

Alice, with feelings she couldn`t express went into the kitchen to make another pot of tea.

Gladys sat, tight-lipped, as if she could say much more, but, with a supreme effort of will, wasn`t going to do so.

James still sat quietly. Evelyn, watching him, knew that he was thinking of his own sons, John and Eddie, out there somewhere, and wondering if the time would come for him to be dealing with what his daughter was dealing with now.

The next day, though, Maureen was in a high cheerful mood. It was as if she`d picked on all the best bits of what people had said to comfort her and was repeating them like a parrot.

“Missing in action,” she said. “It didn`t say *Lost in action* or *Missing presumed dead,* did it? Nothing as definite as that. If there was anything definite, they would have said so, wouldn`t they? He could be lying low, couldn`t he, out of harm`s way, if they got separated from the rest, like Ernest said...”

This, or some similar reformulation, she would repeat, every twenty minutes or so, and those around indulged her and agreed, though they exchanged anxious looks, wondering how long it might be before her mood turned.

The family lived mainly in the back room, the front room being kept for best, for special occasions, though when Evelyn came with Merle, they sometimes used it as a sitting room. Now, Maureen would sometimes sit there alone, or with Marcia in her arms, swaying back and forth as if she was sitting in a rocking chair.

"Do you want me to set a bit of a fire for you, love?" said Alice, popping her head around the door.

"No, I`m all right, mam," said Maureen. "I`ll be through in a minute," though sometimes she would stay there for another hour.

"Let her be," said James, "she has to do it in her own way."

"She worries me to death," said Alice.

"Let`s have a night out," said Evelyn, at Alice`s suggestion.

"No, I don`t feel like it really."

In a way, Evelyn was glad. She wasn`t especially in the mood for having a night out herself. Since the letter to his parents, just before Christmas, there had been no further word from John, though her own cause of anxiety had been much over-shadowed by Maureen`s. Even her own mother said so. "Be thankful you haven`t heard anything bad," she said. "Thank your lucky stars, you haven`t heard what she`s heard."

"But it`s not anything definite," said Evelyn.

Her mother gave her a sideways look, and she knew that it was what they were all thinking, though they did not say so.

Chapter 22

In the middle of April, John turned up, suddenly, on the doorstep. It was ten o`clock at night, and he was already as drunk as a lord. He wanted to see Merle, but she managed to persuade him to come to bed, though he was soon up again and being sick as a dog in the back-yard. Then, when he came back, he was out like a light.

In the morning, though, he was up early, and when she got up he was standing at the door of Merle`s bedroom, watching her.

"Come back to bed," she said.

"I can`t," he said. "I`ve got to get off."

He sat on the side of the bed and pulled on his socks and trousers.

"Why didn`t you write to me?" she asked.

"Do you have any idea of what it`s like where I am?"

She shook her head.

"The things I`ve seen, the things I have to do."

"I`m sure it`s terrible."

"And you think I have time to write bloody love letters?"

"No. I don`t expect that."

"Well, then."

"You wrote to your mum, though."

"I`ve got to get off."

"Can`t you come back in for five minutes. I miss you, John. I miss you so much. Don`t you miss me?"

"Don`t start all that now. I`ve told you, I`ve got to get off."

Five minutes later, he was gone, without the least ceremony or affection. "I`ll call in at home," he said, "then get back."

Half an hour afterwards, two constables from the Middleton police knocked on the door.

"Is your John here, Evelyn?"

"No, why, what`s up?"

"We`ve just had a call put through from Liverpool. He didn`t report back from shore leave yesterday. Are you sure he`s not here, Evelyn?"

"Tell them to come in," her mother called. "We don`t want folk seeing police on the doorstep."

"Come in and have a look."

The constables stepped inside, taking off their helmets. One of them was Roger Barlow, who John had once played football with for the Parkfield AFC.

"Only we`ve got orders to arrest him, and keep him at the station until the Master-at-Arms` men get here. Now, if he`s been here, and if you know where he is, you have to tell us."

"He`s on his way back."

"He was here, then?"

"Yes, but I didn`t know... I mean he didn`t say it wasn`t proper leave."

"He was drunk," said her mother.

"Do you know where he`s gone?"

"He just said he had to get off."

"It`ll be better for him if he makes his own way back."

"I`m sure he will."

"There`ll be a constable on the lookout for him at the railway station."

"He`s gone down to his mother`s house," said her mother.

"Mam!"

"It`s all right, Evelyn. Only somebody might be doing him a favour if they told him to catch bus up to Victoria before we get down there. Meanwhile, if you don`t mind, we`ll take a look upstairs and out the back."

Evelyn threw on her coat and hat, and set off, running, along Cross Street and then down across the Recreation Ground towards Silk Street. At the top of the steps, she saw him at the corner, just about to turn into Kemp Street.

"John!" she called.

He didn`t turn, but she sensed that he had heard her.

"John!" she called again.

This time he stopped, and turned. It was too far to see his eyes, but she was certain that he was looking at her as directly as she was looking at him.

Then, he turned away and hurrying on, disappeared around the corner of Kemp Street.

Evelyn sat down on the top stair of the Recreation Ground steps, and began to cry.

Chapter 23

One Friday night, at half past nine, a neighbour, Ronny Hale, called at 7 Silk Street, and told Alice and James that he thought they should know that Maureen was in the tap room of the Dusty Miller, singing along at the piano, and having drinks bought for her by the regulars.

James put on his hat and coat, and cutting through the backs, began the short walk along the Old Road towards Middleton Gardens. He didn`t like the Dusty, regarding it as a rough town centre pub, but there were men there in the tap room who knew him and respected him, and when he went in the piano player stopped, and the men turned back to their drinks, letting him get on with it without there being a scene.

"Come on, love," he said to Maureen. "Put your coat on."

She came without a fuss.

"What on earth do you think you`re playing at?" he said, when they got outside.

"I was just having a bit of fun. Is that against the law?"

"No, it`s not against the law. But you`re a married woman with a child, and you know what those men were thinking of you, don`t you?"

"I don`t care."

"Well, you should care. It`s your reputation, and your husband`s good name, and mine. That`s what you should care about."

"I`m sorry, dad," she said, capitulating suddenly, and breaking down into uncontrollable sobs. "It`s just that sometimes, I just don`t know what to do with myself. I feel as if I`m going to go mad."

"I know, love, I know," he said.

"Put your arm round me, dad," she said, "I`m feeling a bit dizzy."

"All right, love," he said, doing as she asked. "All right. We`ll get you home."

"Good night, James," said Joe Warburton, the ARP warden for Parkfield, doing his round. "Maureen."

"Good night, Joe. All well?"

"All well."

"I thought she must be with you," Alice said to Evelyn, when she called round the next day.

"No. I went straight home. I thought she had, too."

Maureen was still in bed, the worse for wear.

Evelyn took the two little girls down to the Town Hall fields. She recalled that they`d been here on one of John`s earlier home leaves. Today was a mild spring morning, with a soft wind, and with the sun trying to push through a light grey cloudy sky. On the far side, there was a little blossom on the bushes, and some boys were kicking a football with their coats thrown down as goal posts. She could picture John, playing for the Parkfield A.F.C., with Roger Barlow, the constable who had come to arrest him when he absconded. That was before they were married, even before they were walking out properly, when she used to walk down with a light tread in her steps to catch a glimpse of him.

She let the girls play on the grass for a while, Marcia toddling and falling over, as she tried to follow Merle, who was skipping and pretending to do dance steps that Joan had taught her.

When she got back, she picked a moment to go and talk to Alice in the kitchen.

"Did John say anything, you know, when he was over?"

Alice`s face broke into warm smile.

"He just said he couldn`t stop, not even for a cup of tea, but he said he`d been up to you and seen Merle. It was just nice to see him, though. Maybe it`ll not be too long now."

She turned away to get on with her work at the sink, and Evelyn realised that she knew nothing of him being absent without leave. Nor did she suspect how dismissive and cold he`d been towards her. She also realised, dimly, at that moment, that somewhere beneath the surface, family lines were drawn up. Alice loved her children, and her grandchildren; she only cared for Herbert and herself; she cared for them a lot, because they were her in-laws, but there was a big difference. For the first time since before her marriage, she felt like an outsider.

"What`ve you been up to, then?" she said to Maureen.

Maureen screwed up her eyes, as if in shamed disbelief. "If my dad hadn`t come to fetch me, God knows!"

She laughed.

Then, in exaggerated, throaty, frustrated impatience, "Oh!" she expostulated. "I just sometimes feel I`ll go mad if I don`t do something. Be honest with me Evelyn, don`t you feel like that?"

"Yes, I suppose I do."

There was a long silence."

"At least you`ve seen John," said Maureen, at last.

"He hardly gave me the time of day. He wanted to see Merle, not me."

"Didn`t you...?

Evelyn shook her head, anticipating Maureen`s question. "Wouldn`t even let me get near him. Mind you, he was roaring drunk when he got home."

"Well, I suppose that`s what the war does to people."

"I sometimes feel I don`t know him anymore."

"I think that about Herbert. I sometimes try to picture his face and I can`t. And I try to think of his voice and I can`t remember it. It`s as if he`d never existed at all, as if he was just someone I imagined. If it wasn`t for Marcia, I`d think it was just all in my imagination."

"She`s starting to have a look of him."

"Do you think so?"

"Just a bit. Round the eyes."

"I had a picture of her done. When she was six months. Sent it out to him. I wonder if he ever got it."

"I bet he did. I bet it`s tucked away safely in his wallet."

"Wherever he is. If he`s anywhere."

Evelyn put her hand on Maureen`s.

"I heard a story once," Maureen went on, "about the last war. A man who lost his mind and his memory in all the shelling, and went wandering off, and they found him years later, living in a French village with a wife, and he still couldn`t remember where he came from, or at least so he said. They were going to try him for desertion, and I`m not sure what happened, but I think he got off because the war was so long over. Do you think something like that could have happened to Bert?"

"Bert`d never do that. He`s too fond of home."

"No, but it turns people strange sometimes, doesn`t it. Like you were saying with John. Winnie at work was saying her dad was in France during the last lot, and she said he told her they encouraged the married men to use the brothels so they wouldn`t go off the rails knowing what they were missing."

"I can`t believe that," said Evelyn, though even as she said it, she realised that she could believe it. If Maureen had even let the word `brothel` pass over her lips in Alice or James` hearing, she would, as like as not, have had the sharpest of rebukes, even a righteous slap across the cheek, but in truth there was a whole world of men and war that women could only guess at.

Was it the same in the navy, she wondered, later. When they were in port, did they encourage the men to get it out of their systems by going to the brothels? There was a quaint morality they had all grown up with where such things were unthinkable, except in the world of degenerate men and degraded women, but the war, when you scratched beneath the stiff upper lip of the newsreels, seemed to be opening up a world where clear moral distinctions were blurred and muddy.

Chapter 24

The summer of 1943 brought no further news of Herbert. In North Africa, according to the radio newscasts, the German army was all but defeated, and the Eighth Army had made landings in Sicily, carrying the war into Italy. The Italians had capitulated, the story went, and some of them were now fighting with the Allies. In Russia, too, the Germans had been defeated at Stalingrad and were in retreat. There was constant speculation that the tide had turned and it would only be a matter of time, but the weeks and months dragged by, and the time when things would return to normal seemed as far away as ever.

A letter came from John in September. *Can`t say much but no shore leave for the foreseeable future. That`s just how it is. Maybe the situation will change by the end of the year. Tell Merle I miss her. Take care of yourself and her. John.*

And that was it. No hint of affection. Something had changed him. Maybe it was the war that made men hard and indifferent. Maybe it was just the war.

She walked over to Parkfield. Alice had had a letter in the same post, and it gave Evelyn a perverse satisfaction to know that it was equally concise. Marcia and Merle were playing in the backyard, pretending to be setting up a house, and everyone said that they were more like sisters than cousins. Joan, practising the new skill she had learned from an aunty, was knitting a scarf with intent concentration, and they were saying that whatever she set her mind to, she succeeded in, so determined was she. Later, Nancy stood up to sing `If You Wish Upon a Star` from Pinocchio, getting out of tune on the high notes, though they all tried hard not to spoil it for her by laughing.

Eddie had some shore leave in June and came home for three days. He took Maureen out on the first night, and she had too much to drink and was bad the next day, but Eddie offered to walk out with Evelyn and the girls, to get a bit of fresh air.

It didn`t take much questioning to find out that he knew about John`s run in with the Master-at-Arms.

"It happens all the time," he said, as if sharing common knowledge. "They have a bad time, those boys, up in the Arctic." He whistled and made a noise in his throat, exactly the same as Ernest. "Ice a foot deep on the decks, no kidding, if you touch the metal rails without your gloves on your hand sticks to it, it`s that cold."

"He never says anything."

"Well there`s only so much we can say. I`m probably saying more now than I should. And then, you see some things you just don`t want to talk about. I know that myself."

"It must be terrible."

"They go mad when they get into port, some of those lads." He whistled and made the noise in his throat again, and laughed. "It`s like a proper madhouse in some of those pubs in Liverpool and Belfast, a proper madhouse."

He laughed again and then stalled as if sensing that he might be saying something inappropriate.

"Maureen`s not heard anything more yet," she said, cutting into the silence.

"No. My mam said. Bad do, that."

"What do you think?"

"Who knows. Bad do. Missing in action. Doesn`t happen in the navy that. If you go in the water, you`re either dead already or dead in five minutes. But to be missing five thousand miles away, in the jungle, that`s something different."

"Is that what it is, jungle?"

"That`s what they say. Tropical. Bad with diseases and all that kind of thing. How long` s it been?"

"Six months."

"I`ll tell you what, Evelyn. If I`m being honest, I wouldn`t be holding up too many hopes. That`s the top and bottom of it, as I see it."

"Don`t say that, will you, not to Maureen?"

"Not a word. You can trust me."

"She needs something to hold onto, you know until there`s something definite."

"You can trust me," he repeated. "I`ll not say anything. Quiet as the grave."

They caught each other`s eye, and both laughed.

"Bloody hell," said Eddy. "I didn`t mean it like that."

"When are you back?"

"Tomorrow. I`m going to go up and see Ernest tonight. Take him out for a drink."

"That`s nice. He`ll enjoy that."

"Aye well, anyway, don`t worry, Evelyn. About our John, I mean. It`ll be all right, once this lot is over."

Back at the house, Alice had made some fritters.

"Just the job, mam," said Eddie.

"Joan, go and give Maureen a shake, will you? I don`t know, she`d spend all day in bed, if she could, that one!"

Chapter 25

"I`m going to have your name put on the rent book," said Evelyn`s mother, one morning when they were hanging out the washing.

It was a fine dry morning, with a wind that was rippling the sheets on the line.

"Why?"

"Because if anything happens to me, I want to know you`re right, you and Merle."

They went inside and made a pot of tea.

"Nothing`s going to happen to you, mum."

"Oh, no, I`m going to live forever, I am!"

"What`s brought this on?"

"Nothing`s brought it on. It`s just that I don`t want to go to my grave without knowing that my daughter and my grand-daughter are sure of a roof over their head."

"John`ll look after us."

"John`s not here."

"You can stop this now, mam, I don`t want to hear it."

"Well, you will hear it. The Wilkinsons are the Wilkinsons, and they`re a very good family, and that`s all very well, but I`m not daft, Evelyn, and the last two times he`s been here, John`s not had two good words to say to you."

"How do you know? You don`t know everything."

"He goes out and he gets drunk, Evelyn. And then he runs home to his mam."

"You don`t know everything, mam."

"Well, no, maybe I don`t. I hope I don`t. But all I`m saying is, if your name`s on the rent book, you`re the sitting tenant. Now what`s wrong with that?"

"Nothing, mam."

"Good. That`s settled then."

In September, Merle went to school for the first time. Nancy was still a pupil there, at the little school in Parkfield, in her senior year; Joan had left the year before and now attended a secretarial college in Manchester.

At first Merle didn`t want to go and there were some tantrums.

"I`m not going to school."

"Everyone has to go to school, lovey. You`ll like it when you get there."

"I won`t"

"What if Nancy takes you."

"I want my daddy to take me."

And so it went on, for days, the same dialogue, with variations, petulant childish logic against ineffective adult reason. In the end, overwhelmed by the occasion, she allowed herself to be led quite meekly to the school gate, and as she disappeared through the doorway, like a lamb to the slaughter. It was Evelyn who had to suppress her tears.

"Poor little love," said Maureen at work. "It`ll be Marcia next. I can`t believe it. I just wish her dad could have seen her, you know, he never even saw her when she was little..."

Her lip trembled and Evelyn recognised the onset of one of the sudden troughs of emotion into which Maureen lapsed. The overseer turned a blind eye as Evelyn comforted her. After ten minutes, the worst of it was over.

"Let`s go outside for a fag."

"Is that all right, Billy?"

"Aye, go on. Don`t make habit out of it."

They went over to the little footbridge over the river.

"All right?"

"Yeh, I`m all right now. Silly sod that I am. As if I haven`t had time to get used to it."

"Well, sometimes, it all gets too much, doesn`t it?"

"You know, I used to think my mam and dad had it bad, you know, back in the slump, but that was nothing compared with this. At least then, you knew where people were."

"It`s the uncertainty, the not knowing, isn`t it?"

"We should have another night out, that`s what we should do. Have a good night out. Something to look forward to."

"John and me used to go up to a pub, up Ashworth Valley, on the other side of Heywood."

"That`s the thing, isn`t it, though. John can come back, and Eddie can come back and go out on the spree, and nobody bats an eyelid, But if you`re a woman..."

"Well, it didn`t stop you going to the Dusty!"

"Don`t remind me of that!"

She picked up Merle from Silk Street after work, and took her home.

"How was it lovey?" asked her mother.

"It was nice. Miss Spencer read us a story, and then we made a picture with leaves, and we learned how to press flowers in a book. Then granddad James met me, and grandma made me a special tea because it was my first day at school."

"I`ll pick her up tomorrow," said her mother later.

"There`s no need, mam. It`s easy enough for them. It`s just around the corner."

"They act as if they own that little girl, Evelyn, and you let them do it."

"You know that`s not true, mam," said Evelyn, but she could see the slight setting of her mother`s jaw that always came when she meant business.

But it was true, the Wilkinsons were a dominant force, not in an unkindly way, but dominant nevertheless. And she did let them.

"I`m sorry, mam. I wasn`t thinking. You take her in tomorrow, and meet her and bring her back."

“Grandma says she`s taking me to Southport,” Merle announced, two days later.

“What`s that?”

“On the train. It`s the sea-side there.”

“Yes, I know, love.”

She looked across the room to her mother.

“I haven`t said anything definite,” she said, a little shiftily. “I told you we had to speak to your mum first.”

“We can, though, can`t we, mum?”

“We`ll have to see.”

“I`ll be a good girl.”

“You`ll have to be a very, very good one.”

“I will be.”

Maureen laughed when she told her the next day. “Ask her if she can take Marcia, too!”

They were standing again on the footbridge over the River Irk. The water was a thick grey colour, and there was a slightly acrid smell of dye in the air.

“The thing is,” said Evelyn. “I`m not sure I want to be away from her. Not with everything else. I know it`s daft.”

“It`s not daft, but what harm can come of it? I shouldn`t think Hitler`ll be sending bombers over Southport.”

“No, I suppose you`re right.”

“Come on, we`d better get back in.”

The machines stuttered and chattered on through the afternoon. Two o`clock, three o`clock. The hour between three and four was always the longest. She looked to see Maureen opposite, concentrating on her machine, occasionally looking up for a moment, letting herself indulge in whatever thoughts of the moment came to her. Was she thinking about Herbert, about Marcia? And her own thoughts drifted in and out, thinking of Hooley Bridge, and that short period of her life when everything had seemed sufficient and full of promise.

After four, the clock began to run down, and you started to look forward to going home, to having your tea, a night at home, the simple things, and then the last twenty minutes dawdled along so slow that you thought they would never go.

Chapter 26

It was agreed that Evelyn`s mother would take Merle and Marcia to Southport for a weekend. They were to set out on Friday, catching the train from Victoria at five fifteen.

"We should have a night out, like we said," said Maureen.

"Go on, then," Evelyn agreed. "I`m for it."

"Right. Where to, then?"

"I don`t fancy Middleton. We know everybody."

"Agreed. Let`s have a bus-ride somewhere, then."

"We could go up to Heywood. There`s a Lyons there, we`ll go there and have a bite to eat, or go to the cinema or a pub."

"Like we did at the Kardomah, just the two of us, and then we`ll go and find somewhere and have a drink."

"Suits me."

"Suits me, too."

They caught the bus from Central Gardens at six o`clock: through the town, up Long Street, onto Hollin Lane, up Hebers and then the long run down to Heywood. It was a route Evelyn remembered well, but she didn`t say anything to Maureen about the associations it had.

The menu was limited at the Lyons Café but they had fish cakes and some chips, and a pot of coffee, which, after the chicory and coffee mixture they were used to, was a luxury.

Then they walked up the main street and found a lively enough pub where two women on their own wouldn`t be too obviously noticed.

Maureen had a port and lemon, Evelyn opted for cinzano and lemonade.

"Do you think those two chaps over there are giving us the eye?" said Maureen.

"They`re with someone."

"Maybe they like what they see better over here."

"Maureen!"

"What?"

"You know what."

"Oh, I know. Still, it`s nice to know you can still catch the eye. Shall we have another drink?"

"Go on, then."

It was when Maureen came back from the bar, and was again letting her eye roam through the crowd that she suddenly said, "Oh, God, it`s Ernest."

"Where?"

"Over there in the corner, talking to the chap in RAF uniform."

"That`s not RAF. That`s Canadian."

"He looks a bit of all right, actually."

"Let`s drink up and slip out before he sees us."

Before they could, however, Ernest caught a glimpse of them, and next thing he was calling them over to join him and his drinking companion at their table.

The Canadian introduced himself as Harry Philpotts, a major in the Canadian Air force, stationed at Ernest`s base. Ernest, they soon realised, was already a bit tipsy and he was a little bit foolishly proud of his companion and his rank.

"So you`re Ernest`s sister, Maureen, and Evelyn, you`re Ernest`s sister-in-law. Well, I`m delighted and honoured to make your acquaintance, ladies."

He raised his glass and tipped it slightly to one side. "Here`s to health and happiness... and oh, a speedy end to the war."

"I think we can all drink to that," said Maureen, chinking her glass against his.

An hour later, as the noise level rose in the pub, making conversation difficult, it became clear that Ernest was getting drunk.

"We`d better start thinking of going for the bus," said Evelyn.

"I`ll give you a ride home," said the Canadian. "Looks as if Ernest might be ready for it, too."

His vehicle was a jeep, with a canvas cover, and it rattled and jumped and roared noisily, with a smell of fumes and petrol. Ernest, revived a little by the cold night air, was effusive and talkative for the first mile, but by the time they reached the outskirts of Middleton, he was fast asleep.

Maureen directed him to Elm Street and then they watched as he stumbled towards the door with his key.

"Quick, drive off," said Maureen, "don`t let Gladys see that we`re with him."

"I`ll take you ladies home," he said.

They made their way back into the centre of Middleton and then up Wood Street.

"Don`t pull up outside," said Evelyn.

"No, of course."

"Just turn here, up into Rectory Street, drop us here."

Ten minutes later, there was a discreet knock on the door.

"I believe you left your purse in the jeep, Maureen."

"I didn`t even notice," said Maureen, giggling. "I`d forget my own head if it wasn`t screwed on."

"Well, here it is. Good job I noticed. I left the jeep at a safe distance, by the way."

"Come in," said Maureen. "We were just putting the kettle on."

Evelyn brought the tea through, and the Canadian produced a hip flask with brandy. "I find a drop of this helps the medicine go down. Anyone care to join me?"

Twenty minutes later he had emptied the last of his flask into his own and Maureen`s tea.

"Well, time for me to go to bed," said Evelyn, intending this to be a cue for them all.

"Well, go on, then," said Maureen. "You go up if you`re ready. We`ll only be a few minutes."

"No, Evelyn`s right. It`s time for bed. I`ll just finish this one drink," said the airman in his ever-so-trustful and respectful tone, "and then I will be gone."

Evelyn went up and lay down on the bed, fully clothed, intending not to sleep until she heard the door closing to signify that their visitor had left.

She listened carefully, and then felt her eyes closing.

When she awoke, she was still listening, but what she heard now was a steady low rap, rap, rap from below.

Half way down the stairs, the additional noises, now seeming preternaturally loud, of breathy effort and muffled exhalations confirmed that Maureen and the Canadian Airman were making love.

Chapter 27

A rainy day in Middleton, Thursday – sodden, soaking, miserable, the third such day in succession. For the most part, it had been a steady drizzle, though for a time in the morning it had been stair-rods, so that, walking to work, even if you had an umbrella, the rain sprayed up off the pavement, soaking the ankles and the stockings. Some of the girls had taken off their stocking and were trying to dry them by the side of their machines.

As she got into the rhythm of her work, Evelyn looked across to Maureen, sitting at her own machine opposite. Maureen did not look up.

It was three weeks since the night they had met Ernest and the Canadian Airman in Heywood.

Returning upstairs, she had sat on the side of the bed in the darkness until quietness resumed below. A little later, she heard another sound which she recognised as the latch of the back door. She waited another ten minutes and then went downstairs. Maureen was sitting there, looking at the embers of the fire. She stood for a time in the framework of the door, until Maureen turned to her.

"What`s the matter?" she said, in an off-hand dismissive way.

Evelyn went to sit in the other chair.

"You won`t say anything, will you?" said Maureen with quiet intensity.

"Course I won`t," she said, reaching out, and putting her hand over Maureen`s. Maureen squeezed her fingers tightly.

"It`s just so hard, sometimes."

"I know it is."

"Do you?"

Evelyn squeezed Maureen`s fingers in turn. "Of course I do. More than you know."

"But you wouldn`t have, would you?"

"I don`t know. I can`t say. I might have done."

"But promise me you won`t say anything."

"I won`t."

"Not ever."

"Not ever," repeated Evelyn.

"Not even if Bert comes back."

"No."

"But he isn`t coming back, is he?"

"Don`t say that."

Maureen stared into the dying embers.

And soon after that, they went to bed, and in the morning, up first, Maureen had been brisk and practical.

That was three weeks ago. Since then she had been moody and unpredictable, mainly uncommunicative.

"I was thinking of taking the kids up to Carr Woods for a picnic on Saturday, you know, through Heywood," said Evelyn.

"That`ll be nice. They`ll look forward to that."

It was the afternoon break, and the rain had thinned to the lightest of drizzle, enough for them to go out to the footbridge for a smoke.

"Hope the weather`s a bit better than this."

"Can`t stay like this forever."

"Do you fancy coming?"

"Yeh. Course I will. Make a nice change. I caught our Joan smoking one of these the other day, you know. I said, you`d better watch out lest I tell my mam and dad, and you know what she said, she said, you don`t need to bother, I`ve told them myself already."

"She never!"

"Well, she`s fifteen. Growing up quick."

She wanted to ask Maureen about herself, about how she felt about things now, but Maureen only wanted to talk of superficial things.

"Come on, we`d better get back in," said Maureen throwing her cigarette butt into the river

Evelyn and Merle called at Silk Street at nine o`clock on Saturday morning. Her mother had made up a basket with sandwiches and some apples, and Alice had made biscuits with some ginger and a little sugar she had kept by.

"At least the weather`s improved."

"Yes," said Evelyn. She had noticed it as soon as she awoke, and then again, walking down Cross Street. It was cool, but the sky was a clear pale blue. "Is Maureen not ready?" she asked.

"I doubt it," said Alice, tight-lipped. "She wasn`t in until eleven."

"Shall I go up and see her?"

"I wouldn`t bother. She was drunk when she got in. She`ll be fit for nothing for a while yet."

"Right," said Evelyn.

But the girls were keen and bright-faced, ready to go.

They walked down to the centre, Marcia in the push-chair, and Merle walking alongside. "Hold on to the pushchair," said Evelyn, "then we can go a bit faster."

Merle, with the obedience of one in happy anticipation of a day out which was a treat, held on tightly.

They watched for the sixty three coming down Manchester New Road. The conductor stowed the push-chair in the hold at the back of the platform, and Merle was already half-way up the stairs and before Evelyn could insist otherwise, had disappeared onto the top deck. She followed with Marcia in her arms. Merle had run to the front seat which was empty, giving a good view out, especially after they had climbed Hollin Lane and had open farmland ahead, and beyond that the moors, now tinged red with autumn heather.

From Heywood, they walked, along past Queens Park, and it struck Evelyn that it would serve just as well to have the picnic there, by the boat lake, or down by the river, but she particularly wanted to go to Carr Woods, where they had been that day before the war, the last time they had been out together before they moved back to Middleton.

After the recent rain, the ground was still damp underneath, but they found a bench close to the path, not far from the spot where they had been before, and unpacked their picnic. The trees still had some autumnal beauty, but the leaves were beginning to thin out, gathering below. She tried to picture the scene as it had been, Merle playing on the rug, John having a smoke and then balancing on the stepping-stones until he slipped. They had talked about the war that day, she recalled, though she could never then have conceived of it being like this, going on so long, until it became a way of life.

"Can we go by the river?"

"You`ll fall in."

"We won`t. Just to look."

"Come on, then, I`ll go with you."

Later, they went to the tea-room. The room was empty, but the lady was cheerful and brought a pot of tea, and some biscuits, and lemonade, and there was a little dog who made them laugh by trying to stand up by the table, looking from one to the other of them, with expectant eyes, hoping to be fed.

"Can we come here again?" asked Merle.

"Can we?" echoed Marcia.

"We`ll come here when your daddy gets back. When both of your daddies come home?"

"When will that be?" said Merle, with childish scepticism, as if it was just one of those predictable adult ways of putting things off. Merle, she realised, had begun to lose any sense of John as a real person; Marcia, of course, now talking and beginning to make her own sense of the world, had no memories at all to associate with the concept of having a daddy. As far as she was concerned he could be the man in the moon.

“Can we get the bus?” said Merle, as they made their way back.

“We`ll just walk back to Heywood, and get the bus from there.”

“My legs are too tired to walk anymore!”

She allowed Merle to perch on the front step of the push-chair, where she pulled funny faces to make Marcia laugh, and in this way, she got them back to Heywood.

“Sorry,” said Maureen, when they got back.

They went into the front parlour, whilst Alice fed the girls in the kitchen, and James asked them about their day.

Maureen leaned forward, and whispered in Evelyn`s ear.

“I thought I might be pregnant, but I`m not.”

“Good,” said Evelyn.

“I`m so bloody relieved. I can`t tell you.”

Maureen squeezed Evelyn`s hand. “Promise me you won`t?”

“What?”

“Ever tell anyone.”

“I`ve told you I won`t.”

Maureen took a deep breath, and breathed out again with relief.

Chapter 28

"Why don`t you ask your mother to come over for something to eat on Christmas Day?" said Alice.

"You know what she`s like."

"It`ll not be anything special, but she`s very welcome."

"I`ll ask her, but she`s happiest by her own fireside these days."

"Well, tell her, anyway, won`t you?"

"I will."

"You`ll be here, won`t you, and Merle?"

"We`ll pop down for an hour."

"Will you not stop for your dinner, love?" said Alice, in that slightly plaintive way.

"Better not, really."

"Just as you think."

At work, the girls were talking about another Christmas dance at the baths. She looked across at Maureen and Maureen pursed her lips without obvious enthusiasm. A year ago it had seemed like an adventure, a bit of harmless frivolity, but that seemed a long time ago. Things were different now. Maureen had been out on her own, she knew, telling Alice and James she was going to sit with a friend from work, Helen Betts or Bessie Metcalfe, but going to pubs and dance halls with girls who didn`t care what people thought of them.

James, always sitting with a newspaper, or tuned into the radio, was upbeat about the war, the progress through Italy, the promise of an invasion through France, the incursions of the Americans in the Philippines and other places in the Far East. "The noose is tightening around Hitler`s neck," he would say. "We`ll have all our lads back by this time next year," he said with the fond optimism of one who has only the wise insights of an old man to offer.

Everyone indulged him, no-one really listened.

When she arrived at 7 Silk Street on Christmas Day, she knew straight away, from the animated mood and the voices, that something unexpected had happened. On the peg, on the hallstand, was a sailor`s cap

At first, with her heart leaping, she thought that it might be John; going into the room she saw that it was Eddie.

"Evelyn!" he said, getting up and coming to embrace her. "How are you, kid?"

"How are you, Eddie?"

His breath had a slight smell of whisky.

The whole family, except for Maureen, were sitting there: James in his usual chair by the fire, Alice sitting with Marcia on her knee by the table, Joan and Nancy in the other table chairs.

"Come in and sit down," said Eddie, indicating the other chair by the fire which Alice had vacated for him.

"She can sit here whilst I get on," said Alice. "Marcia, run upstairs love, and give your mum a shake."

Alice went into the kitchen, and Evelyn took her place with Merle, shy in Eddie`s presence, at her knee.

"Well," said James, "we just need John and Bert and we`d have a full house."

"Eddie`s seen John, haven`t you, Eddie?" said Nancy.

A silence went over the room, and it was clear that Nancy had let slip something she wasn`t meant to.

"I just bumped into him in Liverpool," said Eddie, shrugging his shoulders uncomfortably.

"Did he say anything? About coming home?"

"It was in a crowd," said Eddie. "You know how it is. We were having a few drinks."

"Was he drunk?"

"They were just back in, just come on shore."

"And he didn`t say how long he had?"

Eddie shook his head. "As I say, we were just passing. Then I lost him in the crowd."

"Maybe, he`ll turn up yet," said James, quietly.

Ten minutes later, Maureen came down, looking a bit puffy around the eyes, but otherwise none the worse for wear. "Hiya, our kid," she said to Eddie.

"Hiya, kidder."

"Right," said James, "time to get a pot of tea on the go. Alice!"

"What time`s our Ernest coming over?" said Eddie.

John did not come home during the Christmas and New Year period. She waited for him to turn up, but not in any real expectation. Before he went back, Eddie had another quiet word with her. "Don`t feel too badly. They have a hell of a time, those lads, Evelyn. Sometimes when they get in, they go crazy, not just your John."

"What, so that they don`t want to see their wives and their children and their family?"

"Don`t ask me, Evelyn. I don`t know. I`m just saying..."

"I know Eddie, I`m not blaming you."

"I`ll have a sharp word with him, when I see him," said Ernest, on another occasion. "You can be sure of that."

It served to confirm that the family had conversations about it to which she was not privy.

"I always said," her mother remarked, "the Wilkinsons are a clan."

"I`m a Wilkinson," said Evelyn.

Her mother turned away, tight-lipped.

At the cinema, the newsreel continued to follow the campaign in Italy, with news of advances at Anzio and repeated attacks at Monte Casino. The RAF was carrying out successful bombing raids over Germany, they were told, and the constant theme was that it would only be a matter of time. James picked up a story in the newspaper about allied troops taking an airfield at Myitkyina, Burma, an important air base, and he explained that this meant that they were now taking the battle to Japanese, and that they too would soon be on the run.

He told Maureen that this meant that more information would soon be coming back, and he reassured her that she would soon have news of Herbert. Maureen greeted such assurances with a seemingly lethargic indifference, as if she had used up all the emotional energy she had on such repeated speculations, and had none left to deal with anymore. James and Alice exchanged worried looks behind her back, and tried to dissuade her from going out as often as she did, but it was to no avail. Maureen was in a fragile and volatile state of mind, and James`s attempts to take a strong fatherly line served only to inflame the situation further. Ernest`s attempts to reason with his sister met with no more success, especially if Gladys happened to be at his side.

Evelyn was walking home along Cross Street one pleasant Sunday afternoon in the April of 1944, when a car-horn honked behind her, and, looking up as the car drew alongside, she recognised the driver as Charlie Breen.

"Evelyn," he called, brightly. "Long time no see!"

"How do, Charlie?"

"Not bad, not bad at all. Hop in, I`ll drop you off at home."

"It`s only two minutes."

"Never mind. Save your legs. Is this Merle?" he said looking directly at the little girl, who nodded shyly. "Hello, Merle, I`m Charlie. Do you want a lift home with your mam?"

She looked at Evelyn and then nodded.

"Come on, then, jump in."

"Don`t drop us right outside," said Evelyn. "You`ll have people talking."

"I`ll drive a bit up Wood Street, then," he said.

"You can drop us here," said Evelyn, when they reached Top Wood Street.

"Let`s have a bit of a spin," he said, turning off Wood Street onto the lane which ran up over Bowlee. "That's all right, isn`t it? What do you think Merle?"

"I think it`s nice," she said.

"There you are, then. The boss has spoken."

"Just a little way, then," said Evelyn.

"How`s John, then? Have you heard from him?"

"Christmas time, you know..."

"And how`s he doing?"

"Well, they can`t say much, can they, it`s all hush-hush."

"Bad business. Soon have them home, though, by all accounts. Let`s hope so, anyway. I`ll certainly be glad when it`s all over."

She wondered exactly what he meant by this but didn`t question it.

They made their way slowly up the lane, with fields and farmland on each side, until they reached the top.

"It`s nice up here, isn`t it?" she said. "Never walked this far over."

"I`ve heard people say they`ll build all over this, when the war`s over. Re-housing people from Manchester."

"What, from the bombing?"

"Not just that. There are places not fit to be lived in down there. Slums. Not fit for rats. I`ve seen them, you can take it from me, Evelyn. They`ll be shifting them out here in thousands. Irish, mainly. Polish. Russian. The lot. Middleton`ll be a different place after the war."

"Seems a pity to spoil it all."

"Well, there`ll be opportunities, that`s the way I look at it. New people. Supply and demand, that`s the business I`ll be in."

"Is that how you came by the car?"

"Well, I had a stroke of luck there. Not of the horse or greyhound variety, I hasten to add. No, I`m done with all that now. Solid business, that`s what my line is."

They reached the top of the lane.

"Can`t go any further," said Charlie, "there`s an airfield up here now. Top Secret."

"Better get back, anyway. My mother`ll be wondering where we are."

"Let me take you out again," he said, as they came back towards the edge of the town. "Bring your mam, too, if you like, all above board. Probably do her good to have a bit of an outing."

"No, I don`t think so."

"Was it something I said?"

"No. Course not. But you know how it is."

"Enough said, Evelyn. You`ll not have any bother from me. I may not be in Middleton long, anyway, not this time, anyway, you know, if business calls."

"You can drop us off here, if you will."

"I`ll take you just round onto Durnford Street. Then you can cut through the backs."

"Thanks."

However innocent it was, Evelyn could not help but feel a sense of secrecy and impropriety as she got out of the car, as if the curtains were twitching at the sight of herself, Evelyn Wilkinson, married woman of the town, slipping out of a car and hurrying away along the street. Within a few steps, however, she realised she was being overdramatic.

"Did you enjoy that?" she said to Merle.

"Yes. I liked having a spin in a car."

"So did I."

She decided to be up-front with her mother.

"Who?"

"Charlie Breen, he`s a friend of John."

"You`d better not let the Wilkinsons get a niff of it."

"Why! There`s nothing wrong happened."

"You just watch yourself, young lady."

She said it again, later, before they went to bed. "You watch yourself, young lady."

And in a curious way, as she went to bed, at the thought that there was something she had to watch herself over, she felt a curious sense of elation.

Her immediate fear was that Merle would let something slip the next time they visited 7 Silk Street, but as it turned out, Joan called round to say that Marcia had begun to show signs of the chicken pox, and so they decided to keep Merle away for the time being.

"How is she?" she asked Maureen at work.

"A bit fretful. Full of blotches."

"Poor thing."

"They`re terrified at home, because of our Bessie and the diphtheria, but the doctor said it was chicken pox. Couldn`t be mistaken for anything else."

"She`ll soon pick up."

"I expect so."

It was later in the day, during the tea break, that Maureen said, "listen, I`ve got something I want to tell you."

"Go on, then, what?"

"Not a word, mind you."

"Go on."

"I met someone, on Saturday night."

"Bloody hell, Maureen. Who?"

"He`s called Frank. Works at Avrose. Protected occupation. They make the Lancaster Bombers there."

"And?"

"He said he wants to see me again."

"Did you tell him about Bert?"

"Yes."

"And what did he say about that?"

Maureen shrugged and twisted her mouth. "He`s separated from his wife. She was having a baby by someone else. He`s waiting for a divorce."

"Honestly?"

"What do you think I should do?"

"Keep well clear, I would have thought."

"He asked me to go home with him. He`s got his own house. His wife went back to her mother, you know, when they broke up."

"And did you?"

"No, but I was tempted. I wanted to, Evelyn. I tell you, I lay awake half way through the night wishing I had."

"Well, I know what that feels like," she confessed, and they both tittered quietly. "So, what will you do?" asked Evelyn.

"I don`t know. See him again maybe. That`s all, probably. Or not. I don`t know."

"Just take care."

"That`s the thing I envy about you, Evelyn," she said, throwing the end of her cigarette into the river. "You`re always so sensible."

Chapter 29

There was a row going on at 7 Silk Street. Alice and James had arranged to take the family to a guest house in Blackpool for four days over the Bank Holiday weekend, and Maureen was refusing to go. Joan did not want to go, either, but her protest was as nothing compared with Maureen`s vehement objections, and James was holding his ground.

"If you think I`m going to leave you here to get up to God knows what..."

"James!" warned Alice.

"Up to God knows what, I say, then you`ve got another thought coming."

"I`m twenty five, I`m a married woman, I`m not yours, I`ve a right to live my life as I choose."

"You`ve a right to live your life as your husband would have you live it, if he was here."

"But he`s not here. And it`s not your right to take over as if I was a ten year old child again. I`ve told you, I`m not going!"

"Leave her be," said Alice. "Her mind`s set. I`m not having the whole house upset over it. Evelyn can come instead."

"Very well, then," said James, still white with anger in his battle with Maureen`s defiance. "Have it your way. But either she comes with us, or we none of us go. We`ll stay here, the lot of us. And that`s my last word."

With that he went out of the room.

It was Maureen who, in the end, capitulated. "He can have his way this time," she said to Evelyn. "But when I get back, I`m having mine."

"Why aren`t you coming, mum?" Merle asked.

"It`s a guest-house, love, they`ve only so many places."

"I`ll stay here with you, mum."

"Then what would Marcia do without you. Who`s going to teach her how to play on the sand?"

"Will you miss me?"

"Of course I will, love."

"I`ll miss you, too. But I will go if you think I should," she said, a self-sacrifice in which there was no trace of disingenuity to allay the pure pleasure and excitement she felt at the prospect of going.

"She`s a madam, that one is," said her mother when she told her.

"Maureen?"

"Aye, Maureen, who did you think I was talking about?"

At work, the next day, Maureen had a fixed almost smug look on her face, as she worked, and she didn`t look up. Evelyn sensed that she had something up her sleeve.

"I`m going over to stay with Frank," she said.

"When?"

"Tonight, after work."

"Does he know?"

"Not yet."

"What if...?"

"What if what? If it takes him by surprise? It`ll be his choice then, won`t it? But I think I know what he`ll choose."

On Thursday night, they packed Merle`s bag so that she would be ready to go straight from school on Friday.

"I`ll be all right, mum," she said. "Don`t worry about me."

"All right, then, I won`t."

"And don`t worry about Marcia. I`ll look after her, too. So you can have a nice rest, can`t you?"

"I can."

"Right, I`d better get to bed, then," she said, at last. "It`s a big day for me tomorrow."

Chapter 30

Charlie Breen`s car was parked outside the Albion on Wood Street. She had seen it when she walked down into the town in the early afternoon, and it was still there half an hour later when she returned with the few bits and pieces of shopping she had been for.

"They`ll be there by now," said her mother, alluding to the Wilkinson holiday trip to Blackpool.

"They`re lucky with the weather."

Her mother had made some sandwiches for lunch with corn beef. She brought the newly brewed pot of tea to the table. There was no proper milk or sugar, but she had opened a tin of Carnation which she poured liberally into her own cup.

"It`ll be hot on the beach. You did put a hat in for her didn`t you?"

"Course I did. Maureen`ll make sure she wears it."

"I hope she does."

"No thanks," said Evelyn, as her mother offered her the tin of condensed milk. "It makes it too sickly."

"Please yourself."

"Do you want a cigarette?"

"No thanks, love, it`s been getting to my throat."

"I`ll go and stand by the door."

She went to stand by the front door. The road was hot in the early afternoon sun, and some people had already put chairs out on the flags to get the benefit of it.

"Hello, Evelyn."

"Hello, Mrs Blackshaw."

"Merle playing in the backyard, is she?"

"No, she`s gone to Blackpool with her gran and granddad."

"Lucky girl. Be nice for them this weather. Nice break for you, too, I shouldn`t wonder."

"It is, an`all."

She looked quickly down the road, confirming at a glance that Charlie`s car was still outside the Albion. Making a session of it, no doubt, she said to herself.

She finished her cigarette and went inside. Her mother was just finishing washing the pots.

"I would have done that, mam."

"It`s all right. It`s no bother. What are you going to do this afternoon?"

"Thought I might have a walk over to see Mary Rennie."

"Right, well I`m going up for lie-down."

"Are you all right, mam?"

"Course I am. If I`m not down by four, call the undertaker."

"Don`t joke about things like that, mam."

She heard her mother`s steps up the staircase, and tidied her hair in the oval mirror. It was too hot for a coat, but she put a light cardigan round her shoulders, and then, looking at herself again in the mirror, put on the lightest smear of lipstick.

"Evelyn!"

She ignored the call and walked on.

"Evelyn!" It came again, and she knew her walking on was a matter of form, because she could easily have gone up Rectory Street if she`d wanted to be sure of avoiding him completely.

She stopped and turned, putting on a disparaging look.

"Evelyn," he said, crossing the road, "don`t be like that."

"I don`t like being called out to from pub doorways."

"No, course not. Sorry. I was just coming out and caught sight of you."

"Right, I`ll get on, then now."

She turned away and walked on, but she felt the air behind her was electric. She got as far as the Vic Picture House, opposite Wrigley`s Garage, near the bottom of Wood Street, and then heard the wheels of the car, slowing down to pull up beside her.

"Jump in, Evelyn. Where are you going? Let me drop you off."

The next thing she knew, they were driving up past Towncroft Avenue, and turning past the cricket ground onto Hollin lane.

"Wait a minute," he said, pulling over. He got out of the car and pulled the hood down.

"That`s better," he said. "A bit of a fresh air. Nothing like it."

"My hair`ll be all over the place," she protested, though when they got to the top of Hollin Lane, with the open country ahead, the sensation of the warm wind blowing into her face and through her hair was exhilarating. The pleasure was tinged with guilt, but she was glad that she had bumped into Charlie Breen again, and that he had stopped to give her a ride in his car.

They came into the centre of Heywood, and turned into the Bamford Road, soon coming to the dip of Hooley Bridge where the River Roach flowed past.

"Look, there`s our old house," said Evelyn, as they climbed up Hooley Brow. "It seems such a long time ago, When I was pregnant with Merle, and she`s five now. That`s when you stole my ten shillings from me."

"That`s when I invested your ten shillings for you, you mean."

They turned from Bamford Road into Bury Road, and then turned down past the dye-works at Simpson Clough, where John had worked, onto the Ashworth Valley road. They stopped for a few minutes where Cheesden Brook ran under the little road bridge, and then carried on up the steady climb of the lane, passing the hamlet she remembered where the lane wound past of five or six cottages, and a farm-house.

"This is where we used to come walking," she said. "Up here and down in the valley."

"It`s glorious isn`t it? Just look at it. This`d be the life for me. A farmer. Out all day in the sun."

"And the rain!"

"I wouldn`t mind that. Honest work. It`s good for a man to have proper work to do."

"Why don`t you try it? Farming, I mean," she added, correcting an obvious possible misunderstanding.

"There`s no way in, is there? Farms are all in families, aren`t they, father to son, father to son. Besides, it`s all getting mechanised these days, isn`t it?"

They reached the turn into Chapel Lane where the Egerton Arms was.

"Fancy stopping in for one?" he asked.

"We used to go in there, they might remember me. There`s another place a bit further on. Owd Betts."

"Sounds good to me."

They sat in the corner of the lounge, and he brought her a half of shandy, and a pint of mild for himself.

"So, you don`t hear much from him, then, your John."

She shrugged her shoulders.

"You can tell me, Evelyn. Remember I`m his pal. We go back a long way, me and your John."

"He was keen to see me, at first, you know, when he got back, but lately, he just wants to go drinking, or doesn`t come back at all`s more the case."

"Well you have to think how hard it is for them. They must see a lot of things."

"That`s what their Eddie says."

He put his hand over hers, momentarily, in a gesture of consolation, and she was aware, not without a further twinge of both pleasure and guilt, that she was allowing him into an area of confidentiality bordering on intimacy.

“It`ll be all right when it`s all over,” she said, drawing her hand away. “Get back to normal. They say it shouldn`t be too long now.”

“Well, let`s hope not.”

They came out into the afternoon sun. Across the hillside, to the summit of Knowle Hill, a mile away, scattered strings of people were strolling along the winding paths, and there was a smell of heather and new bracken in the air.

“Shall we have a little walk?” he suggested.

“I haven`t really got my right shoes on.”

“Just a little way, then. Seems a pity to waste such a nice afternoon.”

“All right, then, just a way.”

They stepped aside to let another couple with a boy in school uniform pass, and a little further on, where the path widened, he slipped his hand lightly onto her waist.

“No,” she said.

It wasn`t as simple as that, though for one treacherous moment she wished it was….

“My mam`ll be wondering where I am,” she said.

“Come on, then,” said Charlie. “I`ll get you back.”

“I enjoyed that,” she said, as they drove back down the valley. “Thanks, Charlie.”

“Listen,” he said, a bit later. “Some pals of mine are having a bit of a garden party tomorrow.”

“A garden party, that sounds posh.”

“It`s up on Sunny Brow Road.”

“Oh, yes. Just past Parkfield Church.”

“That`s right. I wondered if you fancied coming along.”

“I don`t think so. I don`t think I could.”

“Well, look, I`ll not put any pressure on you, Evelyn. But if you decide you fancy a nice afternoon, I`ll be going up there from the Joiners Arms about one o`clock. I`ll leave it up to you.”

“What`s going on?” said her mother, that night.

"What do you mean?"

"Don`t try to kid me. You couldn`t kid me when you were a little girl, and you can`t kid me now."

"There`s nothing going on."

"Don`t tell me then," said her mother. "In fact, I`d rather you didn`t tell me, then I can put my hand on my heart and say I don`t know."

Evelyn drew a deep breath.

"All right, all right," said her mother. "But you just watch out for yourself, young lady, just you watch out for yourself."

Chapter 31

The last thing Evelyn accepted, as she lay awake in bed that night was that there was any need to watch out for herself. And at the same time, she didn`t see why, after months and years of putting up with the deprivations and loneliness imposed on her by war, she should feel bad or guilty about the little bit of distraction that went with an afternoon out with an old friend, one of John`s old pals.

Images of the day crossed and re-crossed her mind, the drive along to Heywood, the drive past Hooley Bridge, the road winding up through Ashworth Valley, the walk over the moor with the warm wind and the smell of the heather. At last, she fell asleep with these images playing vaguely across her consciousness. When she awoke suddenly, in the indeterminate half-light of dawn, she decided, making an end of the vacillations of the night, that there was no reason why she should not go with Charlie to his garden party. When she awoke again, in the proper light of day, she decided that there were probably good reasons why she shouldn`t go.

It was another fine morning.

As they had breakfast, they heard the Jacksons rowing in house next door – intermittent voices, his angry, stubborn, mordant, hers shrill in pitch and rising to sudden shrieking climaxes.

"They`re always the same when the weather`s like this," said her mother.

"What`s the weather got to do with it?"

"Your dad was the same. Always that way out when it was hot for more than three days together. It was a relief to me when we got a bit of rain."

"My dad hated the rain. He was always complaining about it."

"He complained about everything. Whatever it was, he wanted the opposite."

"I think it`s nice, I might go out for a walk later on."

"Oh, aye? Where to?"

"I only said might. I don`t know yet."

"Will you go along to Mrs Stirk, see if they`ve finished with last night`s paper yet?"

"You should say if you want to read the paper. I`ll buy one for you."

"Well, I don`t mind reading it the next day. Nothing`s changed that much in one day has it?"

"Do you want any more tea?"

"Aye, go on, give us another cup."

"It looks a bit stewed, mam."

"That`s how I like it."

"Do you want me to open a new tin of Carnation for you?"

"Go on, then. Treat me while you`ve still got me. It`ll not be long."

"Mam!"

"All right, all right! Keep your hair on."

"Do you want me to take you to church, mam?" she asked after they had cleared away the pots.

"No. I`ll save it up now, till I see him in the face. It`ll do then."

She spent the rest of the morning sorting through her drawers, and tried on a couple of summer dresses she had bought when they were still living in Heywood.

"That`s nice," her mother said, "I`ve not seen that one, have I?"

It was a pale apricot sleeveless frock, which had short-sleeved jacket to go with it.

"I`ve not worn it since before I had Merle. Didn`t know if it`d still fit me."

"You`re lucky. Nothing ever fitted me after you."

"Thanks, mam!"

"No, you look nice in it, I mean it."

"Why don`t you come with me, mam? We could go up to Jubilee Park. It`ll be nice there today."

"Jubilee Park!" said her mam, with a rich wistful note. "I used to meet your dad there. That was just before the first war started."

"Come with me. You can tell me all about it."

"No," said her mother, emphatically. "I`m better off here, truly I am. You go off and see Betty or June, or whoever, but don`t tell me who it is, then you won`t have to tell me a lie."

"What do you think I should do, mam?"

Her mother looked at her with the clearest and sharpest of blue eyes. "What are you asking me for? You`ll do what you want to do, I dare say. Just make sure you don`t do anything you`ll regret."

"Tell me what you really think."

"You only live your life once. It`s not a rehearsal."

"This is my friend, Evelyn."

"That`s nice name. Evelyn. I`m Melisse."

She offered her hand and held Evelyn`s fingers lightly for a moment.

"Melisse, that`s a nice name, too. Is it French?" Evelyn asked, noting the woman`s accent.

"Belgian. Or at least, I am. From Bruges. Come with me and get a drink, Evelyn."

The speaker, tall and slender, with wavy blond hair which she wore loose, high cheek bones and large blue eyes, was, Evelyn thought, very beautiful. Her slight accent somehow made her English seem all the more elegant.

Charlie had gone over to talk to a chap on the lawn, who was trying to put up a badminton net, with two children, a boy and a girl of about nine, in attendance. The man was about thirty five, and, like the woman, was tall and slim.

The driveway to the house, along which they were now walking, was fifty yards long, and it was separated from the lawn by a line of trees. It was bordered on the other side by rose beds, and beyond, a paddock of rough grass where two horses were grazing.

Dunarden, as the house was called, was one of five rather grand houses along Sunnybrow Road, each in its own grounds, set about with mature trees. To the south, there was an open perspective over the Irk Valley, and to the north and west they backed onto what had been open farmland when they were built, but which was now part of the North Manchester Golf Course.

"It`s a lovely house," Evelyn ventured to say. "We sometimes go to the church at Parkfield, but I`ve never been along as far as this."

"It is. A very nice house. Not ours, though, only one we rent whilst the war is on."

"Oh."

"Our home is in France, near the border with Belgium. When the war started, we came to London, and then here. Robert was brought up near here," she added, pronouncing Robert in the French way, Rob-air.

They went into the house through a rear porch, into an area with a kitchen, a morning-room and a scullery. "Now, Evelyn, have a drink to take outside. This is Pimms, very light, very refreshing on a hot day like this. Have it with a little soda."

"Thanks."

"Now we`ll go out through the hall and the main door so I can quickly show you the house."

The hall was a spacious area, with panelled wood and chess-board tiles and rugs, and with a wide open staircase going up to a first landing with a stained glass window, and then turning to continue upwards. From the hall a double door led into the main lounge which ran along the whole frontage of the house, with two bay windows with leaded lights looking down over the garden, where the game of badminton was now under way. The two children were merrily hitting the shuttlecock as high as they could, and the tall man was presiding at the net, which in fact he seemed also to be holding up. A third child, a little younger, had now appeared, too, and was loudly making it known that she expected her turn to follow soon.

"They`ll soon get bored with it, I`m afraid. We`re going to take them for a long walk later on. A forced march, as they call it."

Evelyn laughed. She noticed that Charlie was sitting at a garden table to the side, with another chap who wore a panama hat and horn-rimmed glasses and a white jacket, and very pretty young girl of sixteen with long auburn hair.

"This room," said the hostess, opening a door on the other side of the hall, "should be the dining room, but Robert has taken it over as his studio, and an artist`s studio is always untidy."

Through the open door, Evelyn saw stacks of canvasses, some rolled, some framed, some piled up, several deep. One, on an easel and still unfinished, was evidently a portrait of the girl she had glimpsed through the window a moment before; amongst the others, Evelyn could not but help notice, were several nude and semi-nude studies of the hostess herself.

"Where`ve you been?" Charlie asked.

"Tour of the house."

"Impressed?"

"You didn`t tell me he was an artist."

"They both are. She`s an illustrator."

"Have you seen his paintings of her?"

"Yes. Good, aren`t they?"

"Charlie!"

"What?"

"Do they let the children see them?"

"Oh, they`re all very bohemian. The kids just think it`s normal. Don`t bat an eye-lid."

"Who's the man with the panama hat?"

"Oh, that`s Quentin. He`s a poet or calls himself one. He`s a bit consumptive, or so he says. If you ask me, it`s all an act. Come on, I`ll introduce you."

Quentin shook her hand rather stiffly, and she sat down at the garden table, whilst Charlie went to get them both another drink. She tried to make some small talk with Quentin, but he was too superior or too shy to make anything more than the minimal responses.

When Charlie came back, Quentin excused himself and went to watch the badminton game.

"He`s in love with Esme," said Charlie.

"She`s the pretty one, I take it."

"Yes."

"She must be half his age!"

"Yes. But she teases him. It`s a standing joke. He`s the only one who doesn`t see it."

"And who is she?"

"Melisse`s sister. Or half-sister."

"And are Melisse and Robert married?"

"Yes. Well, no. Not exactly. They were both married to someone else, in France, but she`s Catholic so no chance of a divorce. They`ve both got a child from their first marriage. The youngest one there, is theirs, if you can follow that."

"My head`s spinning."

"Here, have a smoke of this."

"What is it?"

"It`s a reefer. It`ll help you to relax."

"I don`t need any help. I`m relaxed enough with this, what is it?"

"Pimms. Just take a puff. It doesn`t do any harm."

"So, how do you know them, Charlie?"

"I went to school with Robert. Prep School. Aged ten. My grandfather owned a cotton mill. His grandfather owned a coal-mine. Then I met up with him in Manchester, a few months back. It was me that found them this place to rent."

"You`re a clever boy aren`t you!"

She took a draw of Charlie`s reefer, and passed it back to him. Then she sat back, and allowed herself to take in what a beautiful day it was. The air was full of the scent of something sweet, something rich and humid, almost overcoming the senses.

"Hello, Evelyn."

She opened her eyes. It was the tall man, Robert, the artist, offering his hand.

She smiled and offered hers. He took her fingertips only, as if he was going to kiss them, though he didn`t go so far.

"We`re hoping you`ll come and join in the badminton."

She realised that the children were standing behind him, in anticipation.

"But I`ve never played..."

"Neither have we, any of us, so, if you will play with Thomas, it`s a knock-out. We don`t really know the rules, but we can make them up as we go along."

"Go on, Evelyn, be a sport," said Charlie.

"All right. But what about you?"

"I`ll get us another drink."

They began to play, and Evelyn, very self-conscious at first, did her best to pick up the flight of the shuttlecock and return it when it was her turn. The general mirth, however, soon overtook the seriousness of the game, and she began to enjoy herself.

Esme was sitting at the head of the lawn, where it rose on a shelving bank beneath the bay windows of the house, and Quentin was standing by her, like an awkward sentinel. As they played, Charlie came from the house with Melisse, and they too sat on the bank, watching the game with mock applause.

"Come and sit down, Evelyn," said Melisse, at last. "You deserve a rest."

"Come and sit here," said Charlie. "Here`s your drink."

"The children have now abandoned badminton," announced Quentin, in a slightly pompous intonation, "and now revert to more basic sports."

The others laughed, for the children, having found a pile of grass cuttings which the gardener had left, were throwing handfuls of dried grass at each other and laughing with high shrill laughter.

"It will end in tears," said Melisse. "We must take them for a walk."

"A route march," said Esme, with humorous familiarity.

"I`ll make one," said Quentin. "I`ll show you Schwabe's` Chimney."

"You`ve shown it to us before."

"Quentin is a descendant of the Schwabe family," said Esme, for Evelyn`s benefit.

"Did you know," said Quentin, enjoying a certain amount of attention, "that Emma Schwabe was involved in a *cause celebre* in Paris in 1879. A certain doctor, anxious to purge his daughters of habits which derived from, shall we say, the more Dionysian side of human nature, so deprived them of all human comforts that they died."

"What are Dionysian sides of human nature, Quentin, do tell us," said Esme, archly, evoking laughter which Quentin ignored but clearly enjoyed. "Emma gave evidence in his favour."

"And was he acquitted?"

The conversation went on, in desultory fashion, with witty retorts and laughter and Evelyn felt her eye-lids growing heavy. She closed her eyes, and felt the warmth of the sun on her face, and everything seemed pleasant and agreeable. What would Maureen think, she said to herself, if she could see me now? Wait till I tell her.

She forced her eyes open, and tried to tune back into the conversation. Then she felt her eyelids growing temptingly heavy again.

The next thing she was aware of was that Charlie was next to her running his finger slowly along her shoulder, and because it was so nice, she didn`t want him to stop.

"Come upstairs with me," he whispered.

"Where is everybody?" she said sitting up, suddenly awake.

"Gone for a walk. Just you and me."

"I`d better be getting back," she said.

"Come upstairs with me first."

"I can`t."

"Why not?"

"You know I can`t."

"You can if you want to. Who would know any different?"

"I would."

"Well you would, and I would, but nobody else has to know, do they?"

He started to stroke her arm again, and she didn`t stop him.

"We may never get another chance like this, and who knows what the future holds? Everybody deserves a bit of happiness, Evie, especially in these hard times."

Her heart was beating quickly, and she could feel the pulse of it in her temples.

"It`s cooler inside," he said, slipping his hand lightly over her breast, and she knew that if she didn`t stop him straight away, he would take it to mean that she didn`t want him to stop.

"Will you come upstairs with me, Evelyn?" he said, a short time later.

"Yes, all right," she said.

Chapter 32

When the letter from Bert`s regiment came it so chanced that Ernest was at the house, and he took upon himself the grim task of going to tell Bert`s mother. Joan was sent over to tell Evelyn, and she knew immediately, from the tautness of the girl`s face that something was wrong. For a moment, she thought it was John, and she felt the blood drain from her own face, but then Joan managed to mumble enough to make it clear, and one kind of lurching terror was replaced with another. It was no longer possible, the letter explained, to entertain any hope that Bert was still alive. Statements taken from prisoners liberated from Japanese work-camps confirmed extensive casualties during the action in which Bert had gone missing. On the overwhelming balance of evidence, he was now to be officially classified as missing presumed dead...

Bert`s mother, as Ernest reported, when he returned to the house, simply nodded her head slowly, as if his message had merely confirmed what she had long known already. She sat quietly for a long time, staring into the fire, but she didn`t cry or show any emotion. Sitting there with his hat on his knee, Ernest had not known what to do but then a neighbour called, and made a pot of tea, and eventually he had thought it decent to take his leave.

"I told her you`d go to see her," he said to Maureen, "when you`re feeling right."

"Yes, I will, I`ll go and see her."

Maureen`s mood was volatile. When Evelyn went round, Maureen threw her arms around her and sobbed uncontrollably for five minutes. Then, as if it were an energy that had blown itself out, she sat back, and stared into space, oblivious of everyone else in the room.

"I`ll make some tea," muttered Alice, quietly.

Marcia sat at the table, looking at her mother, her face blank with childish worry, not fully understanding what was going on.

"Do you want me to take her for a bit?" said Evelyn. "She can come and play with Merle."

"No," said Maureen, as if waking up. "Come here, lovey, come here."

Given permission, Marcia slipped gladly from the chair and ran over to her mother, nestling in her arms. Alice brought in the tea and they all sat there, lost in their own thoughts.

The next day, Maureen was up early, and was full of the assertion that everything was to carry on as normal, impatient with anyone she found looking at her with the gentleness of pity. The following day, she insisted on returning to work.

"I can`t sit around here all day," she said.

"You need time, love. Stay here for a bit. They`ll understand."

"No, I`ll go mad if I have to sit around anymore."

"Just give it a couple of days. Or it`ll catch up on you."

"Let her be," said James.

Then, a couple of days later, as Alice predicted, the reaction set in. She sat in the chair for hours on end, as if in a torpor, and would not let Marcia out of her sight, as if she feared some invisible hand would reach out and take her away, too.

"The worst thing," said Alice, talking quietly to Evelyn when Maureen had agreed to go upstairs for a lie-down, "is not having him to bury. It`s just official papers. It doesn`t seem real."

"I`ve heard them say that the vicar will do a service anyway. They did that for men who never came back from the last war."

"It`s not the same though, is it?"

Maureen shook her head decisively when Evelyn mentioned this idea, at work, later in the week.

"It might help just to bring things to a close."

"I can`t picture him, when I think of him. I can`t see his face. I haven`t been able to for a long time. That says something, doesn`t it?"

"I don`t know what you mean."

"Do you think this could be a punishment, a judgement?"

"A judgement on what?"

"On me. You know why. You`re the only one who knows."

"No, I don`t believe that sort of thing at all. Thousands of men are dying, Maureen. It`s because of war. Not because of you, or me, or anyone else, it`s because it`s a war."

Maureen squeezed her fingers. "Thank you," she said. "I think you`re the only one who really understands..."

Evelyn did understand, more than Maureen knew.

She had not told anyone about the day when she had gone to the garden party at Sunny Brow Road, and what had happened, and she could not tell anyone, though she had a shrewd idea that her mother knew. As ever!

For a short time the shame could not have washed through her more thoroughly if she had committed a murder. Then she had put it into a box. A guilty secret either breaks you, or you confess, or you live with it. She had put the guilt, along with the memory to which it was attached into a box, and she had firmly closed the lid.

Charlie, his windfall now spent, seemed to have disappeared from Middleton again.

The memory of that afternoon, a hot summer garden and a cool bedroom, seemed now as remote as if it had happened in another life-time.

And now Maureen`s news had put everything into a new perspective.

James` enthusiastic following, in the newspapers and on the radio, of the landings in Normandy and the progress of the Allied Armies through Europe, was offset by the new fear of the V1 doodlebug bombs attacking London. There was yet a sting in the tail. Would they have the range to reach Manchester?

The immediate sense of loss and mourning for Bert had passed, Evelyn noticed, amongst the Wilkinsons, except inasmuch as it registered with Maureen. They watched Maureen, just as Marcia watched her – if Maureen was upset, they were anxious. If Maureen was all right, then they were happy. That was how it worked.

The Wilkinsons didn't see of Maureen everything that Evelyn saw. A month after the letter had come through, Maureen complained to the overseer at work that she was feeling unwell. Normally Jack Shirt was an uncompromising man with little tolerance for people`s personal troubles, but because of Maureen`s situation, he told her to go home. It was only later that she discovered, through an innocent remark of Merle, that Maureen had not been at home at all until just before tea-time. She decided not to say anything, to quell any curiosity she felt. If Maureen wanted to share any confidences with her, that was her business; for her own part she had no intention of sharing her own confidence with Maureen.

One Friday, during the tea break, Maureen took her to one side.

"If I bring Marcia round to yours tonight, can we stop over till the morning?"

"If you like. Why?"

"I`ve already told my mam. Just for a change and you know how much the girls like it. Your mam won`t mind, will she?"

"No, she`ll be all right."

"She goes up early, anyway, doesn`t she?"

If Evelyn felt some degree of curiosity about Maureen`s scheme, it soon became clear, when she arrived, that Maureen was preparing for a night out. They put the girls to bed at half past eight, and Evelyn`s mother went up half an hour later.

Almost immediately Maureen changed into a smart dress and clipped up her stockings. Then she went into the kitchen and started to put on make-up.

"What`s this then?"

"Going out."

"I`d never have guessed."

"Why not? I`m a widow now. It`s official. A single woman."

"Why all the secrecy then?"

"Oh, you know what they`re like. They never give me a minute`s peace, fussing all the time."

"So, where are you going, then?"

"You remember I told you about Frank from Avro?"

"The chap who`s divorced."

"Yes. Well, his divorce hasn`t come through yet, but it will be soon."

"Was it him you saw the other week, when you went out of work?"

"He had an afternoon off."

"Right," said Evelyn, nodding.

"Will I do?" said Maureen, with a bright smile.

She put on her coat and a headscarf. "Don`t wait up for me!" she said with a pert smile, and then she was gone.

Chapter 33

And then, in the February of 1945, John came home. Not, as Evelyn might have imagined, on a quick flying visit, where the best she might hope for was a couple of hours, sharing him with his pals at the Britannia or the Dusty Miller, but this time, for good, discharged for *incapacity beyond the officer`s control*, as the letter said. Which meant, as James explained, an honourable discharge, though it also meant, that he was no longer fit to serve.

What that meant, they had to wait and see.

Any gladness or hope, or expectancy – for it was surely better than the grim finality of the telegram about Bert - was offset by the reality of John`s arrival home.

He had no use of his legs, and his face was gaunt and drawn. His body seemed shrunken inside the grey demob suit they had put him in, and his hands, one over the other on his knees, twitched with self-consciousness as he endured other people`s reaction to his condition. Only his eyes, with a kind of bitter mirth, expressed a vestige of defiance.

He had been accompanied from Liverpool by a petty officer who brought him to the door of 7 Silk Street in a wheelchair, and who stayed for a cup of tea as if that were a requirement of decency.

"Take care of yourself, John," he said, as he departed, putting his hand on John`s shoulder. "I`m sure I`m leaving you in good hands."

It had been John`s wish to come to Silk Street. Evelyn`s resentment now vied with guilty relief that it somehow took responsibility for him away from her.

"All right," said John, when his companion had gone. "You can stop looking at the animal in the zoo, now."

"John love," said his mother, choking.

"I`d like to sit on my own for a bit," he said.

Alice had made up the front room for him, and James pushed him through.

"Do you want me to stay with you for a bit?" said Evelyn.

"No," he said quietly.

"What was wrong with that man?" said Merle, on their way home.

"He was injured in the war. He's very brave man. A hero."

"Is he my dad?"

"Yes," said Evelyn, stifling a sob in her own throat.

In the days and weeks that followed, John would not speak of what had happened to him. It was only when Eddie came back that they began to piece together a picture.

His ship had been torpedoed, and from what Eddie had heard, he had been lucky to get out of it at all. His legs had been crushed and there was some damage to his spine and his lungs. Most of the crew had perished.

Sometimes, she would sit with him for half an hour, and Merle would play on the floor with her doll close by, but he was testy in conversation, and soon became tired and irritable, especially when the children were there.

In the household, there was a day-by-day dialogue monitoring him.

"He had a good breakfast this morning, his appetite is definitely getting better..."

"He`s getting stronger, he managed to stand up at the toilet door, and sit down himself..."

Joan and Nancy joined in.

"He was in a good mood this morning. Joan told him that joke, the one about the man with a dog who could talk, and he had a right good laugh."

"It was him who told you that joke," said Maureen, who was slightly put out that her sitting room had been taken away from her.

"No it wasn`t," said Joan. "It was Eddie."

"He laughed anyway," said Nancy, regardless.

Sometimes, when Evelyn sat with him, particularly if she talked to him about getting better and coming back home, he grew irritable and shouted. Then, when she came out of the room. Alice would be standing there, with a look of concern and disapprobation on her face, as if it was she, Evelyn, who disturbed the otherwise smooth progress of his recovery.

One day, a mild spring day, she pushed him as far as Town Hall Recreation Grounds.

"I wish things could be as they used to be," he said. "Do you remember Hooley Bridge?"

"I do. And Queen`s Park, and Ashworth Valley."

He snuffed, a half-laugh. "Those were the days."

One evening, when she called round, he was drinking whisky.

"That`ll not help you get better."

"I`m not going to get better," he said. "Don`t you understand that. I`m not bloody well going to get better."

Chapter 34

It was Ernest who came to Wood Street to ask Evelyn if she knew where Maureen was. It was Sunday evening and Maureen had not been seen since the previous day.

"We thought she might have come and stayed here."

Evelyn shook her head. "She does sometimes, but not last night. Has she got Marcia with her?"

"Yes."

"Well, did she not say anything?"

Ernest shrugged his shoulders. "They`ve been knocked sideways with our John the way he is," he explained. "It`s caused no end of trouble, you know, with our Maureen. She just doesn`t see it. How hard it is."

Evelyn took a deep breath. "She didn`t say anything to me."

"Has she been seeing someone, Evelyn?"

"Come in, and sit down, Ernest. I`ll make some tea."

He sat awkwardly turning his hat round over his knee.

"If she has," he said tentatively, "you know, if you think she has, just tell me, for my own peace of mind, so I don`t worry something else has happened. Something worse."

"Tell me something, Ernest. Why didn`t John come home here, so that I could look after him. Why does he reject me?"

"I think it`s maybe because he doesn`t like you seeing him the way he is."

"It`s been that way for longer than that, Ernest."

"I can`t speak for him, Evelyn, he`s never confided in me, I swear. I wish he had, but he never did."

"I think your Maureen has been seeing someone. She sometimes comes here, and goes out. She doesn`t tell me much."

Ernest nodded. "Thanks."

She saw the trouble in his eyes.

"Don`t worry. She can look after herself."

"I dare say."

"Don`t tell her I said anything, will you? I don`t want her to think I`d go behind her back."

"I won`t. Will you let us know if you hear anything? If she gets in touch or anything?"

"Course I will."

"What`s up?" said her mother, who had retired discreetly to the kitchen when Ernest came in.

"It`s Maureen. She`s gone off somewhere with Marcia."

Her mother turned the corners of her mouth down. "Has she been mucking about with someone?"

"She`s met someone. A divorced bloke."

"It`ll be that, then. Look no further."

"Well, she can, can`t she? She`s a widow now."

"I`m not saying anything. Just that if you`re looking for her, that`s where she`ll be."

"I`ll see her at work tomorrow. Find out what`s going on."

At work the next day, Maureen`s position was empty.

"Where`s your Maureen, then?" said the overseer.

"She was a bit poorly over the weekend. I thought she`d be in this morning, though. Shall I go and call round, see if she`s all right?"

"Go during your break if she`s not in by then. I can`t afford to have two machines idle."

At break she put on her coat and scarf and ran across the footbridge, up Booth Street, and then across the main road, cutting through the backs up to Silk Street.

"And you`ve not had any word?"

"No," said Alice.

James sat silently, looking towards the fire, the set of his face that of a man wanting no communication, his world falling apart.

"Can I pop in and see John while I`m here?"

"He`s still asleep," said Alice, with a certain protective resolution.

"I`m his wife, Alice," she asserted.

"He needs his sleep," Alice said, quietly, but without losing a shred of her resolve.

Evelyn turned, walked down the hall and let herself out. On the doorstep, she took a deep breath, screwed her lips tight, and then made her way back to work.

Avro was out through Middleton Junction, on Green Lane. At half past four, Evelyn ran home, checking that her mother had picked up Merle, and that all was well, and then she hurried down to the centre, and caught a 54 bus, past the station, up Grimshaw Lane, and then walked the half mile to the Avro gates.

"I need to have a word with Frank Sharp," she said to the man on the desk.

"Is it important?" he asked, in an officious way.

"It`s family business, yes, important. I wouldn`t come all this way if it wasn`t."

"I`ll see if I can get someone to go over and see if he`ll come," said the man, unsympathetically, as though it was still a matter of chance.

He disappeared, and then a minute later, came back.

"Take a seat there," he said, pointing to a chair, as if it were the one designated for her, and she would lose her opportunity if she didn`t take it.

She complied, and waited.

Five minutes passed, and then ten. The man at the desk still ignored her, as if she had given herself up to a matter of chance in which it was not his role to intervene.

At last there came a sound of footsteps, and a man of thirty five, smartly dressed, appeared. He looked at the commissionaire, and the commissionaire nodded almost imperceptibly to where Evelyn was sitting. The man looked. It was obviously not whom he was expecting.

"She`s my sister-in-law," Evelyn explained. "She`s not been home since Saturday."

"How did you know to come here?"

"She told me. Enough, anyway."

"I`ve not seen her," he said. "Not for a couple of weeks. She was in a right mood, then, I couldn`t get any sense out of her. She was saying we had to get married, but I`d always said to her it was just a thing. No, that`s not true, it was always her telling me it was just a thing. Until she heard, you know..."

"About Bert."

"Yes."

He shrugged his shoulders. "My divorce hasn`t come through yet. I don`t know how long it will be. I can`t even think of marrying anyone else yet."

"And you`ve not seen her?"

He shook his head. She believed him.

"Look," he said, taking a pocket-book from his jacket, and ripping out a page. "This is my address. It`s on Pilkington Street, up past Spring Vale, do you know it?"

"Yes," said Evelyn.

"Well, look, anyway, if you hear anything, or if you need to speak to me, this is where I live. Or if it`s urgent, there`s a telephone number here. People will be grumpy, but if you say it`s important they will get me."

"Thanks."

"So, you`re Evelyn, then. Maureen`s told me about you."

"Has she?"

"Yes. I`m sorry about your husband."

"Thank you."

"Maureen said he was in a pretty bad way."

"Yes, he is."

"It`s a bad look-out, isn`t it, bloody war!"

"Anyway, I`d better get off."

"Right."

She walked back to the bus-stop, and in one sense she felt relieved. She`d had a picture of Frank in her mind, that he was someone who would just take advantage of Maureen, but now she felt sure that he was a decent man, a man that could be trusted.

A plain post-card from Maureen arrived at Silk Street with the first post on Tuesday morning. It was post-marked Blackpool. There was nothing to worry about, she said. She wanted to have a bit of time to herself, that was all. She didn`t give an address.

James was stern, and muttered rebukes under his breath, but there was a sense of relief in the house. At least she had contacted them; they knew she was somewhere, safe. Alice went quietly into the kitchen. She had other things to worry about.

When Evelyn called, John was sitting in the bay window where a little sunlight was still filtering through the net curtains.

"They`ve heard from Maureen," he said.

"Yes, your dad`s just told me."

"Don`t know what she`s playing at."

"How`ve you been feeling?"

He twisted his mouth. "About the same. They wheeled me out into the yard this afternoon. In the sun."

"That`s nice."

"I`ll be glad when it`s over."

"Don`t talk like that."

"Why not. We all know it."

"Let me take you home and look after you."

"Too late for that."

There was a long silence, and then he said, in a dry tone, "I`m sorry I let things go so badly."

"You don`t need to say that," she said quietly.

"The war`s a different world. It makes heroes out of some men. It just made a mess out of me. Scared out of my wits half the time, and drunk the rest."

"Nobody blames you," she said, her own secret buried deeply, a tight wedge of guilt.

"Pour me a glass of whisky, will you, love, before you go?"

"You shouldn`t."

"It helps. Takes the edge off."

"All right."

On arriving home, a card from Maureen was waiting for her, too. Before she could read it, however, Merle was demanding her attention. "Where have you been, mummy? You`re always going off somewhere or being late."

"I`ve been down to see grandma and granddad."

"Is Marcia there yet?"

"No. She`s in Blackpool."

"Has she gone on holiday?"

"Yes."

"Why didn`t they take me?"

"Come on, young lady," said her mother. "Time you were ready for bed." She nodded towards the card. "You`d better read that."

I`m in Blackpool. Can you come over to see me this weekend? I have to talk to you.

There was an address, but she was under strict orders not to reveal it to Alice and James.

"She`s in some sort of trouble," her mother said, when Merle was in bed.

"What do you think I should do?"

"Well, you`ve got two choices. Either you take this down to Silk Street, or you go to Blackpool and see her."

"What do you think I should do?"

"It`s not what I think you should do. It`s what you think you should do."

"And what`s that?"

"You`ll go."

"Will you be all right looking after Merle?"

"If you want. But why don`t you take her with you? Stop her getting bothered."

"No, I`d rather just go and come straight back. If I take Merle she`ll want to stay for a holiday."

"All right."

She caught the 59 - down through Rhodes, Heaton Park, up to Crumpsall, then through Cheetham Hill, to Victoria Station, and booked a day return to Blackpool. There was time for a cup of tea before the train left, but the café was dingy and smelled of stale cigarette and pipe smoke, so she went to wait on the platform, watching the business of the station until the train shunted in.

"Evelyn!"

She looked up.

"Evelyn," came the voice again, and from between the scattered platform crowd appeared the figure of Charlie Breen.

"Evelyn what are you doing here?"

"I could ask you the same question."

"I`m off to try my luck in Blackpool. They say it`ll be booming there when the war`s over. How about you?"

"I`m going to see a friend. Day trip."

"Very nice."

The train came to a halt, and the passengers began to board.

"Do you mind if I...?"

Without waiting for an answer, he sat beside her. She looked out of the window, her eyes on the platform, until the train gave its characteristic little lurch, and slowly, with a creaking and labouring of wheels, the platform began to lessen away. A short time later, moving with the steady rhythmic rackety-rack, and with smoke drifting past the window, they were looking out over the back-yards and roof-tops of Salford.

"They moved back to London," Charlie began. "Robert and Melisse."

"I don`t want to talk about Sunny Brow Road."

"No. Well, fair enough, Evelyn. Point taken. Best left in the past. Cigarette?"

"No thanks."

"Bad news about Herbert."

"Yes."

"How`s Maureen taken it?"

"Oh, you know. Some days are worse than others. She hadn`t seen him for nearly four years, remember."

For a moment she wondered whether it would do any harm to tell him the real reason for her visit to Blackpool, but she decided against it.

"I heard John was back."

"Yes."

"Do you mind if I ask, they said he was in bad way..."

"Yes, he is."

He waited for her to elaborate, but she didn`t.

"Well," he said at last, "he`s away from it now, anyway, time`s a great healer, I`m sure he`ll pull through. I bet he was glad to see Merle."

"He hardly recognises her. It`s the same with everyone. It`s changed him."

"I`m sorry to hear that."

It was eleven o`clock when the train arrived in Blackpool.

"What time`s your train back?" he asked.

"I`ll get the four o`clock or the five thirty."

"Fancy meeting up for a drink before you go?"

"No. I don`t think so, Charlie."

"Well, fair enough. I`ll be seeing you, then. Take care, Evelyn."

It was a quarter of an hour`s walk, through the rows of terraces off Waterloo Road to Durley Road, number 15, the address Maureen had given her. It was, like the other houses in the street, a run-down boarding house, with peeling paint, and yellowing net curtains at the front window.

The landlady, a thin grey lady of sixty, with an impassive but somehow severe expression, led her to the bottom of a staircase. "Third floor," she said. "Room 12."

"She disapproves," Maureen said. "But she`ll not turn custom away."

"Can we go to the sea-side?" said Marcia, obviously glad to see someone from home.

"Come on, then," said Maureen. "Let`s go out for a walk."

Evelyn waited until they were sitting on the sea-wall, with Marcia playing on the sand below, before she broached the subject of what was going on.

"I`m pregnant," said Maureen. "That`s what`s going on."

"Oh, Maureen, no!"

"Oh, yes."

"How long?" Evelyn asked, when the first shock had passed.

"About five months."

"And does no-one know?"

Maureen shook her head.

"You`re not showing much."

"I`ve been hiding it. No-one notices anything at home unless it`s to do with John. Don`t think I could get away with it much longer, though."

She took Evelyn`s hand and held it over her stomach.

They went to a café for lunch, some ham sandwiches and a pot of tea, with a small cup-cake for Marcia.

"I must have been pregnant before I heard about Bert," Maureen explained. "I don`t want anyone to know about that."

"What are you going to do?"

"Stay here. Have the baby here."

"You can`t," said Evelyn. "You`ve got to come home."

"I`ve written a letter to Frank, but I can`t bring myself to send it."

"Why? It`s his responsibility. He`ll have to do the right thing by you?"

"What if he doesn`t, though?"

"It is definitely his, isn`t it?"

"Yes. But he might not believe me. He`s always asking me. He thinks because I`ve been with him, I might have been with others."

"Have you told him about...?"

"No, but that was ages ago. Just a bit of fun. No need to drag that up, is there?"

"No."

They went back to sit on the beach. Marcia was digging a sandcastle, and another girl, much the same age, came to play with her. They worked earnestly together, with that natural instinct for collaboration and friendship."

"Have you got the letter with you?"

"Yes, in my bag."

"Give it me. I`ll take it to him. I`ll talk to him."

"I`m not sure..."

"You`ve got to do something."

"All right."

"Where does he live?" asked Evelyn, somewhat disingenuously, remembering that Frank had told her where he lived when she went to speak to him at Avrose.

"It`s on the envelope," said Maureen, bringing it from her bag.

Evelyn took it and put it in her own bag.

"I`ll go tomorrow, if I can. And I`ll send you a note. But you`ll have to tell them at home, too."

"One thing at a time!"

"Right, I`d better get going if I`m to catch the four thirty."

"Thanks for coming. Come on Marcia," she called. "We`ll walk you to the station."

They began to walk back along the South Beach promenade, and crossed the road towards the station entrance.

"That`s Charlie Breen, over there, isn`t it?" said Maureen.

"Where?"

"Just there, by the news stand."

She looked up and saw Charlie, smiling towards them in acknowledgment. "I bumped into him on the train coming down."

"You didn`t say."

"Didn`t think it was important."

"He looks as if he`s waiting to meet you."

"Hello, Maureen," said Charlie, taking off his hat. "Nice to see you. I didn`t know it was you Evelyn was coming to see."

"Right," said Maureen, turning to Evelyn. "Have a safe journey. I`ll see you soon."

"What`s she doing here, then, Evelyn?"

"Just having a bit of a holiday."

"Right. Fair enough."

"What are you doing here?"

"I told you. Seeing if there`s anything going on to tempt an entrepreneur..."

"No, I mean, what are you doing here, now?"

"Just thought I`d come and see you on your way. Why don`t you come and have a drink?"

"I`ve got a train to catch."

"It`s delayed," said Charlie. "I checked, just before. You`ve got an hour and a half to wait."

She insisted on going to the departures board to check; he wasn`t making it up.

"Look, Evelyn," he said, when they were sitting in the station café. "Why don`t you stop over, make a night of it? We could have a few drinks, something to eat – I saw a smashing looking chop-house just up the road – get a nice comfortable room in a big hotel. They don`t ask any questions."

"I`ve got to get back," she said, firmly.

"Think about it, Evelyn. We could make it a night to remember. Like that afternoon at Sunny Brow Road."

"I told you I didn`t want to talk about that."

"I know. But what`s the harm? Don`t tell me you didn`t enjoy it, because I know you did. Have a think about it, I`ll get us another drink, there`s still plenty of time."

Whilst he was being served, she pictured the lawn at Sunny Brow Road, and remembered the half hour they had spent together in the cool bedroom, on that summer day, nearly a year ago: stepping out of her own life for just a moment, being someone else. Now she had the perfect opportunity to do so again, and the thought of it, in this situation, where no-one could hold her accountable, was tempting.

"I got you a gin and tonic," said Charlie.

"What did you do today, then?"

"Went to see a man down at the Pleasure Beach. It`s all pretty rundown now, but I`m thinking I might make an investment. Once the war`s over, and things get back to normal, it`ll be like a licence to print money, I reckon."

"Sounds all right."

"So, come on then Evelyn, let`s crack a bottle and celebrate! What`s to stop us?"

"They`ve just announced my train."

"You could always ignore it."

“Yes, I could. But I`m not going to, Charlie.”

He grinned, like someone who knows what he was trying was a long shot, and having no hard feelings over it.

“Come on, then,” he said. “I`ll walk you to the platform.”

Chapter 35

She watched the expression on Frank`s face change as he read the letter.

"Bloody hell," he muttered, under his breath.

It was Sunday evening. On arriving home, she decided she had to take her mother into confidence.

"You don`t need to worry about me saying anything, not to the Wilkinsons or anybody. It`ll all come out soon enough, I dare say."

Now she was sitting in the armchair in Frank`s front room on Pilkington Street, waiting for him to finish reading.

"And she`s in Blackpool, you say?" he said, at last.

She nodded.

"Why didn`t she say anything?"

"I think she`s frightened. She just wanted to get away from everything before anyone found out."

"I take it they don`t know at home, then?"

"No. No-one did until she told me yesterday."

"Bloody hell," he muttered again, quietly, under his breath.

"Am I to take her a message?"

"Yes...," he muttered, "...I don`t know. I`ll have to think it out. Look, do you mind if I have a drink, Evelyn. You did say it was Evelyn, didn`t you?"

"Yes, Evelyn."

He went to the cupboard by the mantle-piece and took out a bottle of whisky.

"No thanks," she said at his gestured of offering her a drink.

He sat down again, with the glass in his hands. "I usually make it a rule not to drink in the house except for special occasions. I suppose this counts."

"It`s all right," she said. "It`s the same with us. We keep a bottle just in case."

"That`s right," he said.

"So," she said, at last. "What am I to say?"

"I`ll go and see her. I`ll go tomorrow. You`ll have to write the address down for me."

"All right," said Evelyn, reaching for her bag.

"What is it, a guest house?"

"Yes."

"And she`s got her little girl with her?"

"Marcia. Yes."

"Bloody hell," he muttered again.

"Good luck," she said.

"I think I might need it," he said, swallowing the last of his whisky.

On Monday she saw the overseer and told him that Maureen wanted her cards. She told the other girls that she`d been called away suddenly to look after a sick relative in Gorton.

"Poor thing!" someone said.

"Never mind `poor thing`. I wouldn`t mind a sick relative if it`d get me out of this place!"

"So, who is it, then? I didn`t know she had family in Gorton."

"Right, come on," called the overseer. "Let`s get to work, ladies!"

By lunchtime, other gossip had taken over from Maureen`s absence.

It was on Tuesday, when she visited Silk Street to sit with John for half an hour, that she found Frank already there. It was a family gathering. John was sitting in Alice`s usual chair, opposite James. Alice and Frank were sitting in chairs drawn round from the dining table.

"This is Evelyn. Maureen`s sister-in-law."

"I`ll go and wait in the front room if you like," she said.

"No, it`s all right," said Frank. "You`ll need to hear all this as well."

"He`s got our Maureen with child," said Alice, sobbing.

"As I said," Frank went on, picking up at the point he`d left off, "I`ve been to see her, and I`ve found a proper place for her to stay. Comfortable enough, with a bit of a kitchen and bathroom, and her own door and everything. I can`t marry her yet, because I`m waiting for my divorce to come through, but I`ve told her I`ll see her right, and as soon as I can I`ll marry her, so long as that`s what she wants."

As he was talking, Evelyn looked over at John. His face was grey, the face of a spectre, and there were moments when she thought his eyes were going to close and his head drop forward. She could not help but think that his presence must make Frank`s ordeal more of an ordeal.

"She`s only been a widow for three months," Alice was saying. "I don`t know how you think she could know her own mind so soon, to put her through this."

"I`m very sorry, Mrs Wilkinson, but all I can do is say what I`ve said. I`ll do the right thing by her, if I`m allowed to."

Evelyn realised he could have said more, and admired him a little for not saying things which could have lessened Maureen in her parents` eyes.

"I`ll go and see her," said James. "I`ll talk to her, and get her point of view."

"I tried to persuade her to come back," said Frank. "But she was already set against it."

James nodded. "I believe you`ve done your best, lad. In the circumstances. You didn`t need to come here, but you`ve done what you thought you had to. I`ll see Maureen, and we`ll take it from there."

She helped John up from his chair, and James came to help, too, in the business of getting him back to the front room. He was almost light enough to carry, she thought, but there was hardly any strength in his legs at all.

He sat on the bed, getting his breath back, for several minutes. Then, he seemed to be laughing.

"What?" she asked.

"Good job Ernest wasn`t here," he said, repeating the harsh, wheezy laugh.

"Do you want me to stay with you for a bit?" she asked.

"Think I`ve had enough excitement for one day, don`t you? Poor old Herbert, he`d turn in his grave, wouldn`t he, if he had one."

"Don`t be too hard on her."

"Get me a glass before you go," he said. "She brings me barley water, thinks it`ll get me better. Put something proper in it for me, will you?"

Chapter 36

Maureen had her baby, a girl, in Blackpool Victoria, in August 1945. She decided to call her Joan. Frank`s divorce was completed in the autumn. The wedding was in a registry office in Blackpool. Ernest was there, with his mother. James had stayed at home to be with John. Evelyn was not invited. It was expected that she would be at Silk Street, as required.

After two weeks, Maureen came back, with Marcia and Joan, to live with Frank at the house in Pilkington Street, beginning her life as Mrs Sharp. It was terraced house, with the front door straight onto the pavement, similar to Wood Street, but it was spacious inside, and Frank had done some work on it, decorating and fitting it out with nice furniture.

Evelyn went to visit, a couple of weeks after they came back, with Merle. Frank took the two girls out for a walk.

"He`s very good with Marcia," said Maureen.

"That`s nice."

"I think it suits him, being a father. It`s in his nature. He says he`d quite like Marcia to take his name, you know, so we`re all of a piece, when she goes to school and everything."

Evelyn nodded. Maureen checked that Joan was sleeping and then poured some tea.

"So," she said, "you still haven`t explained what you were doing in Blackpool with Charlie Breen."

"I wasn`t doing anything with him. I told you, I just happened to meet him on the train."

"But he was waiting for you, wasn`t he?"

"I didn`t know he was going to be there."

"But you went for a drink with him, didn`t you? I saw you."

"Maureen! Were you spying on me?"

Maureen shrugged her shoulders. "Either you did or you didn`t."

“Well, what if I did? The train was delayed. I caught the half past five. Where`s the harm in that?”

“I didn`t say here was any harm, did I?”

“No, but you`re hinting at it.”

Maureen sipped her tea, and went silent.

“Well?” said Evelyn, at last.

“I know I`m not perfect, Evelyn, but it`s just when I think of our John the way he is, it`d break his heart if he saw you, meeting up with someone like that at a pub in Blackpool.”

“And what about your Bert? What would he have thought if he`d known what you were up to?”

“That`s not the same thing. He was missing. We already knew the worst. Well I did.”

At that point, Frank came in with the children.

“We went on the swings,” said Merle.

“Any tea left in the pot?” said Frank, cheerily.

“Forget I said anything,” Maureen said, in the hallway, as they were preparing to go. “I`ll never mention it again.”

Evelyn walked with Merle to the corner of Oldham Road, and waited for the bus. Inside, she felt angry at Maureen, not only because of her hypocrisy, but because she was carping at something which had happened when she was going out of her way to help her out of a fix. But underneath, what rankled was that Maureen had somehow elevated the meeting in Blackpool to the level of a betrayal. And what rankled beneath that, was that without realising it, Maureen had stumbled on the truth.

She stayed on the bus a further stop, and called in at Silk Street. John was in better spirits than usual, more talkative, and Merle sat by him and let him stroke her hair.

“I`ve been feeling better today,” he said. “I`ve always liked autumn, I like the smell of autumn.”

“I`ll push you out in your wheelchair if you like. It`s still light.”

"I don`t like people seeing me out in that thing. Makes me feel like a cripple. I`m going to try walking up the street, with my crutches, just a few steps each day, build up the strength in my legs."

"That`s good."

"I think maybe I should get away from here. It closes round me like a cobweb at times, what with my mother fussing and all. If I can get a bit of strength back in my legs, I was thinking I could come back with you, we could even think of renting a place again. I sometimes think how good it would be to be together in a big double bed again. Do you remember that?"

"Of course I do," she said, squeezing his hand.

On the way home, in the growing autumnal dusk, her eyes were filled with tears. His gentleness hurt her more than his indifference. His hope hurt her more than his despair.

She put Merle to bed, and talked to her about her dad, and about Marcia`s new dad. Then, she said to her mother that she was tired and was going to go up for an early night.

"You go up, love," said her mother, somehow wordlessly in tune with her mood. "I`ll bring you up a cup of tea."

In the middle of the night there was a knock on the door.

It was James.

"You`d better come," he said.

Chapter 37

When she opened her eyes, she struggled for a moment to know where she was. James was sitting opposite, his head bowed to his chest in sleep; Alice was sitting by the bed, awake but still as a statue. John`s breath seemed easier now; the steep, harsh gasps had now become more restful, less distressing: when she had arrived at the house, at three o`clock, she had been certain that he was about to die.

The first cold light of dawn was beginning to creep along the edges of the curtain, and through the slightly open door, the steady ticking of the clock in the next room could be heard. It struck the hour with six small chimes, and Alice stirred.

"You come and sit by him," she said to Evelyn. "I`ll get ready for the girls getting up.

She went quietly out of the room, and Evelyn took her place by the bed, touching John`s shoulder, just as his mother had before.

On the walk across to Parkfield, James had told her that he had begun to complain of being short of breath in the evening. The doctor had come, and he had given him something for the pain, but at the doorway he had explained quietly to James that there was nothing more he could do for him. He had managed to sleep for a time, but then had awoken with cramps and tightness across his chest. Then he had begun to lapse out of consciousness and they thought he was slipping away. It was then that Alice had told James that he must go and bring Evelyn.

There was the sound of feet on the staircase, Joan and Nancy getting up. Hushed voices came from the next room, and then the two girls came to the doorway.

"Go in, and give him a kiss," said Alice.

Evelyn stood to make way, as the girls obeyed, first Joan, then Nancy, leaning over to kiss John`s forehead, both white-faced and suppressing tears.

"Now, come on, and have some breakfast. Then you must go to tell Maureen and Ernest, Nancy, and you must go to work, Joan."

"I can`t go to work, mum!"

"You must. There`s nothing you can do here."

Footsteps were passing by the window now, people on their way to work. For the rest of the world, a normal day was beginning. The daylight was full outside, and James stood to put out the electric light.

A short time later, the front door opened and closed as Joan and Nancy left the house. Alice brought in a tray with tea and some toast.

"You must eat something, both of you," she said, though neither of them did.

"Go upstairs and lie down for half an hour," Alice said to James. "It might be a long day."

She took Evelyn`s place by the bed. "Do you want to go and see to Merle?"

"I`ll just pop over, and see she`s right. I`ll come straight back."

She put on her coat, and let herself out, turning left, and hurrying up the steps and across the Rec., the quickest way. She knew that her mother would look after Merle, but in truth, she felt a guilty relief to be away from the house, from the silent intensity of the death-bed room. It felt like a terrible kind of freedom.

"Have you been to see my dad?" said Merle, who was dressed and ready for school.

"Yes."

"In the middle of the night? Is he very ill?"

"He`s sleeping now."

She looked up. Her mother tilted her head, posing a question. Evelyn shook her head quickly. Her mother seemed to understand both of the intended meanings.

They walked down together, escorting Merle to the little school in Parkfield.

"Who`s picking me up?" said Merle.

"I am, sweetie," said her mother.

"Are you going to stay with my dad?"

"Yes."

Merle seemed happy with this and went off into the playground.

"I`ll have to tell them at work," Evelyn said.

"I`ll go," said her mother. "You go and do what you have to do. You`ll only have this one chance. It`s a bad business, but you`ll only get your peace of mind if you see it through."

"He`s much more peaceful now," said Alice, when she went back into the room. "Listen."

His breathing now was steady and quiet, almost inaudible. She leaned forward to listen. Alice smiled. What was she thinking, Evelyn wondered. Did she still somehow cherish the thought that he would yet recover, or was it a stage in the process of grief?

James came down from his rest. Evelyn went into the kitchen and made another pot of tea. Then they sat and chatted quietly, almost normally, remembering things – when John had played for the Parkfield AFC team, when he had first told them about Merle, when he come back for the first time in his navy uniform. Little stories, affectionate details, things that even made them laugh.

And then, at quarter to ten, just when there was an illusion of a pleasant normality that had hours to run yet, John`s breath began to rattle in his throat. It went on for twenty minutes, and then, suddenly, he opened his eyes, wide open, clear and pale blue, and then his breath, which had become quiet, stopped altogether.

Chapter 38

Ernest took care of the funeral arrangements.

It gave him something to do, something to keep him from the falling into the abyss of his own thoughts.

The undertaker came in the early afternoon to lay out the body, and immediately a first veneer of formality was imposed. The coffined figure, dignified in his navy dress uniform, was much less awful than the exhausted body lying in his soiled and crumpled sheets. There was a sense now that his pain was gone. The vicar came and said a quiet prayer with the family and accepted a small glass of whisky, and then the doctor, who, having formally pronounced the fact of death, now brought the certificate he had prepared. Ernest took it to the registrar, and the vicar stayed to talk to James and Alice about the service.

Maureen came later in the afternoon. For a minute or two, she and Evelyn were alone together in the room. Maureen stepped forward to look down at John, and Evelyn was aware of the soft sniff of tears held back. She said nothing to comfort Evelyn, or to commiserate; when she turned to go, their eyes met for a second, and whilst Evelyn looked for condolence, Maureen`s expressed only a kind of cold repudiation. Soon after, she left to go home, and they did not see her again until the day of the funeral.

Some neighbours called, to express their sympathy, and those who so wished were allowed to see him and pay their respects. The family all moved about the house with a strange detached quietness, like ghosts themselves.

And so the day passed. James wrote a letter to Eddie, and they planned how to keep the wake for the first night.

"You go home, now," said Alice to Evelyn. "Go and see to Merle. We can manage here."

It was not unkindly, but underneath, Evelyn felt that the family wanted to close its ranks without her there.

It was something of a relief.

"Nancy came, then?" she asked when she got home.

"Yes. Poor lass. She could hardly get it out."

"Does Merle know?"

"Not yet. I thought it was best coming from you. She`s fast asleep now. I should leave her until the morning."

The following day, Ernest took the train to Liverpool to report John`s death personally to his ship`s HQ. He was kept waiting for an hour in a dingy waiting room by an orderly who had not fully grasped the nature of the situation but then he was apologised to profusely by an officer who had mugs of tea brought in, and then produced a flask of brandy. There was a process of application, he explained, in response to Ernest`s enquiry, for the Royal Navy to endorse a gravestone or memorial with its insignia, and with an inscription that stated death from wounds sustained in service.

"If I can take down the details from the death certificate," he said, trying to decipher the doctor`s scrawl. "That should be fine, Mr Wilkinson. I`ll just give you this form, and this one, and if they could be returned to this address in Portsmouth, it should be a mere formality. It usually takes two to three months, but experience suggests that most Parish Cemetery Commissions advise a similar period before the erection of a monument to avoid the possibility of settlement."

"We weren`t actually thinking of a monument," said Ernest who had fondly imagined that if he tried hard enough the gravestone and the committal would be almost simultaneous.

"A standard gravestone does classify as a monument, Mr Wilkinson," said the officer, with kindly condescension, offering a further small measure of brandy to Ernest`s mug.

"Right," said Ernest.

"Bloody awful business," said the officer, as if wanting to let his guard down. "So many young men. At least your brother died at home, with people he loved around him. Some men joined the navy because of what they heard about the trenches, but a death in the sea can be a terrible thing. I have to see a lot of people where there`s no body, you see, terrible ordeal for them, no real closure, you see…"

"My brother-in-law was lost, presumed dead, in action in Burma."

"Well, there you are, Mr Wilkinson," he said, emptying the last drops of his flask into his own and Ernest`s mug, "you already have a taste of what that feels like."

"Have you been drinking?" said Gladys, when Ernest arrived home, and collapsed into a chair.

"No, just tired," he replied. "Tired. Tired. Tired."

The day of the funeral dawned bright but by ten o`clock a steady drizzle had set in, and after the service at All Saints, in Rhodes, the mourners stood at the graveside clustered under the black umbrellas of those who had had the foresight to bring them. Two naval people from Liverpool came and introduced themselves to James and Alice. Eddie, granted compassionate leave for the day, was in his uniform. Maureen stood with Ernest and Gladys; the two other daughters, Joan and Nancy stood with their parents; Evelyn stood in a loose group which comprised the two men from Liverpool, some neighbours, and others from the neighbourhood who regularly attended funerals whoever it was.

Afterwards, they returned to Silk Street, and Evelyn helped Alice serve refreshments, and for a short time, with the help of some of James` whisky for those who were so inclined, the sombre atmosphere was alleviated with reminiscences, and philosophical and religious reflection.

Maureen was the first of the family to leave, and it seemed to Evelyn once again that she had deliberately avoided being left alone to talk to her. Later, Evelyn slipped out quietly, saying to Alice that she thought she should get back to see Merle. Later, Ernest called round.

"I`m sorry I didn`t get a chance to say goodbye this afternoon, I didn`t realise you`d gone."

"It was all a bit much, Ernest. I wanted a bit of time to myself."

"Well, that`s understandable, Evelyn. I just hope, well, you`re still family, and you must let us keep on seeing Merle."

"Of course I will, Ernest. What makes you think I wouldn`t?"

"I don`t know. Nothing really."

"Maureen`s a bit off with me sometimes. I don`t know why."

"That`s just Maureen. Ever since she got married again she`s been hoity-toity with all of us. She`s got a lot of memories she wants to scrub out, I think."

"I suppose everybody`s trying to make a new start, one way and another."

"Yes, well let`s hope the world`s a better place, now that it`s all coming to an end. God knows, people have paid the price for it."

Chapter 39

VE night in Middleton, as in towns up and down the land, was a matter of riotous and exuberant celebration, all day and well into the night. Crowds gathered in the Gardens and danced with strangers, drunken revellers sang patriotic songs, and some of the more foolhardy doused themselves in the fountain.

"There`ll be some headaches tomorrow morning," Evelyn said to her mother.

"Aye, and a few more headaches in nine months` time, I shouldn`t wonder."

Next day the clearing up began.

Three months later, victory in Japan was declared, and from then onwards the sense that the war was truly over began to take hold.

There were street parties on Wood Street, tables set out, end to end, in the middle of the road. Similar celebrations took place throughout the town. There was a sense of excitement about when all the boys would be coming back, but like most expectations, such as the end of austerity, the hopes of things getting better, it was a slow process. Normality returned, but it was a normality that wasn`t much less grey than the normality which had existed before.

In November, on a crisp morning, with just a hint of mist, Evelyn walked with Merle as far as Rhodes, and found to her surprise that John`s headstone was in place. It was a white tablet, three feet high, with the symbol of the navy, an anchor and chain engraved in a circle at the top, and a cross below. The inscription was simple: *He Gave His Life For Those He Loved, And Those He Loved Remember.*

She tried to explain the significance to Merle, and the little girl stood solemnly for a moment, with tearful eyes, trying to take it in. Then she went off to play, looking for flowers amongst the graves, and Evelyn stood at the grave, in silent communion.

"Why didn`t you tell me?" she asked, calling in at Silk Street on the way home.

"It`s only been there a week. We`ve hardly seen it ourselves yet. I think Ernest was going to call round, didn`t he say he was going to call, Jim?"

"I think so. I would have come round myself, but I thought we`d be seeing you anyway."

They were indulgent of Merle.

"You must bring her down every Saturday, or Sunday, leave her for a couple of hours, if you like. Then, if Maureen brings Marcia, they can play together. They`re like sisters, really."

Frank, she was told, had bought a little business in Middleton Junction, a newsagent and tobacconist`s shop, with live-in premises. They were going to be moving in soon, and Maureen was going to take a hand in the business. Frank had ideas, it seemed, about how to expand it and build up the trade.

Later in the year, her war-widow`s pension came through and it was back-dated to the date of John`s death when his disability service pension had stopped.

"You`ll be comfortable now," Alice said. "He would have wanted that, for you and Merle."

She walked home with a slightly uncomfortable sense that the pension somehow put her under an obligation to them.

"What they want," said her mother, "is for you not to meet anyone else and get married again. The devoted widow, bringing up their grandchild, that`s what they want, if you ask me."

"What do you think I should do?"

"You`re thirty two," said her mother. "And you`re flesh and blood. Find another husband, that`s what I think. And it`s what you think, too, if you`re honest with yourself."

Chapter 40

One Sunday, almost a year after John`s funeral, Evelyn called in at Silk Street to find that Joan had brought her sweetheart home to tea. He was a neat fresh-faced young man, handsome enough, with jet black hair, not much more than twenty, and he had been demobbed just a couple of months before, having been up through Germany after the surrender, helping to get the mess sorted out, as he said.

"This is my sister-in-law, Evelyn," said Joan, full of herself. "This is Ronny."

"Hello, Ronny."

"And this is my niece, Merle."

Merle, shy, hid behind Merle`s skirts, but was soon peeping out at the stranger, who waited for her to peep and then winked at her, so that it soon turned into a game.

They sat down to tea. It turned out that Ronny was the son of Joe Warburton, who managed Coombes the cobbler`s shop in the town centre, and who had been the Parkfield A.R.P. during the war. The young man had started work at Ashton Smethurst`s building yard, but he had been at the Grammar School before joining up, and it seemed that he had good prospects of getting on.

He had also become pals with Eddie, who had arrived back on civvy street at about the same time. They`d been over to the dog track at White City for a night out, and to Manchester Racecourse down in Salford, and Joan confided that she was worried some of Eddie`s fecklessness would rub off on Ronny, but to Evelyn he seemed a steady enough lad, and she doubted he would let himself get led very far astray.

Ernest now had a job at the offices of the Borough Council, and every Friday night, his routine was to have some tea with the family at Silk Street, and then call to see Evelyn and Merle, before catching the bus going back home, and taking Gladys out for a drink at the Liberal Club.

"I wish our Eddie would get himself settled down," he said, on one such occasion.

"I expect he`ll find his feet," Evelyn suggested. "I`ve heard about others who`ve taken time to get the war out of their system."

"He`s talking of going to Blackpool now."

"Blackpool?"

"He was talking to someone in the pub, one of John`s old pals, Charlie Breen, and apparently he was saying there`s work to be had there."

"Really," said Evelyn, suppressing a moment of panic at the thought of Charlie talking directly to one of John`s family.

"I think what our Eddie sees is not work but one long holiday, that`s the trouble," said Ernest, grinning and clicking his tongue in that peculiar way he had.

After he had gone, Evelyn took a deep breath. She reassured herself that Charlie would not let anything slip, especially to Eddie, who, she had no doubt, would make short work of it if he thought any slight was being offered to John. On the other hand, she wondered how it would be if Charlie Breen`s name came up in conversation in the family when Maureen happened to be there, whether Maureen might say she suspected something odd was going on when she saw Charlie waiting for her outside Blackpool Station.

The next few times she went to Silk Street she was on tenterhooks, but it passed off easily enough. Eddie had taken a job at the Cromer Mill, and was seeing a girl he met there, Beatrice, and so for the time being there was no talk of Blackpool.

Then, as is often the way, one kind of relief leads immediately into another kind of trouble.

She came home one afternoon, after picking up Merle from school, and found her mother slumped in a chair, with a cup of tea spilt over her lap, and the cup on the floor at her feet.

"I`ll just make a cup of tea," she had said, as Evelyn went out. "I`ll have five minutes, then I`ll get her tea ready..."

Merle, with a child`s intuition that something is deeply wrong, began to cry. Hurriedly, Evelyn took her to the neighbour, and asked them to send out for the doctor.

Going back into the house, she got out the smelling salts, but it was to no avail, and she became aware, as she tried to minister to her, that her mother had soiled herself in the chair. Before the doctor arrived, Evelyn had already begun to feel the chill of death spreading through her body.

"Heart failure," the doctor said. "It could have happened at any time. Would you like me to arrange for her to be taken to the chapel of rest?"

"I don`t know," said Evelyn. "It doesn`t seem proper somehow."

"More and more people are doing it that way, these days. And with just yourself and a child in the house."

Evelyn nodded. "Yes, then, if you would."

She took Merle down to Silk Street.

"Oh, no!" said Alice, in shock. "Sit down. Jim, give her a drop of brandy. I`ll put the kettle on."

"Right," said James.

"Poor love," said Alice, turning to Merle. "Come with me. I`ll see if I can find you something nice in the kitchen."

"Are they laying her out?" asked James.

"I said I`d have her taken to the chapel."

"To the chapel?" said Alice, bringing in the tea.

"The doctor suggested it, with it just being me and Merle in the house."

Alice nodded and glanced towards James.

"Well, I suppose it makes things easier," she said, with a slight hint of disapproval which Evelyn chose to ignore.

Ernest called round the following night. "I`m so sorry, kid," he said. "If there`s anything I can do, anything at all."

"I`m going to have her cremated," she said. "Up at Rochdale. Next Tuesday. I don`t want a lot of fuss. Tell your mum and dad for me, will you? I don`t suppose they`ll approve."

"Well, it`s nothing to do with them," said Ernest, in an uncharacteristic show of disloyalty. "Do you want us to come?"

"Yes. Will you tell your Maureen?"

"Course I will."

"She knew my mam. They always got on."

"I`ll go over there tonight."

Ernest came to the crematorium, with James and Joan. Alice was not feeling well, James explained. There was no sign of Maureen.

A week later, she went up to Rochdale with her neighbour, Myrtle, to pick up the ashes.

"What are you going to do with them? Put them on the mantle-piece?"

"I don`t know."

"You can have them put in a graveyard. Some people scatter them, in the woods or at sea. I`m not sure how that works out at the day of judgement. If you ask me, I`d rather have me body in one place, full of worms or not, but I suppose that`s just old fashioned."

"Well, I`ll think of somewhere for her."

"I`ll tell you where she`d want to go, your mam. She`d want them putting in the yard outside, just by the back gate where she can stand and hear a right load of gossip!"

Chapter 41

"Your name`s on the rent-book," said the landlord, "and that`s all right by me, so long as the rent`s forthcoming, so to speak. There`s not any problem over that, is there?"

"No," said Evelyn. "I`ve got a bit of a pension from my husband, so I should be all right. I can go back to work when Merle`s a bit older."

The landlord nodded. He was not particularly concerned with personal details; he liked to get his money and steer clear of trouble and messy dispute.

"Now that I`m on my own here, with just my daughter," said Evelyn, broaching a subject which her mother had prompted on several occasions before she died, "how would it be if I were to take in a lodger, to help out, if need be."

"You want to be careful," said the landlord, "you don`t want any trouble or complications."

"No, but could I, according to my terms?"

"I`d rather you didn`t, but if you have to, make sure you draw up an agreement with a week`s notice specified. I don`t want a sitting tenant if you choose to up sticks."

"No, I`ll make sure there`s no inconvenience. Not that I think I`ll have to do it anyway, but just in case."

"That`s right. Now, I have to get on, so unless there`s anything else..."

"No," said Evelyn.

She had meant to mention the bit of damp that was coming through in the back bedroom where the gutter was dripping, but she decided to let it pass, for this time at least. She felt she had gained enough. She didn`t want to tempt providence.

"I`ll ask Ronny," said Joan, when she mentioned the problem of damp when she was next at Silk Street.

A couple of days later, Ronny came round with a ladder and some cement, and he repointed the brickwork under the gutter.

"That should dry out, now," he said.
"Can I have my own room, now?" asked Merle.
"Yes, all right."
"And can Marcia come to stay with us?"
"We`ll have to see," said Evelyn.
"You`re always saying that,"
"What?"
"We`ll have to see."
"Well, we will, won`t we!"

"Can I walk to school on my own?" asked Merle, one morning, just after her seventh birthday.

"Yes, all right," said Evelyn. "As long as you go straight there, I don`t want you wandering off, mind!"

"I won`t."

She took her across Wood Street, and then watched as she made her way along Cross Street towards the school. There were plenty of other youngsters making their way to school alone, so it wasn`t a worry.

That night, Merle was full of her own independence.

"Can I walk down to my gran`s on Saturday? On my own I mean."

"You won`t get lost will you?" she teased.

"Course I won`t. I`ve been there hundreds of times."

So, that Saturday, she saw Merle across the road, and watched her on her way before going down into the centre of the town to do some shopping. Whilst she was there, she dropped off some shoes at Coombes, for soling and heeling, and it was Joe Warburton who served her at the counter.

"Sorry to hear about your mother, Evelyn," he said, putting a tag on the shoes. "We used to have a right good chat when she came in."

"Oh, aye, she was always one for a bit of a chat."

“We`ve been seeing a bit of your Joan, too, what with her and our Ronny.”

“He came over and did a job for me a couple of weeks ago.”

“Trying to impress, eh? I wish he`d do a few jobs here from time to time,” he joked.

“He`s a very nice young man.”

“Thanks, Evelyn. He`s not a bad one, when all`s said and done.”

“Get away with you, Joe, you`re proud as Punch of him!”

“Well, maybe I am, at that.”

When she got back to the house, she heard the sound of giggling from upstairs, and when she called, Merle`s face appeared at the landing, with Marcia`s beside her.

“Marcia!” she said. “What are you doing here?”

“Come to play,” the little girl answered. “Merle brought me.”

“I held her hand all the way,” said Merle.

“Does your mum know you`re here?”

“She wasn`t there.”

“Gran said we could play out if we didn`t go far.”

“We`d better get you back before she starts worrying. Come on, get your coats on.”

Before they could set out, however, there was a knock on the door, and an irate Maureen walked in.

“What`s going on?” she said.

“What do you mean? There`s nothing going on.”

“I left her with my mum for half an hour. And when I get back she`s gone off with your Merle. She`s not old enough to go wandering off.”

“She`s safe enough here.”

“That`s not the point.”

“Well, I`m sorry. I was just about to bring her back. No harm was meant.”

“Right, then.”

"Stay and have a cup of tea while you`re here. I hardly see you these days."

"I haven`t time. Frank`s expecting me back, and I`m already late."

"Right. Well, she`s got her coat on."

After they`d gone, she found Merle sitting on her bed upstairs.

"What`s up, love?"

"Why was Aunty Maureen angry? Was it because I was bad bringing Marcia here?"

"Course you weren`t bad, love, she was just in a bit of a rush to get home. You weren`t to know."

"Marcia said she was going on holiday to Blackpool, with her mum and dad and baby Joan."

"Did she?"

"And gran and granddad Jim. Can we go on holiday, mum?"

"We`ll see."

"You`re always saying that."

"We`ll have to save up."

It was that weekend that she decided to put an advert in the newsagent`s window offering lodgings. She sat down to word the card so that it was clear she wanted a respectable person, a working or professional person with no family attachments.

"It`ll give me a bit extra," she said to Myrtle, the neighbour. "I could do with it."

"You`re doing the right thing," said Myrtle. "Who knows, maybe you`ll get an eligible young man."

"Not a chance," said Evelyn. "I`m done with all that."

"No-one`s done with all that!" said Myrtle. "Least of all those who say they are!"

Chapter 42

"He`s says he`s going to get Marcia`s name changed," said Ernest, when he called round, on Friday night, a couple of weeks later.

"How do you mean?"

"Legally, you know. Adopt her, so that she has his surname."

"What does Maureen think?"

"She`s all for it. She`ll do anything he says, if you ask me. But maybe it makes sense."

"Poor old Bert. He never even saw her, and now they`re taking his name off her."

"Well, the world rolls on."

"I suppose it does."

"I`m sorry they didn`t take Merle away with them, Evelyn. I told them, I said to my mother it wasn`t right."

"Well, they can`t take everyone. Anyhow, I`m hoping to take her away on holiday myself in a bit."

"Well, that`s grand."

"Have another cup of tea, Ernest?"

"Go on, then. One before I get off."

The next time she was at Silk Street, she hinted that she would like to take Marcia with them to Blackpool in a few weeks` time.

"Just a long weekend," she said. "They`ll be good company for each other."

Alice seemed pleased, but as the time approached, she didn`t say whether or not she`d asked Maureen, and Evelyn decided not to press the point.

"She`s only little, anyway," said Merle, dismissively. "I`ll have more fun with you."

They were lucky to get one of the finest weekends of the summer. Evelyn got a deckchair on the crowded beach, and Merle bathed in the sea. In the evening they went to a show at the Tower, and the next day walked down to the funfair, where business seemed to be picking up now that the war was over. She wondered if Charlie was still working there, and kept half an eye open, but there was no sign of him.

Getting back home, she took out the card she had started to write for the newsagent`s window, copied it out with one or two little changes on a fresh card, and the following day took it across to Whittaker`s. On the way back from the shops, she stopped to look at it, now posted in the window and wondered if she would get any response.

There was nothing for a week. Then, a young couple came who were getting married, and wanted a room until they could find their own place. Then, there was a man in his fifties who had been transferred to the Middleton Post Office, and who said he would only take the room if there was an assurance that the little girl could be relied on to be quiet. She had to tell both of them that she considered them unsuitable.

Finally, there was a Miss Owen, who had taken a teaching position at the Durnford Street School, and she seemed ideal.

She was quiet and kept herself to herself, most of the time, her main preoccupations being marking her books and ironing her blouse and skirt for the next day, but after a few weeks she began to come out of her shell, and sometimes, on Friday nights, she would sit and chat to Evelyn, and in that sense it was nice to have a bit of company. On Saturdays, she usually went home, to her parents in Urmston, which gave them a break too, so, all-in-all, it seemed the perfect solution.

Then out of the blue, one day just after she had returned from the Christmas vacation, she announced to Evelyn that she was getting married.

"It was someone I knew at college," she explained, "but he was engaged to someone else. That`s fallen through now, and he asked me. I said yes, straight away."

"Do you love him?"

"Yes, I think so."

"You think so?"

"Can I tell you something, Evelyn? When we were at college, after graduation, we had a sherry party, and, afterwards, I let him have his way with me. Well, I say it like that, but I wanted it, too. Now, he says that`s he broken off his engagement, because of that, and that he couldn`t stop thinking about me. Do you think that`s a bad start for agreeing to get married."

"Not necessarily," said Evelyn, realising how confused and rusty her own thoughts were about marriage and sex. "You have to follow your heart, I suppose."

"You should find someone else, Evelyn. You`re still young, still very attractive."

"Such flattery!"

"It`s not flattery."

"Can I tell you something, Sue? When my husband was away in the navy, I had a bit of a fling with another man. I didn`t know then that my husband was going to die, but I knew he had fallen out of love with me."

"It must have been hard, what with the war and everything."

"I`ll tell you what, shall we have a glass of sherry?"

"Go on, then. Just one. I don`t suppose it`ll do any harm…"

After Susan`s departure, Evelyn found herself missing the routines which had built up around her comings and goings, the meals, the occasional chat in the evening, sometimes over a glass of sherry. She thought about putting her advert back in the window of the newsagent`s, but held back, thinking to herself that she might not be so lucky next time.

"Are we going to have another lodger?" asked Merle.

"Why?"

"I didn`t think I`d like having a lodger, but Sue was nice. I liked her."

"Yes, she was, wasn`t she?"

"Could we have Marcia as a lodger?"

Evelyn laughed. "I think Marcia`s already got lodgings."

"Yes, but she wouldn`t have if she ran away."

"Why would she do that?"

"Because she hates her new dad. That`s what she told me at grandma`s. She said she wants to come and live with us."

"Does she tell your gran this?"

"No, just me."

"Well, you must tell her she`s got to try and like her new dad, because he`ll look after her."

"She doesn`t like baby Joan, either. She says she`s just a nuisance."

Evelyn laughed again. "Is there anything she does like?"

"She likes Aunty Joan, because she shows her how to dance and she says we can have her old tap shoes when our feet are big enough."

For a time they settled back into living alone in the house, just the two of them, but she soon began to notice the difference, when her own rent was due at the end of the month, and it was this that persuaded her, after three months, to have another go.

It was a windy night in March, about half past eight, when there was a knock on the door. Merle ran down the stairs, calling that she would see to it, and then she came into the room from the hall.

"It`s a gentleman, mum," she said.

Evelyn went to the door.

"Charlie!"

"Evelyn."

"What is it? What brings you here?"

"Aren`t you going to ask me in?"

"All right, you can go back upstairs," she said, catching Merle`s eye. "This is Charlie. He was one of your dad`s friends. Come in. I`ll put the kettle on."

She brought the tea-pot through and began to pour.

"I thought you were still in Blackpool."

"I was until the end of the season. But to tell you the truth I`m looking for something new."

"Was it not what you wanted?"

"It was all right, for a time. But I thought I`d give Middleton a try again. Always calls me back."

"Anything in particular?"

"Well, I`ll find something to tide me over, and keep my eye open for a business opportunity. They say laundrettes are going to be the big thing soon. Or cars, maybe. I know cars."

"I remember."

"Yes, lovely little machine that. Had to let her go in the end, but I reckon I`ll have another one soon."

"Sugar?

"Two please. Lovely."

"There you are."

"Thanks. Well, I suppose I`d better get down to business."

"Business?"

"Yes. I saw your advert in the newsagent`s window. I`ve come about the room. I`m looking for lodgings."

"Oh, I don`t know about that, Charlie."

"Why not? I can give you cash up front. It`ll not be a problem."

"It`s not that."

"I don`t mean any funny business, Evelyn. I`m staying with a pal at the moment. But just temporary. I was looking for some proper digs, and I saw your notice. It`s as simple as that."

"I`m still not sure."

"I`ll not be any problem. I`ll probably be out most of the time, anyway."

"I`ve had one or two other people round," she said, a convenient fiction for not answering him directly. "I`ll have to give it some thought. I`d prefer a lady really, you know how people talk."

"Right," said Charlie. "I see. It didn`t say that on the card."

"No, well, as I say, I`ll have to give it some thought."

"Right, then. Well, thanks for the cup of tea. I`ll not outstay my welcome. I`ll call by in a couple of days, then, see if you`ve made a decision."

"Right."

She let him out at the front door.

"Goodnight, then, Evelyn."

"Goodnight, Charlie."

As soon as she had closed the door, Merle came down the stairs.

"Is he the man who took us out in a car once?"

"Yes."

"I thought so. I didn`t remember at first, but then I did."

"He came about taking the room."

"Sue`s room?"

"Yes."

"Did you say he could?"

"No, not straight away."

"Why not?"

It was obvious that Merle`s childish point of view saw him as the man who had taken them out for a car-ride, not as someone about whom there might be gossip.

"I don`t see why you shouldn`t take him on," said Myrtle.

"You don`t think people would talk?"

"What if they do? You`re a widow woman, there`s no shame in taking in a lodger. Have you had any other takers?"

"No."

"Well, there you are, then."

Myrtle, of course, knew nothing about her fling with Charlie, that afternoon at Sunnybrow Road, but even so, her reassurance helped put things into perspective.

"If he comes back, we`ll take him on, on a trial basis, shall we?" She said to Merle.

"On a trial basis. See if he comes up to scratch."

Evelyn laughed, and immediately hoped that Charlie would come back.

A week passed. Two. She wondered if he had taken the message and gone off.

Two weeks later, the man from the Post Office came back.

"I saw you were advertising again. I`ve been somewhere but it`s not entirely satisfactory. "

"I`m afraid the situation is already taken."

"Oh. In that case you might be so good as to remove the advert."

"Yes I will. I`m sorry to have inconvenienced you."

She took the advert out of the window, concluding that she had said enough to put Charlie off altogether.

Visiting Silk Street, Evelyn noted that a photographic portrait of John, in his full navy dress uniform, had taken pride of place over the mantelpiece.

"We had it done at Halkyard`s," said Alice. "You can take the plate, if you like, if you want to have one done yourself."

"Yes," said Evelyn. "Thanks."

She already had a small copy of the photograph on the dressing table of her bedroom at home. John had given it to her after his initial training in Liverpool, but she had not realised that there was an original plate, or that he had left if for safe-keeping with his parents.

"He`s done us a nice frame, hasn`t he? Very reasonable. He can do the same one for you, if you want me to ask him."

"No, I`ll see him about it myself," said Evelyn, "if I`m taking the plate in."

It was the following Friday night, stopping by on his usual rounds, that Ernest said his mother had mentioned the photograph, asking if she had yet taken it to Halkyard`s. As ever with Ernest, there was a hint of tension, a sense that he had been sent on an errand.

"I haven`t had time, yet. Does she want the plate back?"

"There`s no urgency," he said, going on to change the subject.

After he had gone, she took out the plate from its wrapping, and looked at the image with its inverted tones. Then she went upstairs and looked at the small photograph on the dressing table. She looked at the picture for a long time, wondering what life would be like now if he had come back safe. Better or worse, John? she asked. Better or worse?

At last she made her mind up.

"I`m not having you staring down at me from the mantelpiece, John," she said, replacing the photograph on the dressing table. "You`ll do here."

When Ernest came round the next Friday, he asked again about the plate. "You can take it back," she said, giving him the package. "I`ve got a print of it. Will you give it back to your mother?"

"Right," said Ernest. "I`ll be seeing them on Sunday. Will you not be over this weekend?"

"Merle`s had a bit of a snuffle, I think I might keep her at home, this weekend."

"Right you are, then. I`ll get off. Be seeing you, chuck."

"Be seeing you, Ernest."

Chapter 43

"If Joan and Ronny get married," said Alice, one Saturday, "they`ll go and live with Peggy and Joe. Well, they`ve got plenty of room there, it makes sense."

"Yes, I suppose it does," said Evelyn.

"Well, Eddy`s promising to go away, too. Now that he`s finished up with her, Beatrice, he`s all for getting himself over to Blackpool again."

"Well, he`s been hankering after it since he came back."

"He has, but, anyway, the thing is, as like as not, there`ll be room here for you and Merle."

Evelyn tried to disguise her inner reaction.

"I would have thought you and Jim would want a bit of peace and quiet rather than more of us round your neck."

"Well, it`s family, isn`t it? It`d save you a lot on your rent an` all, when you think about it."

"Yes, I will. I`ll give it some thought."

"Any road up, it`ll not be for a while yet."

"They`ve not named the day yet, then," said Evelyn, with some relief.

At that point, James came in, with some paraffin he had managed to get from the Lamp Oil shop on Union Street. "It`s raining cats and dogs out there," he said, taking off his wet coat and hat.

"Here, give those to me," said Alice. "Don`t you be dripping all over the floor."

James looked at Evelyn, and rolled his eyes. He was beginning, bit by bit, she thought, to get back some of his lightness and mirth, to get back to his old self.

"Put the kettle on, Alice, love, while you`re in there!" he said, winking at Evelyn, and clicking his tongue, just the way that Ernest did.

She stepped back, and saw herself in the scene – living here, in John`s old home, helping Alice with the chores, pretending to put on looks of disapproval at James` jokes; in later years, looking after them as they grew older. In some ways, it had a charm – it would make life easy and comfortable, it would be good for Merle to have people around her, it would take the pressure off her, financially. It had a lot to recommend it. And yet... another part of her froze at the thought of being bound to such a role. She was just over thirty. A big part of her adult life had been overshadowed by the war, but she still wanted to have some aspirations for herself, something to look forward to besides being a dutiful mother and housekeeper for her mother and father-in-law.

Sipping her tea, she glanced up at John`s photographic portrait; if she came to live here, she reflected, she would be constantly under its gaze. It made her shiver. If he had come back whole and well, it would have been difficult enough, she surmised, to have woven back together the unravelled ends of their lives; that would have been one thing; the last thing she wanted now was to be in thrall to the impassive gaze of the icon that he had become in the house.

On her way home, she stopped by at the newsagent`s and wrote a new card for the window, advertising for a lodger.

Chapter 44

Eddie and Ronny had been to the greyhounds at Belle Vue and had come home drunk. Ronny was in the doghouse with Joan, who had also given her brother`s ear a lashing for leading him astray. Ernest, as ever, was trying to mediate between the parties.

Maureen and Gladys were keeping aloof, disdainful of the petty altercations of the young. Alice was serving tea. Marcia and Merle were playing in the yard outside. Baby Joan, now nearly six months old, was fast asleep. Frank had taken James to the Church Inn for a half to get away from it.

It was Nancy`s birthday.

That was the reason for the family gathering.

And Nancy was miserable, because everybody else`s problems were dominating the occasion. Besides which, she was sixteen and not a single boy had yet shown any interest in taking her out.

The newsagent`s business, Maureen was telling Gladys, was enough to drive anyone to distraction, with its early hours, and organisation of paper deliveries and unreliable paper boys, but they were beginning to do well, yes, very well, indeed, thank you very much, and Frank was thinking of applying to the GPO for a licence to open up a sub-post office.

Gladys listened with a rather tart look on her face. After the war, when Ernest had moved to a job with the Borough, she`d hoped it might lead on to better things; but it had turned out to be just another clerical job, and he seemed content to plod along with that, and with his other routines.

"He`s such a hard worker," Maureen was saying of Frank. "Up with the lark, and then never stops till the night. Seems to thrive on it. He`s a good father, too. He dotes on Joan, and on Marcia, too. As if she was his own."

"She doesn`t always seem to appreciate it," said Gladys, slyly.

Maureen looked up, and at that moment caught Evelyn`s eye. In days gone by, there had been a confederacy between them as far as Gladys was concerned, but that had gone now. Maureen, she now suspected, wanted to distance herself from the war years when they had spent so much time together, and from the knowledge Evelyn had of her during that time.

She was glad, at last, to get away. It was beginning to drizzle as she walked along Cross Street, but she didn`t bother with her hood. They quickened their step, making a game of it, putting in hops and skips, and managed to reach Wood Street just as the downpour started. Sheltering in the door of the shop opposite, Charlie Breen was waiting.

"I saw the advert had gone back in the window," he explained when they were inside. "I`m back in the lodging stakes, if you`re interested."

"I can`t offer any tenancy agreement. Just a week`s notice."

"That`ll suit me."

"I`ll have to get you to sign to say you agree to that."

"If you want me out, just tell me and I`ll go."

"It has to be on a proper business footing, you see, otherwise my landlord won`t like it."

"Right."

"I`ll show you the room, then. Breakfast`s included in the rent, but if you want anything to eat at night, that`ll be extra."

"Right. That suits me."

"You can have the front room to sit in, if you want, of an evening, but no visitors unless you give me warning, and no-one after ten o`clock. I`ll give you a front door key, but if you come in late and make any noise that`ll be it."

"Understood."

"Right, then. When will you be wanting to start?"

Chapter 45

In some ways, Charlie Breen was an ideal tenant. He was up and out of the house by eight o`clock each morning, and he seldom returned before nine in the evening, and on most occasions, after he had had a cup of tea, he went straight to bed. What the nature of his business was, she was never quite clear, but he paid his rent in advance, and in the main kept himself to himself.

"Well, that`s how you want it, isn`t it?" said Myrtle. "Does he not have a lady friend or anything?"

"I don`t think so."

"Well, it`s funny old world. Maybe he prefers the company of gentlemen."

Evelyn laughed. "What do you mean?"

"Well, he dresses nicely, doesn`t he? They say that`s sometimes a sign."

"A sign of what?"

"Never mind. A sign you`ve got nothing to worry about, anyway."

Evelyn laughed again.

"I`m sure I haven`t."

Ernest continued to call round on Friday evenings, on his route back from Silk Street.

"You`ve taken on another lodger, then?" he said.

"Yes,` she said, brightly, inconsequentially, though she was glad Charlie wasn`t there. "It all helps."

Ernest nodded. She could tell he was uncomfortable, and sensed that there had been some discussion at Silk Street.

"It`s a gentleman, is it?" he asked.

It was obvious that word had travelled. She ought not to have been surprised. She thought she`d better seize the nettle. "It`s an old pal of John`s. Charlie Breen."

"Oh, aye," said Ernest, though not with any particular meaning.

"Just short term, probably. A few weeks. I think he`ll be moving on."

"Oh, well, as you say, it all helps."

The next time she went to Silk Street, she sensed the atmosphere.

"Are you sure it`s right?" said Alice, "with a little girl in the house."

It was obvious that Alice thought it wasn`t.

"It`s just a business arrangement. He keeps himself to himself."

Later, she heard Alice gently quizzing Merle, in the kitchen.

"He`s all right," Merle was saying. "He used to have a car. He took us out for a drive once. During the war."

"Oh, that`s nice," said Alice.

Evelyn squeezed her eyes shut for a moment. When she opened them, Maureen was looking directly at her.

"If it`s a problem," Charlie said, when she told him. "I`ll go. I told you I wouldn`t put you to any trouble, and I won`t. Tell me if you want me to go, and I will."

"No, there`s no need for that. I can`t be making all my decisions by what they think at Silk Street."

"Well, they`ve always been a bit clannish. Even your John used to say that."

"What happened in Blackpool, Charlie? Did it not work out?"

"Well, I trusted a man who didn`t deserve it. Let me down badly, actually. Had money from me on me on a bad business venture, and then did a bunk."

"Was there nothing you could do?"

"Not legal. Your only resort is the heavy mob in cases like that, and then you get in so deep you can`t get out. I walked away from it."

"You did the right thing."

"Story of my life. But, anyway, things are looking up now, I reckon, and it`s all on the level, too."

"Well, that`s for the best."

He nodded his head.

There was a silence between them, a thoughtful silence. She wondered if he might allude to the afternoon at Sunnybrow Road. It was long ago enough now, she reflected, for it to be acknowledged.

"I wanted to ask you something, Evelyn," he said, as if reading her thoughts. She took on an attitude of attentiveness.

"Yes," she said, adopting a neutral tone.

"I wondered if it would be all right if I brought a lady friend round for an hour, next Friday night."

"Of course it is," she said, without giving out the slightest signal of how crestfallen she felt.

Chapter 46

She was the fool, she reflected. She had been vain enough to think, underneath, that he carried a bit of a flame for her. The afternoon at Sunnybrow Road, and again when he had asked her to stay over at Blackpool: she thought there was more to it, but now she realised it wasn`t so.

He was simply a man who thought he might be onto a good thing, taking his chance. It was what men did. She understood that. It was simply in the past.

She walked with Merle to school on Monday morning, and then got on with the wash: filling the tub, scrubbing the stains with a bar of soap, then working it all round the tub with the posser, whites first, when the water was clean and at its hottest, then the rest. Then, it was time to put the mangle over the tub, before hanging it all out on the line. That was the only thing to do, just get on with things. It was dreary work, hard and physical, too, but it took you out of your mood, and by dinner-time, when Merle was due back from school, she was in good spirits. She ran down to Morton`s, the baker, and brought home two meat and potato pies, Merle`s favourite.

In her encounters with Charlie during the week, she was suitably cool and distant, though he showed no sign of noticing.

On Friday she cleaned and dusted the room, and made sure everything was proper.

"I`ll introduce you if you like," said Charlie.

"No, that`s all right, thanks. I`ll stay in the kitchen. You can take the radio through, if you like."

"Thanks."

"I`ll make you a pot of tea at about half-past eight. You can come through and fetch it."

"Right, thanks. Well, I`ll get off then. Be back about eight."

From the kitchen, she heard them come in, and was tempted to go and catch a glimpse but she overcame her curiosity. She waited quarter of an hour and then made the pot of tea, and waited for him to come through.

"It`s all right to smoke, isn`t it, Evelyn?"

"There`s an ashtray on the sideboard."

"Thanks."

He went back in with the tray, and she heard the faint sound of dance music from the radio as the door opened and closed.

Then, at ten past ten, the door opened again, and Charlie popped his head round the kitchen door. "I`ll just see her home, then, won`t be long."

Twenty minutes later, he came back in, and brought the radio through. "Thanks," he said. "And thanks for the tea. Well, I`m dead beat, I`ll turn in I think. I reckon I might have a bit of a lie-in in the morning, so I`ll not be wanting breakfast. Are you all right, Evelyn?"

"Will she be coming again?" she asked, meaning it to sound practical, but realising that it sounded far from that.

"What`s up? You should have said if you minded."

"No, it`s all right. You`ve every right to have visitors. It`s none of my business."

He sat down.

"To tell you the truth, Evelyn. She`s just a pal. Nothing more than that. I know people talk. I thought if I brought a lady friend back a couple of times, it might put a stop to any gossip."

"Is that it?" she said. "Is that all?"

He nodded, and she realised she was beginning to cry.

"Don`t tell me you were jealous, Evie."

A moment later, she was in his arms.

"I`ve had no life of my own, Charlie. Not since the war started. Just that afternoon at Sunny Brow Road, that`s the only bit of life I`ve had."

"I thought you`d just put it in the past."

"I had. I thought I had."

He stroked her hair, and kissed her brow. Then she tilted her face upwards and they began to kiss.

"I`d better get back to my own room," he said, when the first light was beginning to filter through the curtains. "Before Merle wakes up."

"Don`t go yet," she teased, nuzzling up to him.

They drowsed for a while longer in each other`s arms.

"Bloody hell, Evie," he said, at last, "you`d better let me go or I`ll not be answerable."

"All right, then," she said, pushing him away playfully. "Go on. Get off with you!"

He pulled on his shirt and trousers, then sat on the side of the bed, and leaned over to kiss her.

"Is it just a one-off, this, or are we to make a go of it?"

"Are you really asking me that, Charlie Breen?"

"What do you say?"

"Not a one-off. I hope not anyway. I`ve not done with you yet."

"That suits me," he said.

Chapter 47

"I already know," said Myrtle. "These houses are built solid, but there`s a limit to how thick they can make walls."

"I hope we didn`t disturb you."

"Don`t worry about me. After his snoring for thirty years, there`s nothing keeps me awake."

"You won`t tell anyone, will you?"

"I won`t. But you`d better mind, these things have a way of getting out. What does Merle know?"

"Nothing. Not yet, anyway."

"Don`t be too sure of it."

Evelyn nodded. It was something she had thought of. It was three months now, and they had been careful. Merle seemed quite fond of Charlie, and she hadn`t asked any awkward questions, but it only needed her to notice something and let it slip down at Silk Street, and the cat would be amongst the pigeons.

"You should get him to marry you," said Myrtle. "If he`s keen. Why not? "

"I don`t know how well that would go down."

"Your husband`s dead. You can get married again. In church, too, if you want. There`s no-one can stop you."

"I`m not sure I`m ready, Myrtle. Not for all that again. Not yet anyway."

A couple of days later, Charlie came home just after dinner.

"I`ve got to pop over to Liverpool for a few days. Little business opportunity, but I`d be a fool to let it go. I`ll keep paying you the rent, of course."

"I wasn`t thinking of that," she said.

"I`ll just throw a few things in a bag."

"Do you want something to eat before you go? Let me get you something."

"No, I`ll be all right. I`ll get something at the station."

"Are you sure?"

"Look, Evie, I`ve got an hour before I have to get off. I thought we could go upstairs for a bit, if you fancy it."

"What sort of a woman do you think I am, Charlie Breen!"

An hour later, she woke up from a light drowse, and felt his nearness and warmth, his arm around her.

"Why don`t we get married, Charlie? Then it could be like this all the time. It wouldn`t have to be a secret."

"I like the sound of that. We`ll have to talk about it when I get back."

"When will that be?"

"Like I said, a couple of days, three at most."

"Promise?"

At that moment, the sound of the front door opening and closing was heard.

"Mum?"

"Christ!" muttered Charlie.

"They must have left them out of school early. Quick. Just get back into your own room."

"Mum?"

"I`m just up here, love. I was having a lie-down."

"I forgot my pumps. I`ve come back for them. Do you know where they are? I`ve got to get back quick or I`ll be for it."

"I`ll be down in a minute, love," she said, dressing herself all the time. "Have a look in the kitchen."

"Is Charlie here?" Merle asked, when she came down the stairs.

"Why?"

"His coat`s over the chair in the kitchen."

"He`s got to go over to Liverpool. He came back to get some things. Here`s your pump bag. Now, you`d better get back before you get in trouble."

By the time Charlie came down, she`d made a pot of tea.

"Is it all right?"

"I think so. She saw your coat but I don`t think she suspected anything."

"Good."

"We can`t have things like that happening, though, Charlie."

"No."

"Sooner or later, she`ll put two and two together."

"I know. We`ll have a talk, when I get back. We`ll get it sorted out. But I`ll have to get off, now, Evie, or I`ll miss my train."

"Have a cup of tea, at least."

"No, I haven`t time."

That night, Evelyn went to bed early, and slept well. She awoke at five o`clock with the luxury of sleep still wrapped around her, and pulled the spare pillow into her arms as if it were him. His distinctive scent was there. A mixture of shaving soap and tobacco. She breathed it in, savouring it.

"Oh, Charlie Breen," she murmured. "I miss you. Come home, soon. Come home, soon."

"You`re cheerful, mum," said Merle.

"Am I?"

"You`re humming songs. That usually means you`re happy."

"Well, maybe I am."

"Why are you happy?"

"Do you need a special reason to be happy?"

"Has Charlie gone forever, or is he coming back"

"Coming back, I think."

"I hope he is."

"So do I. Now come on or you`ll be late for school."

"Right."

She went about the usual household chores with a light heart, humming one tune after another. Upstairs she tidied his room and changed the sheets. Then, in her own room, she wondered what changes she might make if it became their room together. How would Merle take it, she also wondered, if she married Charlie. At Silk Street they were saying that Marcia still hadn`t accepted Frank, and that the two were often daggers drawn. She doubted Merle would be like that; she liked Charlie, she`d said as much, though obviously it would be a bigger thing if he became her step-father.

She picked up John`s photograph. John in his navy uniform, looking self-assured, self-possessed. All the memories were still there, the good times and the bad – the year at Hooley Bridge, the rows when he had been out drinking, the sense of rejection during the war years, the loneliness and the guilt. But the emotion had gone from those memories now, almost entirely.

As usual, Ernest called round on Friday night.

"I see they`re building on the spare ground at the bottom of Rectory Street," he said, by way of conversation. "Nice little houses they look, too. Toilet and bathroom upstairs. Very nice!" He made the clicking noise in his throat. "That`s the future. Never mind going out to the yard in the middle of the night, eh? By the time Merle`s grown up, they`ll take all that sort of thing for granted."

"How`s Marcia? I haven`t seen her for a bit."

"She`s turning into a pretty little thing. Like your Merle. I reckon they`ll both be breaking a few hearts before too long!"

He stayed a little longer than usual, and she suspected he felt more comfortable knowing that Charlie was away.

When he went, she went up to see Merle. She was reading a book and had already put herself into bed.

"Good girl," she said, kissing her brow.

By ten o`clock she was in bed herself. Four days, she said to herself. Four nights.

So far, lying in bed, missing him, had been a kind of luxury, a kind of self-indulgence. She had half-expected him to arrive back today. Tomorrow would be five days, and he had said three. Surely, he would be back before the end of the weekend.

And then, on Saturday, and again on Sunday, when he did not come back, she wondered if she had scared him off.

Or rather, he had taken what he wanted, and had had enough of it.

Emptiness, and anger, resentment and jealousy began to invade her thoughts. And then, as the next week passed by, day by day, she tried to order her thoughts by imposing indifference on them.

"Right," she said to herself, "I`ve learned my lesson. From now on, I trust no-one."

Chapter 48

James had started to develop a trembling in his left hand. If he placed his hand a certain way on the chair arm, his hand tapped on the wood like a claw.

"Stop tapping," Alice said.

"I`m not tapping. It does it of its own accord."

"Well, stop it."

"I can`t stop it."

He tried to turn it into a joke. "It must be the DTs."

"It`s not the DTs."

"I`ll hold it still for you granddad," said Merle.

She stood by the chair holding his hand still. "Is that better now granddad"

"Oh, aye, that`s champion, that is. Can you stop there all day?"

"Not all day!"

"I`ll have to get Marcia to take over, then."

"There now," said Merle, after two minutes. "You`ll be all right, now. If it happens again, just see if you can hold it still yourself. Or put it on your lap so it doesn`t tap on the chair and annoy gran."

"Right," he said, dutifully putting his hand in his lap, and clicking his tongue, "I think it`s stopped now."

"Has he seen the doctor?" Evelyn asked Alice, in the kitchen.

"He says it`s just his nerves. Says he needs rest, but I don`t know," she said, shaking her head gravely.

"Perhaps a bit of sea air would do him some good," she said, when Ernest called round on Friday night.

"The doctor`s given him some new tablets for his nerves. We`ll see how he gets on with them."

She poured him a cup of tea.

"Thanks, Evelyn. Just the job. No sign of your lodger returning, then?"

"No," she said, matter of factly. "He may have decided to stay in Liverpool, for all I know. To be honest, I don`t care, as long as he pays his rent."

"He`s paid up, then, has he?"

"Well, till the end of the month."

"Well, maybe it`d be no bad thing, if he stops away, I mean."

She didn`t ask him to explain, but she knew that the family took a dim view of her having a male lodger.

When Ernest had gone, she switched on the radio. It was a concert of popular American music, the kind they had been broadcasting more and more since the war. It was no more than ten minutes later that the door opened, and Charlie popped his head round the door.

"Is that a pot of tea on the go, Evie? I`m gasping! What`s the matter, you look like you`ve seen a ghost."

"Maybe I have!"

"How`s tricks then?"

"You`ve just missed bumping into Ernest."

"I know. I saw him in the town, waiting for the 59. I thought he must have been here."

"Did he see you?"

Charlie shook his head, and then smiled. "Have you missed me, Evie, love?"

"Three days you said, Charlie. It`s been nearly a fortnight."

"I know. I`m sorry. You know how it is."

"Do I?"

"I kept thinking, I`ll get away tomorrow, I`ll get away tomorrow... but it dragged on. That`s the way it is with business sometimes. But look, I`ve got your next month`s here, and a bit extra."

"You did all right, then?"

"I did more than all right. And listen, I had this idea that we could go away for a few days, you and me and Merle..."

"Don`t be daft, Charlie?"

"What`s daft? We could have a little cottage for a week, on the coast, near Rhyl. I`ve heard it`s lovely out there."

"I can`t go away with you, Charlie, you know that. My name`d be mud."

"You could if we got married, though?"

"Married."

"Weren`t you saying as much, before I went?"

"I was. Well, I said we`d talk about it. It`s all a bit sudden this, though."

He took on a moody look and sipped his tea in silence. Like a little boy, she thought, a little boy who has everything planned out to suit himself, and then goes into a mood when other people don`t fall over themselves to fit in with it.

He wanted to come to her room that night, but she didn`t let him. Or the next night. But when Merle went off to Sunday school, she took him a cup of tea in bed, and quite as she planned, one thing led to another.

"I missed you like mad, Evie," he said. "I thought about you every night."

"Just at night?"

He laughed.

"I missed you, too," she conceded.

Chapter 49

Charlie`s business ventures tended be short term, and to end up with fallings-out and accusations of skulduggery. There were times when he was flush, as he called it, and there were times when he was strapped. When he was flush, he was the life and soul of the party, and generous with it, and money left his wallet quickly, especially if he treated himself to an afternoon at Belle Vue or Castle Irwell. When he was strapped and full of the miseries and would spend long dinner-times in the tap-room of The Dusty Miller or The Commercial bemoaning his lot over two or three drawn out halves of mild, but he was never down for long. He would spruce himself up and go up to visit his aunt in Alkrington, try to beguile her with a bit of his easy charm, and usually there was something, a share dividend which had come in, or an annuity which she could be persuaded to part with. He had been more or less disinherited by the respectable part of the family, but his aunt now seemed to have forgotten how many times she had been disappointed by his bright promises that the money was being set to a good purpose.

"Who knows," he joked to Evelyn, "she might leave me something one of these days. She can`t have that much longer left."

"Charlie!"

"I`m only joking. The longer she keeps toddling along, the better, as far as I`m concerned."

And so it went. With a bit of capital, as he called it, in his pocket, he would set out looking for a new opening, and the circle would begin again.

From time to time, his ventures took him away, to London or Liverpool, and Evelyn got used to him being away longer than he said he would, though it was usually only by a day or two. When he was in a warm, sentimental mood, he returned to the topic of marriage, making promises that the right combination of factors was just around the corner, and she learned to take it with a pinch of salt, though she was glad he didn`t forget it. And she was glad he didn`t up sticks and leave. On the whole, the domestic situation wasn`t disagreeable. Merle liked Charlie, and the two of them had their own confederacy of jokes and ribbing. Once or twice a week, he came to her room and asked her if she would let him come into the bed, and though there was a kind of fiction that he was asking a favour that she might well be expected not to grant, in fact, she looked forward to his visits more than she admitted.

"A word in your ear," said Myrtle, one morning, when they met in Jacques`, the grocer, on the corner of Cross Street.

"What is it?"

"Not here. Come round for a cup of tea."

She went home and unpacked her bag, then went to Myrtle`s back door by the yard.

"I`m not one for tittle-tattle," said Myrtle, "but I wouldn`t be a proper friend if I didn`t tell you what I've heard people saying."

"I don`t think I`m going to like this."

"It`s not anything in particular, but you know what folk are like, with their side remarks and nods and winks."

"About me?"

"What do you think? You and your lodger."

Evelyn nodded. She was not entirely surprised.

"Mind you, people`d talk even when there`s nothing to talk about, but in the circumstances, I thought I`d better put you on your mettle."

"What sort of thing do you mean, Myrtle?"

"Got his slippers by the door, you know, that sort of thing, comes home at odd times during the day..."

Evelyn took a deep breath. "Right."

"I say, have you nothing better to bother your heads with, she`s my neighbour and if anything was going on, I`d know about it, it`s a load of squit, but that`s just me, that`s the way I am."

"Thanks," said Evelyn, though she wondered, momentarily, if Myrtle`s protests might add rather than detract from speculation.

"A load of old gossips!" Charlie scoffed when she mentioned it to him.

"Well, maybe they are, Charlie, but it`s my good name, isn`t it, and it spreads, and it`s not smoke without fire, is it, when it comes down to it?"

"I`ll stop coming back in the afternoon, then."

"There is another solution..."

"I know Evie, and I promise you, we will, as soon as we can."

"Honestly?"

"Honestly. There`s nothing I want more."

"But what?"

"But we have to get it right, you know, have a bit of money behind us."

"I thought you were doing all right, you know, what you said when you came back from Liverpool."

"Well, I was, but I had a few debts to pay off. I`m straight now, but I`m strapped as far as ready cash is concerned.

"We don`t need that much, do we? We`re all right."

"I`ll be honest with you, Evelyn, I`ve had a chequered past, as you well know, easy come, easy go, that`s been me, but if we`re going to pitch in and make something of it together, I want to have something a bit more solid as a base, something more steady."

She waited for him to continue.

"I`ve been asking around. Trying to find a position, like I said, something steady. Putting irons in the fire."

"Right," she said, prepared to concede that his motives were right.

"But I`ll not come back during the day if it`s causing gossip. Just have to be a bit more patient, a bit more discreet. Unless you want to kick me over the touch-line, that is. If you do, I`ll take myself off, you only have to say the word, Evie."

She reached over and put her hand over his wrist.

"Just say the word, and you can be shut of me."

"I don`t want that, Charlie."

"We`ll manage somehow," he said.

Chapter 50

Towards the end of October, Charlie had another trip over to Liverpool, but this time, true to his word, he was back within three days, and once again he was flush.

"Was business good?" she asked.

"Not bad, but to tell you the truth, Evie, I went over to Haydock Park and had a bit of a flutter, and it came up."

"You shouldn`t gamble, Charlie. You never see any poor bookies, isn`t that what they say?"

"Spot on," he laughed. "But it doesn`t do any harm, once in a while. Anyway, there`s a bit extra for you. Get yourself a new dress, something nice."

"I don`t need anything. I`m all right."

"I want my missus to have nice things," he said, putting his hands round her waist from behind.

"Am I your missus, Charlie?"

"Course you are, Evie."

"I haven`t got a ring on my finger, Charlie."

"That can soon be remedied."

"It`s not just a piece of jewellery I`m talking about."

"I know that."

"Well, then..."

"All right, all right. Give me a chance. I haven`t even unpacked my bag yet!"

"Go and do it, then. And give me your dirty washing, don`t just leave it in a drawer, or under the bed."

"Bloody hell," he said, kissing her ear. "You`ve got me under your thumb already, haven`t you?"

"Get away with you," she said. "I`ll put the kettle on."

When Ernest called, the following Friday, he told her that the doctor had said that he was considering a diagnosis of Parkinson`s disease for James.

"Can they give him anything?"

Ernest shook his head. "It`s progressive. Just a question of how fast it develops. I mean, I see him getting worse week by week, but the doctor says he`s not bad, by some standards, so we`ll just have to see."

"I`m sorry, Ernest, I am. How`s Alice taking it?"

"Well, you know her, she sets her face against bad news, won`t let it throw her off course."

Evelyn nodded. That kind of resilience had always been part of Alice`s make-up, ever since she had known her. What can`t be mended has to be coped with...

Charlie had managed to get himself a job with an Estate Agent, showing prospective buyers around various properties. It didn`t pay much, he said, but it gave him a knowledge of the property game, a stepping stone or a spring-board.

"If I had a bit more capital," he said, "I think I could do something big, I really do."

On the subject of setting a date for a wedding, he was typically evasive, always waiting for something to happen first.

"We need to get a good start. Get away from here. Get somewhere new. Somewhere that`s just our own."

He never said anything you could disagree with, seemed at times almost more enthusiastic than she was, but it was always hedged about with conditions.

Eddie was back from Blackpool for a few days. He was shocked to know what the doctor had said about his father, and wanted to know why he hadn`t been told before.

"Oh, aye," said Alice, quietly, "and what would you have done about it, lad?"

"Well, what is being done? Has he seen a specialist?"

He was angry and in denial, blaming everyone for their complacency, and in the end it took Joan, now growing confident and mature, to put him right. Eddie withdrew, and sulked, and then went out to the Joiner`s Arms for solace.

The day before he went back, he took Evelyn to one side.

"What`s going on, Evelyn?" he said.

"What do you mean?"

"I`ve been talking to our Maureen. She says you`ve got Charlie Breen lodging with you."

"And what`s the problem with that? I need a lodger to make ends meet, Eddie. I`m a widow. It`s not easy."

"As long as it`s just that."

"Just what?"

"Just a lodger."

"Eddie, I hope you won`t take this the wrong way, but is it really any of your business?"

"It`s family business."

"I don`t know what your Maureen`s been saying, but listening to gossip and tittle-tattle isn`t family business. Maybe it`s her you ought to asking questions of if you`re doing a sort out of family business."

"All right, all right, Evelyn. Sorry if I`m out of order, but we`ve been through a lot."

"We`ve all been through a lot, Eddie."

Charlie was reading the newspaper with his feet up when she got back home.

"Eddie had a go at me," she said. "About you know what..."

"He was always a bit of a hot-head," said Charlie. "Like your John in that respect.

"That`s not the point Charlie, the point is people are whispering, and it`s getting about."

"They`ll soon get tired of it."

"I`m not so sure about that."

"Do you remember when we went on that drive up to Bowlee during the war, Evie," he said, changing the subject, "what I was saying about them building up there?"

"Yes."

"Well, it`s all going ahead. All over the paper, about the legal stuff. Land registration and all that kind of thing. They reckon Wood Street`ll become a proper main road, bus route and all."

"Don`t know that I like the sound of that."

"Well, it`s progress, isn`t it? And like I said, there`ll be opportunities. I was talking to a bloke in the Boar`s Head this afternoon who reckons there`ll be big contracts for building and plumbing suppliers. Worth thinking about, that is."

"What were you doing in the Boar`s Head? I thought you were working."

"I gave in my notice. It was only ever a short term thing."

"When was this?"

"A couple of weeks ago."

"And when were you going to tell me?"

"I`m telling you now."

"Charlie!"

"Don`t go off on one, Evie. I didn`t want you bothered over it, and like I said, I`ve been talking to a few blokes, and it could be the start of something if I play it right."

She went into the kitchen and started to make the tea. It was so typical of Charlie she was determined not to make a row over it.

Later he went out for a walk down into the town, and after Merle was in bed, she sat listening to the radio and began to wonder if the time hadn`t finally come to tell him to move on and get lodgings elsewhere. She wanted it to work, because she was in her thirties and she didn`t want to be alone, and because she liked Charlie and she wanted more from him, but it was getting to the stage when she was putting everything else at risk because of him, and he seemed not to realise that.

At half past nine, she switched off the radio, and stoked the fire down, getting ready to go to bed. She had just switched off the light in the kitchen, when the front door opened, and a moment later, Charlie came through.

There was a dark bruise at the top of his cheek bone, and his left eye was almost closed.

"What`s happened, Charlie. Are you all right? Come here, let me bathe it for you."

"I`m all right," he said. "It looks worse than it is."

"What happened, did somebody jump you?"

"Did somebody jump me? Your Eddie, that`s who."

"Eddie?"

"He was in the tap-room at the Dusty. Somebody said something, and the next thing I knew, he was going for me. I think someone was egging him on."

"About me?"

"Well, yes, about you, and about me. Ouch!"

"Keep still. If you don`t let me bathe this, it`ll be closed up for a week."

"It stings."

"It`s meant to."

"I`ll move out, if you want. If that`s what it takes."

"It`s a bit late for that, now. How`s that?"

"Thanks."

"Do you want a brandy?"

"I wouldn`t say no."

She pulled out a chair to stand on, reaching the bottle from the top shelf of the cupboard.

"Do you want me to do that?" he offered.

"No, I`m all right."

"Do you know what, Evelyn, you`ve got nice legs. They could be a film star`s legs, they could."

"Get away with you. Here you are. Go on. You pour."

"Are you having one?"

"Just a small one, then."

He poured the drinks and sat down opposite. "Well, chin-chin, here`s to the future!"

"Can I ask you something, Charlie?"

"Fire away."

"You do like me, don`t you, Charlie?"

"What sort of question is that?"

"Only if you do, why won`t you marry me? Nobody could say anything, then. We`d be proper."

"You know I want to, Evie."

"But what?"

"You know what`ll happen, don`t you, the minute you get married to me?"

"What?"

"They`ll take your widow`s pension off you. Have you thought about that?"

"I suppose so."

"But have you, have you really, Evie? Have you thought how you`d cope?"

"I thought we`d cope together."

"Well, that`s how it should be, and that`s how I`ve always wanted it to be, but at the moment, well, you know how it is – I`m hard pushed to find the rent."

"You shouldn`t have given up your job, Charlie."

"It wasn`t leading anywhere. I need something that`s got a future. That`s what I`m trying to do now, trust me, Evie. With a bit of luck, by next summer, we`ll be able to move out of here, and have a place of our own, up on Alkrington, somewhere nice."

"Do you mean it, Charlie?"

"Course I mean it. Why wouldn`t I?"

She reached across the table, and put her hand over his.

"Will you have a cup of tea, Ernest?" she said, when he called, that Friday.

"No," he said. "I`d better just say what I have to say and get off."

"That sounds very ominous, Ernest."

"I`m sorry, Evelyn," he said, mortified and apologetic, "you know I`ve always held you in the highest regard and affection, but I think it`s better if you don`t come down to Silk Street any more, not at present."

"Is that what you think, or is it what they`ve sent you to say, Ernest?"

"You know why, don`t you?"

"My lodger comes home with a black eye because he`s met your Eddie in a pub, I think I know why."

"I`m sorry Evelyn."

"He`s lucky he wasn`t reported to the police, your Eddie, for common assault."

"He would have deserved it. But it doesn`t change it though, does it?"

"Change what?"

"Look Evelyn, if you tell me, straight, and I mean straight, that there`s nothing going on, I`ll go back and tell them."

"I`m sorry, Ernest, but you can`t hold me to account like that, not on the strength of something someone said in a pub."

"All right, Evelyn, I`m sorry it`s come to this, I am. I`ll say goodnight, then."

"`Night, Ernest."

She saw him to the door, and when he had gone, she closed the door and leaned back against it, closing her eyes. When she opened them she saw Merle, sitting at the top of the stairs, looking down.

Chapter 51

It was in the autumn of 1947 that she heard from Margaret, a neighbour who was a regular at Parkfield church, that Joan and Ronny were to be married just after Christmas.

"Can we go and watch?" said Merle.

"I don`t think so."

"Marcia`s going to be a bridesmaid."

"How do you know that?"

"I saw her."

"Where?"

Merle had been upset at first, about not going to Silk Street, but she had soon brightened up, taking it into her stride. Until now Marcia had not been mentioned. "Where?" she repeated, seeing some hesitancy in Merle`s face.

"I went up to their house. Last Saturday when you were having a lie-in. They`ve got a shop."

"Was your aunty Maureen there?"

"Yes."

"Was she all right?"

"Yes," said Merle, with effortless inconsequence. "She said we could have some sweets."

Evelyn nodded and decided to say no more about the visit.

"I`m sorry you can`t be a bridesmaid, too."

"I don`t mind. Marcia says she doesn't want to be one, really. She`s only doing it because she has to."

Evelyn smiled, detecting the conspiracy to agree between the two cousins.

On the day, they went and stood at the back of the small crowd outside the church.

"Doesn`t she look pretty?" said Merle, as Joan and Ronny came out of the church. The family came out, singly and in pairs, Alice and James, Ernest and Gladys, Maureen and Frank,

Nancy, Eddie. Passing, Joan caught her eye and half-smiled. Marcia grinned at them broadly. Ernest, seeing them, looked awkwardly away. Gladys kept her eyes steadfastly ahead.

She took Merle`s hand, and lead her away. The wedding party was gathered at the bottom of the approach, posing for a photograph.

"Come on," she said, "we`ll walk a little way down Sunnybrow Road. I`ll show you a house where I went to a garden party once."

She heard, in due course, that Joan had given birth to a son, Paul, and that Ronny had a got a job with a firm of architects and surveyors in Manchester. One day, she bumped into Joan at the corner of Rectory Street and Wood Street. It was an awkward moment. Joan, embarrassed, looked as if she wasn`t sure whether to stop or push her pram onwards.

"Can I have a look?" Evelyn asked.

Joan nodded, and smiled.

The baby, now six months old, had a shock of black hair.

"He takes after Ronny," said Evelyn.

"That`s what everyone says."

"Well, it`s true. He`s lovely."

"We`ve moved into one of the new houses on Rectory Street," Joan said. "Only renting, but it`s nice to have our own place."

"Course it is. It`s a good start."

Joan smiled, and she smiled back. Then the moment passed, and Joan pushed her pram onwards.

Chapter 52

Charlie had been away for just over a week. She wasn`t sure exactly where he`d gone, and he hadn`t said precisely when he intended to be back. Lying in bed, feeling pleasantly drowsy, Evelyn wondered if, one of these days, he would take off and not come back at all. It was over two years since she had first let him share her bed here at Wood Street, and she sensed that the novelty had worn off for him. She was nearly thirty four, no spring chicken, and she had little doubt that he had an eye for the girls. She doubted she would find anyone else now, a woman in her thirties, with a ten year old child, and a dubious reputation. She had got used to loneliness during the war years, and had accustomed herself to the little private ritual which was its compensation, but it wasn`t the same as having real man in your arms, a man urgent for you, and who made you excited with his keenness. She would miss that.

"I`m going out, mum!"

It was Merle`s voice from the bottom of the stairs.

"Wait while I get you some breakfast."

"I`ve had some."

"What?"

"Bread and butter. And some barley water."

"All right. Be back for your dinner."

"I will."

She knew that she would be going to call on Marcia, or to meet up with her somewhere, but she knew also that to interfere would make no difference. Both girls had wills of their own.

She set her mind to getting up, and getting to the shops in good time, but then she felt her eye-lids growing heavy, and began to slip into a half-world of sleep.

She heard the door-latch go below, and called, "Is that you back, Merle?"

Waiting for a reply, she slipped back into her drowse. The next thing she knew, Charlie was in bed beside her, and within less than a minute, abandoning herself to the glamour of his nakedness, and her own, they were making love.

She waited five weeks before she went to see Doctor Gourley. He confirmed what, by then, she already knew.

"It`s not for me to pass any judgement, Evelyn, and I don`t, but you have to be practical, and I can put you in touch with people who will organise adoption for you, if that`s what you want, of course."

"No, that`s not what I want. It`s my child."

"Very well. Come back to me if you change your mind."

"Bloody hell," said Charlie. "Are you sure?"

"I`m three months."

"Bloody hell!" he repeated.

"You could say you were pleased!"

"I am, I am. It`s just a bit of a shock, that`s all."

"We have to get married, Charlie."

"Right."

"If I lose the pension, we`ll just have to cope."

He nodded.

"Bloody hell."

"Stop saying bloody hell, Charlie. I need you to be strong."

"Right."

"We`ll have to get a move on, Charlie. It`ll be showing soon. I don`t want people talking."

She confided in Myrtle.

"I thought something was up. You`ve had that look about you. You can always tell if you look close."

"I hope not too many people are looking close."

"So what`s he going to do?"

"He said we`ll get married."
"About time, too. So when`s the happy day?"
"He`s gone over to Liverpool on business. We`ll go up to Rochdale when he gets back, get it fixed."
"Registry Office?"
"Yes. Can`t see me doing another white wedding at Parkfield!"
"Have you told Merle yet?"
"Not yet. I think she`ll be all right with it, though. They get on well."
"Step-father and a brother at one go."
"Or a sister."
"No, you`re due a boy. She`ll think it`s Christmas."
"It will be, more or less."
"When are you due?"
"January."

It was two days later that the police came round asking for Charlie. They weren`t the local bobbies, but plain clothes men from Manchester.
"He was questioned in Liverpool last year. He gave this address."
"Yes."
"He`s just your lodger, is he, Mrs Wilkinson?
"Yes. What`s it all about?"
"When did you last see him?"
"About five days ago. He said he was going to Liverpool, on business. What is it?"
"Just an enquiry, Mrs Wilkinson. A few questions we`d like to ask him. I`ll leave you my card. If he turns up, tell him to get in touch. It`d be better for him if he does."

Later that night, Charlie came back.
"The police have been here," she said.

"I know. I was watching. I`ve been waiting out behind the yard. In case they came back."

"What`s going on, Charlie? What`s going on?"

"Look," he said, "I`ve got involved in something, I`ve been stupid. I`ve got some money, here. I`m going to put it in the outside toilet, up in the rafter. Once the fuss has died down, you can use it. But wait a bit before you do. If they`re suspicious, they`ll come and look. Otherwise you`ll be all right."

"Charlie!"

"I`ve got to go now. I`m going to turn myself in. That`s for the best. They`ll go lighter on me if I do it like that."

It was a matter of handling stolen goods.

He was remanded in custody, but bail was refused, because there was money involved, and he didn`t cooperate.

The police came to the house again, and searched. They didn`t find anything. When his case came up, he was found guilty and sent down for two years.

On the 20th January, 1950, in Oldham General, Evelyn gave birth to a boy. Two weeks later, she registered him, at Rochdale, as Charlie Wilkinson.

Part 4

Chapter 53

Charlie Wilkinson was nearly a year older than me. He was taller than me by four inches or so, and seemed worldly-wise, clever. You came across older, cleverer boys all the time, and you had to be clever in your own smaller boy way, to make sure they didn`t take advantage or just poke fun.

Charlie was interested in my football. It was one I had got as a Christmas present, and I had meticulously applied dubbin to it, so that it had a burnished, shiny, professional look to it.

He wanted to have a kick about on the street, but I said no as it would scratch the leather – it could only be used on grass.

We went down to the Town Hall fields and kicked it around, and I was pleased to discover that he was, for all his eleven months age superiority, a much less accomplished footballer than I was. And I felt a bit sorry for him because he kept making up excuses for himself, which I could see through, and in an odd way, by the time we walked back I felt that it was him who was trying to impress me.

"What does your dad do?" I asked him.

He shrugged his shoulders. "Don`t see that much of him really."

I tried to fathom this.

"He`s away most of the time. London. Liverpool. Other places like that. Doing business."

We reached the corner of Wood Street and Rectory Street.

"You can come in for a drink of Tizer, if you want."

"I don`t know," I said. What with the Butlers and Miss Fitton, I wasn`t that keen on going into other people`s houses.

"If my mam`s in, she`ll give us a tanner, get a couple of wagon wheels from Paiges."

I was tempted. A wagon wheel was a generously sized biscuit covered in chocolate with soft fudge inside. There were things you would put up with to get the chance to work your way through a wagon wheel.

"Go on, then."

We went through into the kitchen, and he produced a bottle of Tizer. "Cup or just swig?"

"Just swig," I said.

"You go first. I`ll wipe it with my hand."

I took a swig, being careful because I knew if you overdid it Tizer could fizz up and come back through your nose, and handed it to him.

"What mischief are you up to?" came a woman`s voice, appearing at the kitchen door from the yard. "Oh," she said, when she saw me.

"This is Johnny Warburton," Charlie announced.

The woman had a look on her face which somehow told me that she already knew who I was.

"Can we have sixpence to go up to Paiges?" he asked.

"Go upstairs and fetch my purse, then."

As soon as Charlie had disappeared, she sat down in front of me and stroked her hand over my hair. I didn`t mind. She wasn`t young, like my mum, but she wasn`t old either, and there was something pleasant about her, something I liked.

"So, you`re John," she said.

"Yes."

She put her fingers under my chin and tipped my head upwards. She nodded slowly and her face slowly spread across with a warm smile.

I made the mistake of telling my mother later that Charlie`s mum had given us sixpence each. She told me off, saying I shouldn`t accept money from people, but I knew it was really something else.

Later, I heard her muttering something to my dad, and it was when I put it all together, that I realised that the woman I had met, and who had said my name in such a particular way, was Evelyn.

Later that year, we moved up to Alkrington, and the year after that I went to Grammar School in South Manchester, distancing myself even further from the old Middleton I had grown up in. It was a Middleton that was already changing, losing its shape in the seismic shifts of post-war social and industrial change. New housing estates had started their inexorable spread over the surrounding farmland, the mills were closing down, and it wasn`t to be long before the older parts of Parkfield were being knocked down to make way for the new Arndale Centre.

Aunty Gladys died sometime in the early sixties. She dropped dead, as the saying was, but in this case literally. My uncle Ernest heard the sound of her hitting the floor; the doctor said she was probably dead before he heard it. In 1968, Ernest himself had the first of a series of heart attacks that would eventually kill him. I went to visit him, at his house on Elm Street. They had moved a single bed down into the front room. He had ten Capstan full strength lined up on the table beside his chair.

"I`m cutting down," he said.

There was a calendar on the wall with a picture of a young girl with shapely and pertly uplifted breasts. I was shocked. I thought it was only me who thought thoughts like that.

Eddie Wilkinson spent the rest of his life in Blackpool. We went to see him once, with my grandmother, Alice – a couple of years before she died – he was running a cocktail bar at a hotel. I found out, many years later, that more than once he had spent time in the hospital special unit at Blackpool, being treated for alcoholism.

Alice died in 1966, peacefully, sitting alone in the chair by the hearth at 7 Silk Street, with John looking down from his photographic portrait. The last two members of the Wilkinson household.

Merle, John and Evelyn`s daughter, was married in 1961, and soon afterwards, I later learned, they emigrated to Canada.

In my teenage years, I recall Marcia and her fiancé regularly visiting my mum and dad at our house in Alkrington, and they went to dances with them, and other couples who were friends of my parents. There was always an understanding that Marcia and her step-father, Frank, had never got on.

My brother Paul and I were ushers at her wedding in 1965. They had a flat in Middleton Junction, above her husband`s family business. I went there with a friend, to visit them at Christmas in 1968, when I was seventeen. We all smoked and they let us have some whisky. Walking home, my friend and I, slightly tipsy, agreed that Marcia was just about as fit as you could ever hope to meet.

She had a daughter a couple of years later, and in the same year I went off to university.

When I came back to live in Manchester in 1978, and when I was getting married myself, I fully expected Marcia to be on the guest list. My parents said not. There had been some kind of falling out.

I never saw her again.

She died in 1984, aged 43, a cardiac arrest following an operation that was supposed to be minor. It was shocking, and in my own way, I grieved; though because life was so full all about me at that time, I did not grieve deeply or for long.

It was much, much later, that I tried to find out what had happened to Evelyn.

She was in a home, I discovered, suffering from dementia.

"Both her children are in America," the carer explained.

She was sitting in a chair, with her head drooped, and her eyes slightly glazed.

"This is John," the carer said, quite loudly, "come to see you."

The glazed eyes tried, with difficulty, to come to focus.

"John," she said. "Not my John. Not my John."

And then her eyes softened, just as they had on that day when Charlie took me back to their house.

"John," she said, repeating the carer`s words, "come to see me."

When my grandmother, Alice Wilkinson, died, they said that the whole area was soon to be condemned; but in the fullness of time, when they rebuilt the centre, the side of Silk Street with the odd numbers remained, a last bastion of old Parkfield, facing the backside of the Arndale Centre and the car-park of the Archer Public House.

And there it stands to this day.

June 24th, 2013

Also by John Wheatley:

MARCIA, a Middleton novel – tells the story of a first-love that continues to haunt two people long after their lives have gone in different directions. Recording the rituals and intimacies of courtship and marriage, the novel evokes the changing faces of Middleton in the second half of the 20th century.

CANKY`S TRADE – a novel of old Middleton. Set in 1811, when Lord Byron was a guest at Hopwood Hall, when the practice of grave robbing was rife, and when the frame-breakers were setting themselves against new labour-saving technology, Canky`s Trade is a dark comic tale of Middleton at the dawn of the industrial era.

John Wheatley`s Anglesey novels include:

A GOLDEN MIST
FLOWERS OF VITRIOL
THE WEEPING SANDS
THE PAPERS OF MATTHEW LOCKE
THE EXILE`S DAUGHTER

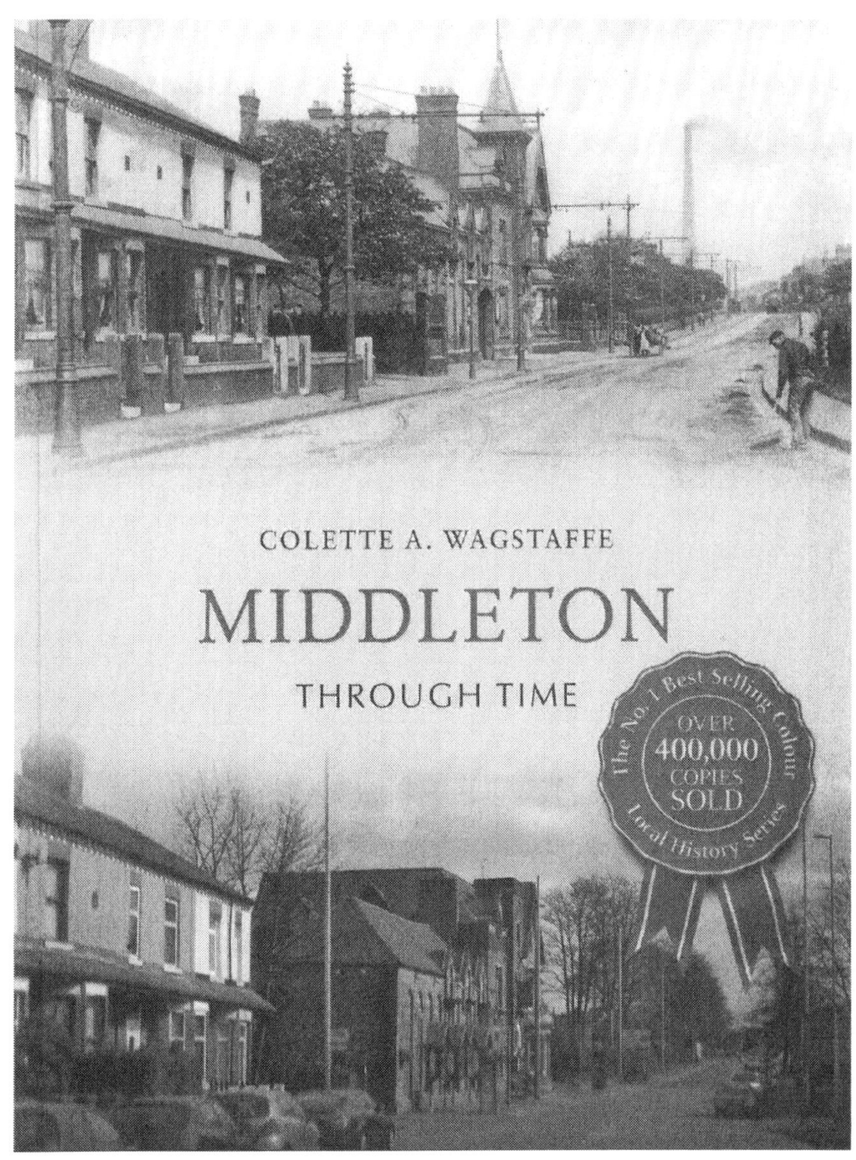
COLETTE A. WAGSTAFFE
MIDDLETON
THROUGH TIME
The No. 1 Best Selling Colour Local History Series
OVER
400,000
COPIES
SOLD

Printed in Great Britain
by Amazon.co.uk, Ltd.,
Marston Gate.